SIGNET MYSTERY

AN APRIL SHROUD

by
Reginald Hill

D0001892

A SIGNET BOOK

NEW AMERICAN LIBRARY

PUBLISHER'S NOTE

This novel is a work of fiction. Names, characters, places, and incidents either are the product of the author's imagination or are used fictitiously, and any resemblance to actual persons, living or dead, events, or locales is entirely coincidental.

© Reginald Hill, 1975

SIGNET TRADEMARK REG. U.S. PAT. OFF. AND FOREIGN COUNTRIES
REGISTERED TRADEMARK—MARCA REGISTRADA
HECHO EN CHICAGO, U.S.A.

SIGNET, SIGNET CLASSIC, MENTOR, ONYX, PLUME, MERIDIAN and NAL BOOKS are published by NAL PENGUIN INC., 1633 Broadway, New York, New York 10019

First Signet Printing, April, 1987

1 2 3 4 5 6 7 8 9

PRINTED IN THE UNITED STATES OF AMERICA

Contents

. . . the melancholy fit shall fall
Sudden from heaven like a weeping cloud
That fosters the droop-headed flowers all
And hides the green hill in an April shroud . . .
                                    —*John Keats*

De'il and Dalziel begin with ane letter
The de'il's nae guid and Dalziel's nae better.
                                    —*Old Galloway Saying*

CHAPTER I

Epithalamium

No one knew how it came about that Dalziel was making a speech. Pascoe had with great reluctance let himself be persuaded into a church wedding, partly by the argument sentimental (*Mum's looking forward to it*), partly by the argument economic (*Dad's paying for it*), but mainly by the suspicion, hotly denied but well supported by circumstantial evidence, that Ellie herself wanted it.

But they had been agreed about the reception. *A pint and a pie*, insisted Pascoe. *A glass of sherry and a sausage on a stick*, Ellie translated to her mother. In the event, they were drinking champagne and eating creamed chicken canapés, but at least they were on their feet, able to mingle freely, and no one was going to start reading telegrams and making speeches. Especially not Detective Superintendent Andrew Dalziel.

"I reckon I know Sergeant Pascoe, *Inspector* Pascoe, *Peter*, as well as anybody," proclaimed Dalziel.

"It can't be the drink," murmured Pascoe. "He never gets drunk. Not so you'd notice."

"That's on scotch. Dad says he's sunk two bottles of champagne so far," said Ellie.

"He's counting, is he?"

"*No!* He just noticed, mainly because merry Andrew there keeps calling it perry. Which hurts when you've paid for genuine non-vintage champers."

They giggled together and drew some reproving glances from a group of elderly relations who clearly believed that Dalziel's speech was the first reassuringly normal thing at a wedding where the bride had not worn white and there was no sit-down meal at the reception. *If you do it standing up, it doesn't count* was a maxim which could carry a decent body through nearly all of life's tribulations.

"He's a good policeman," Dalziel assured the elderly relatives. "He'll go far. Deserves every success. I've encouraged him from the start. And I don't flatter myself when I say I've managed to give him a bit of a leg-up . . ."

He paused and mopped his brow with a huge khaki handkerchief. The bald patch, uncompromisingly visible through the grey stubble of his hair, shone with sweat. He smiled now as he lumbered towards a dirty wedding joke, and with his shining face, broad smile, broader paunch, and the champagne glass held perpetually at the ready a foot from his lips, he should have been a figure of Pickwickian jollity. Instead, he looked as if he had just kicked the door down and was demanding that no one move as he had the place surrounded.

". . . a bit of a leg-up in his career," he resumed. "But he'll have to manage by himself tonight."

"Oh Jesus," breathed Pascoe.

The elderly relatives didn't much care for the joke but were still willing to give marks for effort.

"Ellie I don't know so well. But she'll do very well, I'm certain. My old Scottish grand-dad used to say, when you're picking a lassie, start at the bottom and work up. Broad hips for the bairns, broad shoulders for the housework, and a broad smile for good-nature and a peaceful life. Ellie, now . . ."

Some early-warning system must have told him that he was heading into troubled waters.

"Ellie," he repeated. "It's a hard job being a policeman's wife. Not every woman can do it. But if she can, and I'm sure Ellie can, then it's a grand and rewarding task. There's nothing better for a police-man than to be well looked after at home. Nothing. I can tell you . . . I've been looked after in my time . . . once . . ."

"In every Toby Belch there's an Andrew Aguecheek trying to get out," murmured Ellie. "I think he'd have been better droning on about my big mouth and huge bum."

"So I give you," cried Dalziel, explosively recover-ing from his introspective lapse, "the happy pair! May *their* lot be a happy one!"

"The happy pair!" echoed the assembled crowd of about forty relations, colleagues, friends, while Pascoe and Ellie looked at each other with love and specula-tion in their eyes.

Later as they ran across the car park of the Three Bells to Pascoe's ancient Riley, it was Dalziel who trotted alongside them, using a Martini table-parasol to fend off the rain which had been beating down unremittingly on Lincolnshire for twenty-four hours.

"Good luck," mouthed Dalziel at the passenger window. To Ellie he was almost invisible through the running glass. She smiled and waved. Her par-ents and the other guests had not risked their wed-ding finery in the downpour which meant that at least they were spared the usual primitive valedic-tory rites. It also meant that she couldn't see anyone to wave at except Dalziel and even he had moved out of their way round the back of the car.

"Let's go," she said.

Looking back, she saw him standing in the middle of the car park, waving the umbrella in a gesture of farewell and (accidentally, she hoped) menace.

"You're sure he doesn't know where we're going?" she asked Pascoe anxiously.

"No one does," he replied with confidence.

"Thank God for that. I wouldn't put it past him to decide to spend his holiday with us." She relaxed with a deep sigh, then suddenly laughed. "But he was funny, wasn't he? *Leg up!*"

Pascoe laughed with her and they even managed to laugh again five minutes later when they were stopped by a police Panda driver, curious to know why they were towing a police helmet, a police boot and a banner inscribed Hello! Hello!! Hello!!!

"I thought it went very well, George," said Dalziel. "Very well."

He sounded self-congratulatory as though he had arranged the ceremony himself.

"I suppose it did," said Detective Inspector George Headingley, glancing at his watch. He and Dalziel were the sole survivors of five policemen who had travelled down from Yorkshire for the wedding. In fact they were the sole survivors of the entire wedding group and it was only his awareness of their profession and status which prevented mine host of the Three Bells from pushing them out into the gloomy damp of a late spring afternoon in Lincolnshire.

"Stop looking at your watch, George," said Dalziel. "Have another drink."

He had abandoned the pernicious "perry" and obtained a bottle of the true Hippocrene, Glen Grant straight malt, two large doses of which had restored him to his customary dignity and composure.

"I really mustn't, sir," said Headingley. "It's all right for you, but I've got to drive back this evening. God knows what's happened back there with all the best minds down here!"

"Mondays are always quiet," pronounced Dalziel. "One for the road. A small one."

Headingley knew better than to resist when Dalziel insisted. He watched the broad strong hand pour another measure of scotch into his glass. There was no unsteadiness, no wastage. "A small one" to Dalziel was the precise equivalent of a Scottish pub double. Dalziel's ancestry had long been subsumed by his Yorkshire upbringing, but in some matters he was true to his heritage. He tended to become very sad at the sight of an English small whisky and very irritated when people mispronounced his name.

Headingley had known him, or known of him, all his working life. Dalziel had been a sergeant when Headingley joined the mid-Yorkshire force and his reputation was already established. *Thick as two short planks*, opined the scions of the uniformed branch. *But if you get hit by two short planks, it doesn't half hurt.*

His rise to his present rank of Detective Superintendent had not been meteoric, but it had been inevitable. When the hippo comes up for air, the lighter creatures of the surface impede the process at their peril. These lighter creatures had included his wife.

Headingley did not like the man, but in his own interests had developed a protective shield of long-suffering diffidence which passed for a relationship. He usually contrived to be on the move in Dalziel's vicinity and letting himself be pinned down like this was an error and attributable to champagne and post-wedding sentimentality. And also, he suspected, to a reluctance on Dalziel's part to be left to himself.

"Do you think they'll make a go of it?" he asked suddenly.

"What?" said Dalziel.

"Pascoe and his missus."

The fat man shifted his bulk, not visibly affected by several months of intermittent dieting, and fixed his wide, short-sighted gaze on Headingley.

"Why shouldn't they?" he asked aggressively.

He feels protective, thought Headingley. Mustn't say anything against his precious whizz-kid, must we?

Absurdly, he realized he felt jealous.

Downing his drink, he pushed himself out of his chair.

"No reason," he said. "Must be off now, sir. Quiet or not, some of us will be back at work tonight."

"This is the first holiday I've taken in God knows

how long," answered Dalziel. "I'll be back a fortnight today."

There was a plaintive note in his voice which
alarmed Headingley more than aggression.

"Have you decided what you're doing yet?" he
asked cautiously.

"No." The grizzled head shook ponderously. "I'll
just drive around a bit. Look at the countryside if I
can see it for this bloody rain."

"Oh."

Headingley's voice was studiously neutral, but
Dalziel shot him a malicious glance.

"Of course, if I get bored, I might just come back
early. Take you all by surprise. Give you all your
sticks of rock where you're not looking for them."

"That would be nice," said Headingley. "Enjoy
yourself, sir. See you the week after next."

Dalziel slowly screwed the top back on his bottle
after Headingley had gone. Next he rose, not un-
steadily but with a slowness which in another man
might easily have become unsteadiness. He had taken
the precaution of booking in at Orburn's main hotel,
the Lady Hamilton, situated only a couple of hundred yards from the Three Bells. A short brisk walk
was just what he needed now. It would blow, or in
this weather wash, the stuffiness out of his mind,
set him up nicely for a good solid meal. These buf-
fets were all right but they didn't give a man anything to get his teeth into, especially a man who had
resolved to forget his diet while on holiday.

But at the hotel he met a set-back.

"The restaurant does not open for another hour,
sir," said the shiny under-manager who to Dalziel's
jaundiced eye looked as if he had been anointed
with Mansion Polish. "It is, after all, barely five-
thirty."

"Is that so?" said Dalziel. He stepped close to the
under-manager and bared his teeth in a humourless
smile. "In that case, there'll be time for me to take a
good look round your kitchens, won't there?"

*   *   *

Despite this inauspicious start the meal turned out to be almost as good as had been promised by the hotel publicity. And afterwards in the bar just to add a little spice to the evening there was a scene.

A tall blonde girl, who had caught Dalziel's attention in the restaurant because she wore a deep plunging dress without showing the slightest evidence that she had breasts, punched one of her two male companions on the nose. It was no mere feminine slap, nor even a piece of robust horse-play, but a whole-hearted punch, starting from behind the girl's right ear and ending with a squelchy thump on the point of the man's nose. It was a good blow for such a skinny fighter and it drove the recipient backwards over his tall bar-stool, setting up an interesting chain reaction along the whole length of the bar.

Dalziel sitting at a table by the door grinned with delight. The girl, who looked nineteen or twenty at the most, now casually picked up her bag and walked away from the bar. Dalziel stood up and opened the door for her.

"Well done, lass," he said, genially peering down her dress. "I really enjoyed that."

"Did you?" she said. "Let me double the pleasure."

Dalziel was on his feet and much more solidly built than her first antagonist. Nevertheless the blow drove him backwards on to his table, shattering his glass and spilling the ashtray to the floor.

"Jesus!" he said, gingerly feeling his nose and looking after the girl's disappearing back.

He glowered round the room, defying anyone to be amused by his discomfiture, but most eyes were focused on the attempts to restore order at the bar. The floored young man was bleeding slightly but looked more puzzled than pained. He was in his early twenties, fair-haired, tall, athletically slim, a type Dalziel associated with the three-quarter lines of fashionable rugby teams composed mainly of young men called Bingo and Noddy. His companion was of an age, but shorter and stouter, in fact far too stout for someone so young.

He seemed to be the only person at the bar who had preserved his drink intact and he surveyed the others with a faintly complacent grin.

"Charley," he said. "You really ought to buy all these people a drink."

"You buy them a drink," said Charley. "She's your bloody sister."

Someone came through the door behind Dalziel.

"What seems to be the trouble?" said a voice in his ear.

He turned and looked at a small middle-aged man wearing an old pin-stripe suit of such hideous cut that it could not even be said to have seen better days.

"Trouble?" said Dalziel.

"I was in the restaurant. One of the waiters said something about a fracas."

"Did he?" said Dalziel. "I saw nowt."

He turned and left, pleased for once in his life to have been a sufferer of, rather than from, witness blindness. No one but a sadist or a newspaper reporter would have let a rumour of a fight drag him out of the Lady Hamilton's dining-room and Dalziel had no wish to start his holiday as a comic paragraph in some local paper. Come to think of it, he had pretty little wish to start his holiday at all. It was supposed to do him good, to rid him of the irritability and fatigue which had begun to dominate his working life in the last few months. But it was the time away from work, the time he spent by himself, which he feared most, and all a holiday would do was give him more of that. But it had to be tried, he recognized that. Otherwise . . . well, there was no otherwise he cared to contemplate.

Tomorrow he would set off like a good tourist to explore the highways and byways of the Lincolnshire countryside. Peace and quiet away from the mainstream of traffic, and in a fortnight he could return to work revitalized. Perhaps.

Meanwhile, as he had done for many nights now, he set about postponing the moment of switching off his bedroom light until he was on the very brink of sleep. He poured himself a carefully measured dose of scotch and put it on the bedside table. Next, clad in pyjamas suitable in pattern and size for the fitting of three or four deckchairs, he climbed into bed, placed his reading spectacles gingerly on his still throbbing nose and picked up his book. It was Bulwer Lytton's *Last Days of Pompeii*, which he had stolen from the hotel where he spent his honeymoon and had been reading and re-reading off and on now for thirty years.

CHAPTER II

A Bridge to Nowhere

The countryside was brimming. The rain had continued all night and he had woken several times to hear its monotonous pizzicato on the tiny metal balcony which some ironical builder had positioned outside his unopenable window. It had taken several medicinal malts to get him a couple of hours of dreamless sleep and he had been packed and ready for breakfast by eight o'clock.

He collected his bill at reception just as the under-manager passed without speaking. Dalziel, however, was not a man for childish grudges and he addressed the other cheerfully.

"Listen," he said. "Two things I don't do. I don't pay VAT on a service-charge and I don't pay a service-charge on VAT. You get it sorted."

It took a little time to get it sorted but he was still on his way shortly after nine-thirty.

Orburn was a country town of about seven thousand souls and had been neglected by development and history alike. Nothing earth-shaking had ever happened here nor did it now seem likely that it would. Dalziel, in a conscientious rather than enthusiastic attempt to prepare himself for his touring holiday, had read in a Guide to Lincolnshire of the fine broach spire of the small Early English church in which Ellie and Pascoe had been married, but the thing itself hadn't done much for him. The Guide had found little else to say and the only choice left to Dalziel now was one of direction. The main road (if so it could be called) through the town ran east to west. His car was pointing west so that was the direction he chose. A few miles farther on he hit the north-south trunk road and was faced with another choice. North would take him to Lincoln which he ought to visit. But it was also the direction in which home and work lay and he had the feeling that once he started north he wouldn't stop till the anguished faces of Inspector George Headingley and his colleagues told him he was home.

He turned south, spent ten minutes crawling in the blinding wake of a convoy of huge lorries and angrily turned off the main road and began to work his way back east along a network of narrow country lanes. It was only now that he realized how wet it really was. His morning paper had talked of serious flooding in some parts of the country but in print this made as little impact as shooting in Ulster or air disasters in the Andes. Now, however, as more and more frequently he encountered troughs of brown water wherever the road dipped, he began to realize that the weather was likely to be a key factor in his plans. Finally he stopped, partly because the next trough looked suspiciously deep, and partly because a signpost indicated a road coming in from the left; or rather, where the road ought to be. A hump-backed bridge rose over the stream which, running parallel to the road he had been following, was the source of most of the overspill. But now it was a bridge to nowhere. The land must have dropped away on the far side, the stream had completely broken its banks and the bridge descended into water.

Dalziel got out of the car and looked at the signpost. Another mile in his direction lay High Fold while in better weather the bridge might have led him to Low Fold, two miles away, and (here he laughed humourlessly) Orburn only twelve miles away. He glanced at his watch. It had taken him more than an hour.

He strolled to the top of the hump and gazed out over the flooded fields. The rain he realized to his surprise had stopped, though the atmosphere was still very humid. It was quite warm and there was even a dirty orange glow behind one threadbare section of the low cloud cover where presumably the sun was self-destructively trying to suck back into the air some of the moisture of the recent downpour. Curls of mist and vapour were beginning to form *art nouveau* designs in the more regular pattern of trees and hedgerow breaking the surface of the level waters. Patches of high ground too rose serenely from the floods. On one of these about a quarter of a mile away it was possible to make out a house to which design and distance gave the outline of a story-book castle. Someone had been lucky or wise in his choice of site. Farther than this the damp air made it impossible to see, but the floods certainly stretched as far as the visible horizon.

There is something ineffably depressing about water where it shouldn't be. Dalziel peered down from the bridge and it seemed as if the brown depths were full of dead things. Leaves and branches drifting on the surface were all he could see. Presumably fish and other aquatic creatures survived below. Presumably also the floods had killed as they invaded the dry land, hopefully not humans, but livestock and wild animals certainly.

If, thought Dalziel staring down at the turgidly flowing water, if I saw a body floating by, what would I do? Ignore it and go on with my holiday?

He shook his huge head gloomily. He had been wise enough in his life not to bother trying to plumb the depths of his own motivations and make-up, but he knew too well he'd probably risk lumbago, beriberi and God knows what wading about in this filthy muck to pull the cadaver out, and then he'd hang about to the embarrassment and annoyance of some local jack till he was satisfied of the cause of death.

Floods would be a good chance to get rid of some unwanted relative, he thought sagaciously.

No! Sod it! This wouldn't do at all. The holiday was the thing. Fresh air, commune with nature, bathe in beauty, pay homage to history. An English holiday, tired policemen, for the revitalization of.

Any corpse comes floating this way, I'll say Hello sailor, and goodbye, avowed Dalziel and as an act of both symbol and necessity he descended to the water-lapped limit of the bridge, unzipped his flies and began to pee in the flood.

He had just finished when a noise made him look up. It was a long, creaking noise followed by a gentle splash. It came again from behind a wedge-shaped copse of beeches rising stoically from the water about fifty yards to his left. The mist seemed particularly thick here and he strained his eyes in an effort to penetrate the grey barrier. Then through the haze appeared a shape. The sound sequence was heard once more. And into full view glided a rowing-boat. Hastily Dalziel began to fasten his flies.

The boat pulled by him, the oarsman taking long, leisurely strokes. He had the look of an old country-man, weathered and fit, anything between fifty and a hundred but able to row for ever. In the bows, like a reverse figurehead sat another old man of more determinate age, about seventy, with a profile fit for a Roman coin. But it wasn't either of the men who held Dalziel's eye.

Sitting on the thwart bench was a woman. She was clad all in black, even to a black veil over her face. Her head did not move as she passed, but Dalziel had a feeling that the eyes moved and saw him from behind the veil. So riveting was the tab-leau in the boat, that Dalziel did not instantly take in the most macabre detail of all.

The rowing-boat was towing something behind it, a small flat-bottomed boat.

On it was a coffin.

It was unmistakably a coffin. The brass handles gleamed against the dark mahogany sides and three wreaths splashed white and green along the lid. Even the oarsman's evident expertise could not keep the tow-rope perfectly taut and this strange piece of freight proceeded jerkily, its momentum almost bringing it up to the stern of the rowing-boat at the end of each stroke, as if it were in pursuit. But the woman never turned and Dalziel stood perfectly still, his attitude compounded of astonishment and the conventional deference of one who meets a cortège in the street.

But now a new sound came from behind the copse. Splashes again, but not the soft splashes of expertly wielded oars, and commingled with these were voices chattering and the occasional shout.

Another craft emerged through the mists but if the first could have been created by Lord Tennyson this one owed more to Jerome K. Jerome.

It was a large punt, the kind once used in duck-shooting with a stove-pipe gun mounted in the bows, rusty through neglect and non-use but still menacing for all that. Did they neglect the licence also? wondered Dalziel.

There were six people in the punt, which was perilously low in the water. The gunwale had no more than an inch of clearance at best, and water slopped over the sides with each thrust of the pole by the punter whom Dalziel recognized instantly as his companion in assault the previous evening. The breastless girl was seated in the punt alongside the fat young man, who still wore the same complacent expression. Opposite him was a boy of about sixteen, slim and pensive but with sufficient of the fat youth's features to look as if he had just got out of him. And by the boy's side was a young woman whose straight jet black hair and impassive, high-cheekboned face made Dalziel think of an Indian Maid (Pocahontas in the Board School history book rather than Little Red Wing in the rugby ballad, his only source-texts).

Finally, in the bows, resting nonchalantly against the gun was a dark, ugly-looking man probably in his twenties though it was difficult for Dalziel to be certain as the man's black hair seemed to be in a state of insurrection and only the high ground of his nose and the valleys of his eyes were putting up any real show of resistance.

Despite the impious exchange of views taking place between the girl and the youth with the pole, it was clear that this vessel was in convoy with the rowing-boat. The nearest any of them got to full mourning was the black turtle-neck sweater worn by the boy, but they had all made an effort. The fat youth wore a black armband round the sleeve of his tweed jacket, the hairy man had a black rosette pinned to his *University of Love* shirt, the Indian Maid wore a white blouse and slacks but looked as if she had been specially carved for a funeral, and the breastless girl had tied a length of black crape round her straw boater. Their only protection against the probable resumption of the rain consisted of two umbrellas and a parasol, carried at the slope by the men, except for the punter whose contribution to the solemnity of the occasion and his own dryness was a black plastic mackintosh under which he seemed to be dressed for cricket. Swimming would have been a sport more suitable, thought Dalziel, watching his efforts at propulsion. Basically, he had a not inelegant style, tossing the pole high and sliding it into the water with a casual flick of strong, supple wrists. The trouble was, deduced Dalziel, that the pole was then plunged two or three feet into sodden earth and his efforts to drag it out acted as a brake, so that the punt moved even more jerkily than the coffin.

The Indian Maid spotted Dalziel first and drew the attention of the others to him. The fat youth said something and they all laughed except the young boy. Dalziel was ready to admit that the sight of a portly gent apparently about to walk in to four feet of water was faintly comic, but none the less laughter in these circumstances struck him as a breach of decorum.

The rowing-boat was now out of sight and Dalziel

watched the punt till it too disappeared. Then he
walked back over the bridge and tested the depth of
the water on the road. It was just within the limits of
safety and he edged the car through it with great
caution.

The road now rose again, following the skirts of
the relatively high ground to his right which acted as
a block to the flooded stream. From the crest of this
small slope he could see for quite a way. The road
dipped once more and about a hundred yards ahead
it was flooded for a distance of thirty or forty feet.
But presumably thereafter it rose steadily away from
flood level, for just on the other side of the water
stood a hearse and two funeral cars. The oarsman
was in the water, pushing the coffin ashore where
the top-hatted undertaker and his assistants were
trying to grapple with it without getting their feet
wet.

Dalziel halted and once more settled down to watch.
Finally all was finished, the punt party reached shore
safely, dividing themselves among the two cars, in
the first of which the woman and the old man had
presumably been seated all along, and the sad pro-
cession drove slowly away leaving only the oarsman
seated on the bows of his boat rolling a well-earned
cigarette.

When the cortège was out of sight, Dalziel started
his car once more and rolled gently down to the
trough below, humming "One More River To Cross."
There was nothing like the sight of someone else's
funeral for making life look a little brighter.

Half-way through the trough, he suddenly realized this was much deeper than he had anticipated.
At the same moment the engine coughed once and
died. Dalziel tried one turn of the starter, then
switched off.

Opening the window he addressed the uninterested oarsman with all the charm and diplomacy he
could muster.

"Hey, you!" he shouted. "Come and give us a
push."

The old boatman looked at him impassively for a moment before he slowly rose and approached. He was wearing gum-boots which came up to his knees but even so the water lapped perilously close to their tops.

When he reached the open window he stopped and looked at Dalziel enquiringly.

"Yes?" he said.

"Don't just stand there," said Dalziel. "Give us a push."

"I han't come to push," said the man. "I've come to negotiate."

He proved a hard bargainer, totally uninterested in payment by results. It wasn't till he had folded the pound note Dalziel gave him into a one-inch square and thrust it deep into some safe apparently subcutaneous place that he began to push. The effort was in vain. Finally Dalziel dragged his own scene-of-crime gum-boots out of the chaos in the back of the car and joined him in the water. Slowly the car edged forward but once it reached the upslope its weight combined with the water resistance proved too much.

"Sod it," said Dalziel.

They sat together on the rowing-boat and smoked. Dalziel had already had the one post-breakfast cigarette he allowed himself nowadays, but he felt the situation was special.

"They'll be coming back soon?" he asked between puffs.

"Half an hour," said the boatman. "Not long to put a man in the earth."

"Good," said Dalziel. "I'll beg a lift from the undertaker. Who're they burying?"

"Mr. Fielding," said the boatman.

"Who's he?"

"Mrs. Fielding's husband," was the unhelpful reply.

"Mrs. Fielding was in the boat with you?"

Dalziel reached into his pocket, produced the emergency half-bottle he always carried with him in the car, took a long draught and offered it to his companion.

"Ta," he said, and drank.

"You didn't make that in your garden shed," he added when he'd finished.

"No. Are you Mrs. Fielding's . . .?"

He let the question hang.

"I work up at the house. Most things that need done and can't be done by lying around talking, I do."

"I see. Not a bad job if you play your cards right," said Dalziel with a knowing smirk. "Have another drink. That was Mrs. Fielding's family, was it?"

Why he should have been interested in anything but getting his car out of the flood and back into working order, he did not know. But time had to be passed and the habit of professional curiosity was as hard to change as the habits of smoking or drinking or taking three helpings of potatoes and steamed pudding.

"Most on 'em. The old man's her dad-in-law. Then there's the three children."

"Which were they?" interrupted Dalziel.

"The two lads, Bertie, that's the older one, him with the gut. Then there's Nigel, the boy. And their sister, Louisa."

"The thin girl?"

"You've got bloody good eyes, mister," said the man, taking another drink. "Must be this stuff."

"What about the others?"

"Friends. Visitors," he grunted.

"For the funeral?"

"Oh, no. They were here when he snuffed it. Not that it made much difference to 'em, mark you. Not to any on 'em. No. They just carried on."

"Oh, aye?" said Dalziel, thinking that the trio he had observed in the Lady Hamilton the previous night had hardly comported themselves like grief-stricken mourners.

"What made you take to the water?" he asked. "Couldn't the funeral cars get round to the house?"

"It'd be a long way round. They checked first thing this morning after last night's rain. Couldn't afford the time. They've a lot of work on in this wet weather. So it was either the boats or wait. And they wanted shot of the coffin quick, you see."

"Well, I suppose it's a bit deadly having it lying around the house," said Dalziel charitably.

"Oh yes. Specially when it's on the billiard table," said the other.

There was no answer to this and they finished their cigarettes in silence.

"What did he die of, anyway?" asked Dalziel, growing tired of the unrelenting lap of water.

"Some say his heart stopped," said the boatman. "And some say he was short of breath."

With difficulty Dalziel restrained himself from bellowing *don't you get funny with me!*

"What do *you* say?" he asked instead.

"Me? What should I know about it?"

He relapsed into a silence which plainly rejected breaking by any conventional social means. Dalziel walked along the water's edge a short way and stood inspecting the punt gun. It had been a formidable weapon, but looked very long disused. While the metal had probably never been bright (why give the poor bloody ducks even a chance of a chance?), now it was rusty and dirty and a spider had spun a few hopeful strands across the muzzle.

It began to rain again and after a few moments he returned to the shelter of the car. The boatman ignored his invitation to join him and remained where he was, even his cigarette appearing impervious to the downpour.

Nearly half an hour later the first of the funeral party returned. It was the blond youth, alone and on foot.

"Shit!" said Dalziel and clambered out of the car once more.

"Hello," said the youth as he approached. "You're stuck in the water?"

Dalziel smiled his congratulations.

"Yes," he said. "Where's the funeral cars?"

"I was just telling Pappy, there's a lot more water on the road about a quarter of a mile round the bend. They weren't very happy about taking their shiny limousines through it on our way to the church and now they reckon it's even deeper, so I was sent on to bring the boats a bit farther along."

He grinned amiably, apparently unresentful of the task. Dalziel could guess who had elected him to it. Anyone who let a woman punch him on the nose without setting matters right between them very quickly was saddling himself up for a hag-ride.

The boatman was casting off already.

"Hang on," said Dalziel. "I'll get my stuff."

The level of the water seemed perceptibly higher as he waded back to the car and unloaded his old cardboard suitcase. As he returned cautiously to the dry road, he saw to his chagrin that the rowing-boat was already on its way, leaving him to the uncertain mercies of the punt.

"He's in a hurry," he grunted as he placed his case carefully on one of the seats. The floor looked as if a halfpenny dropped from three feet would blast a hole through it.

"A devoted retainer," said the other with enough of mockery in his voice to give Dalziel some hope for him. "I'm Charles Tillotson, by the way."

"Andrew Dalziel."

"Dee-Ell," echoed Tillotson. "Dee-Ell. Spelt D-A-L-?"

"Z-I-E-L," finished Dalziel.

"How impressive to be pronounced differently from the way you are spelt," said Tillotson, flourishing the pole. "It's sort of a test for people, isn't it? Perhaps I should drop the ILL, Totson. What do you think?"

"How about Tit?" said Dalziel. "Are we going to move or shall we sit here getting wet all bloody day?"

Gingerly he seated himself next to his case and closed his eyes as Tillotson thrust off stylishly, got the pole stuck instantly and almost dislodged himself in his efforts to pull it out.

By the time they had followed the bend of the road and got the rowing-boat back in sight, it had reached the new landing-point and the rest of the party were already embarking. To Dalziel's dismay the funeral car then began to move off.

"Hey!" he bellowed, drawing the attention of the mourners and frightening a small batch of teal who were exploring their new-found territory. But the black limousine purred disdainfully on its way and was soon out of sight.

"Sod the bastard!" said Dalziel savagely.

"Pappy must have forgotten," surmised Tillotson.

"Sod him too."

Some explanation of his presence must have been required and given on the rowing-boat for when they drew level, no one showed much curiosity about him.

The woman, Mrs. Fielding he presumed, was sitting in the stern with the old man. The stout youth had taken an oar and was seated alongside Pappy who returned Dalziel's accusing gaze blankly. The boy was in the bows, curled up like the Copenhagen mermaid. And the other three were crowded in the flat-bottomed boat lately occupied by the coffin.

"I think some of you must go back with Charley," said Mrs. Fielding in a firm, rather deep voice. Her veil was lifted now, revealing a strong almost masculine face which grief and hard weather had only been able to sting to a healthy flush.

"Oh no," protested the thin girl, Louisa. "Bertie's rowing too, and we can't weigh much more than a coffin."

"Nevertheless," insisted her mother.

"I'll go," said the dark hairy man who was taking some shots of the floods with an expensive-looking camera. He stood up and stepped into the punt with the ungainly ease of a sailor.

This seemed to satisfy Mrs. Fielding's distribution problems for the moment. She now addressed Dalziel.

"I'm sorry the car went before Pappy could speak with the driver. If you'd care to come to the house, you can phone from there. Alternatively, we can leave you here and phone on your behalf."

The man called Pappy started rowing and Bertie quickly picked up the stroke as Dalziel considered the alternatives. The rain was coming down harder. The occupants of the rowing-boat were concealed almost completely by a carapace of umbrellas which brought to mind the shield-wall of a Viking ship.

Dalziel turned to Tillotson.

"Follow that boat," he said.

CHAPTER III

A Nourishing Broth

The teal had dropped back to the surface and followed at a safe distance.

"I had a friend," said the ugly man in a pseudo-American accent, "got badly hurt trying to screw a duck."

"Oh, yes?"

"Yeah. He had this thing, you know, about having relationships with the whole of creation. But the duck didn't see it that way. Took half his nose off. After that he changed his scheme, went for the spiritual communion thing more, you know."

"Just as well perhaps," said Dalziel. "He might have had trouble with ants."

The other laughed approvingly.

"That's true, man."

He thinks he's tested me, thought Dalziel. Now I've passed his little shock test, he'll try to patronize me.

"Charley there, the boy with the wooden whanger, now he goes in more for this kind of kick."

He squatted behind the punt gun and made firing noises more appropriate to a howitzer.

"No, Hank, you've got it wrong," protested Tillotson amiably. "I like a bit of sport, that's all. I say, these floods are rather jolly though. I bet a lot of birds will come back. It must have been fine fowling country, this, before they drained it."

"See what I mean?" said the other. "He's just aching to get this old phallic symbol jerking off again."

At last Dalziel had penetrated through the pseudo-mid-Atlantic flip speech style to a couple of recognizable vowels. He liked to know where he was with people and basic information about background was a good place to start. It gave him something to occupy his mind, to keep out the greyness which threatened to seep in whenever he relaxed.

"Not many ducks in Liverpool," he said. "My name's Dalziel. Who're you?"

The dark man looked at him assessingly before replying, "Hank Uniff."

Dalziel laughed, a short sharp offensive bark which acknowledged that there hadn't been much chance of his interlocutor being called Jim Smith or Bill Jones.

"Pleased to meet you," he said. "How was the funeral?"

"Full of images, man," said Uniff. "Hey, Charley, great funeral, huh? I mean, when they dropped the coffin in the hole, well, it was just about water-logged. Cheerist, what a splash!"

"Yes," admitted Tillotson as he passed them in practice of his new technique which involved thrusting the pole into the water off the bows and walking the whole length of the punt. It was inevitable, thought Dalziel, that one so obviously born a victim would sooner or later step over the side.

"Yes," repeated Tillotson, "it *was* rather like a burial at sea. Full fathom five, Tom Bowling, all that. Did you get some good pictures, Hank?"

"I shot off a whole roll," replied Uniff. "But did I get the light right? It wasn't easy to judge and that creepy preacher man didn't help by complaining."

He cradled his camera protectively as if an attempt were being made to wrest it from his hands.

"Didn't Mrs. Fielding object?" queried Dalziel.

"Bonnie? Hell, no. I mean, why, man?"

"Hank's an artist," explained Tillotson, passing them again at a smart trot. His new technique was certainly moving the punt along much faster, but at the expense of direction if one assumed that the rowing-boat was taking the shortest route home. It was now almost out of sight and several points to the nor'-east

Dalziel pulled his coat collar more tightly round his neck and resisted the temptation to take charge of the vessel. He was the super-cargo, not the captain. But something of his feelings must have shown to Uniff who grinned maliciously at his discomfiture and began to whistle "The Skye Boat Song."

"What kind of artist are you, Mr. Uniff?" asked Dalziel.

"What kinds of artist are there, man?" replied Uniff.

"Well," replied Dalziel, irritated, "there's con-artists, and there's shit-artists, and there's . . ."

But his catalogue of abuse was interrupted by the forecast disaster. Tillotson drove the punt forward into a half-submerged hedge, the bows rose in the air, Tillotson screamed and went over the side, Uniff and Dalziel fell together in a tangled heap from which Dalziel recovered just in time to see his suitcase slowly toppling into the water.

Furious, he rose and put his huge hand into the face of Tillotson who was trying to clamber back on board.

"My case!" he yelled. "Get my bloody case!"

Recognizing that this was an essential condition of readmittance, Tillotson pursued the case which had floated only a few feet but was sinking fast. Dalziel took it out of his hands and tried to drain it as, unassisted, the blond youth dragged himself on board, his exertions freeing the punt from the hedge. Uniff all the while took pictures, including one of the pole which for once had not become embedded in the mud but was floating away at a distance of some twenty feet.

Dalziel banged his case down with a force that nearly brought on a new disaster.

"Mr. Dalziel, sir," said Uniff, still photographing. "By the ancient laws of the sea, I elect you captain. What now, man? Are you going to run a tight ship?"

Dalziel swallowed the anger which he realized would not be particularly productive at the present time.

"I might just marry you to this goon," he said, "and see if you could fuck some sense into him."

Instead he swung his wellingtoned foot at the narrow planks which formed the cross seat and his fierce onslaught quickly loosened one sufficiently for it to be torn free. Then, using this as a paddle, he sent the punt in pursuit of the pole.

Uniff now put away his camera and rescued the pole from the water. Tillotson with the natural gallantry of the aristocrat offered to resume his post, but Dalziel with the equally natural bluntness of the peasant told him to keep his hands on his knees and his bum on the floor and not to move on peril of his manhood.

Uniff stepped to the back of the punt and with a vigorous driving stroke which more than made up in efficiency what it lost to Tillotson's in style, he sent the punt scudding over the surface at such a rate that they were only fifty yards behind the rowing-boat as it reached the farther boundary of the water.

There was a lake here, Dalziel surmised, which had overflowed its banks and joined its waters with those of the stream running parallel to the road more than a quarter of a mile behind them. A small landing-stage, waterlogged by the rise in the level of the lake, led to some steps set into a steep sloping garden which rose to a substantial nineteenth-century house in a state of dilapidation not wholly explained even by three days of incessant rain. It was the house he had noticed earlier from the bridge to nowhere and, though close to it lost most of its fairy-tale-castle quality, it still had a solid, fortified look about it.

The other party had disappeared into the house by the time the punt reached the landing-stage and Dalziel did not stand upon ceremony but, using Tillotson's head as a support, he stepped ashore, strode grimly up the garden steps and entered the house without waiting for an invitation. Now he paused, not because of any late revivings of social courtesy but because it was far from clear to him where everyone had disappeared to.

A large entrance hall stretched before him. What might have been elegant wood-panelling had been ruined by the application everywhere of dark brown paint. It was to Dalziel like a nightmarish blow-up of the narrow lobby of his grandmother's house which family loyalties had required must be visited every Sunday although the Presbyterian conscience forbade that anyone should gain pleasure from such a visit. Momentarily he felt like Alice, reduced in scale to a position of total vulnerability.

A door opened. Instead of a monstrous grandmother, Mrs. Fielding emerged and made for the staircase.

Dalziel coughed and she stopped.

"Yes?" she said. "Oh, it's you. There's the telephone. Help yourself."

She turned to go but Dalziel detained her with another thunderous cough.

"I'd like to dry my things," he said. "Get changed. A hot bath would be welcome too."

She looked at him with puzzled, rather disdainful eyes.

"Look, we're *all* wet, but this isn't a hotel," she said. "You might find a towel in the kitchen."

Again she turned.

"Hold on," said Dalziel.

She ignored him and started climbing the stairs.

"Look!" he bellowed after her, losing his patience. "I've been punched on the nose by your daughter, I've been stranded by your boatman, and I've had my case dumped in the water by that long streak of nowt you left in charge of the punt!"

She stopped four stairs up. He couldn't see her face in the shadows, but he got the impression that she was smiling.

"It was your choice to accept the lift," she said reasonably.

"Lady," he answered, "I didn't know what I was doing. But you did. You must have known I'd have had more chance of getting here safely if I'd set out to walk across the blasted water."

Now she laughed out loud.

"We're warned about turning away angels unawares," she said. "I see how easy it could be. Come along, Mr. . . . ?"

"Dalziel," said Dalziel and followed her upstairs, his case leaving a trail of drips which ran parallel to that cast by his sodden coat.

On the landing she paused uncertainly.

"We're a bit crowded at the moment," she explained. "It's a big house, but half the bedrooms haven't been used for years. I wonder . . ."

She opened a door and went in. The room was in darkness but a couple of moments later she opened wide the curtains and beckoned Dalziel in from the threshold.

"You're not superstitious, are you?" she asked. "This was my husband's room. Well, it's got to be used again, I suppose. You don't mind?"

The last question might have been ironical as Dalziel had already opened his suitcase and begun to empty its damp contents on to the bed.

"Not at all," he said. "Very kind."

"There's a bathroom through that door. It communicates with my room, so if it's locked, it'll be because I'm in there."

"Thanks," he said, starting to remove his coat. But she did not leave immediately.

"You said something about being punched on the nose," she prompted.

"It was nothing," he said generously. "A misunderstanding."

"I see. Well, our children seem determined to be

misunderstood, and usually it's someone else who gets hurt. Don't you agree, Mr. Dalziel?"

"I'm not married," said Dalziel, unpeeling his huge sports jacket and revealing broad khaki braces. "And I've no kids."

"Oh. The last of the line, Mr. Dalziel?" she said.

"Aye. You could say. Or the end of the tether."

With neat efficient movements, she gathered the damp clothing from the bed, an act of conservation as well as kindness.

"I'll see to these," she said. "You look as though you could do with a hot bath straight away."

Dalziel was touched by this concern with his health till he saw her gaze fixed on his right hand which had unconsciously unbuttoned his shirt and was presently engaged in scratching his navel.

"Thanks," he said and began to take off his shirt.

The water in the antiquated bathroom was red hot both to the touch and to the sight. Having seen the brown peat water used in the manufacture of the best whisky, Dalziel did not anticipate harm from a little discoloration and wallowed sensuously in the huge marble tub, his feet resting on the brass cherubim taps which time and neglect had verdigrised to a satyric green.

From what he had seen so far of the house, he surmised that the Fielding family had been going through bad times. You needed a lot of cash to keep up a place like this these days. This didn't necessarily mean they were poor, not by his standards. It did mean that probably they had been living beyond their means, or rather that as far as the house was concerned their means had lagged behind their rapidly growing expenditure. He was rather surprised to find himself being so charitable towards the idle rich but whatever the failings of the younger members of the household, Mrs. Fielding had struck him as a pleasant intelligent woman. And handsome with it. Not a word much used of female attractiveness nowadays. You couldn't call loose-haired kids with consumptive eyes and no tits handsome. But Mrs. Fielding was. Oh yes.

One of the cherubim seemed to leer at him with unnecessary salaciousness at this point. A trick of the steam. He got out and towelled himself vigorously.

Back in the bedroom he discovered that his tin of foot powder had become a runny blancmange, so he opened the bathroom cabinet in search of a substitute. There was a mixture of male and female cosmetics and a variety of pill bottles. Either Mrs. Fielding or her late husband was a bit of a hypochondriac, thought Dalziel. It was difficult to tell from the scrawl on the labels. Even the printed words were difficult. Boots of Piccadilly he could manage. But Propananol . . . could that be for athlete's foot? Piles, more likely. There was a tap on the communicating door.

"Just finishing," he called.

"Your trousers were soaking," Mrs. Fielding answered, "so I've put them with the rest to dry. You'll find some things in the wardrobe to wear for the time being if you like. There're hot drinks downstairs."

"Ta," he called. A kind and thoughtful woman, he decided. Once she had made up her mind to be welcoming she carried it through.

Mr. Fielding had clearly not been as fat as Dalziel but he had been tall and broad-shouldered. The trousers wouldn't fasten at the waist, but a long nylon sweater stretched over the cabriole curve of his belly and covered the shameful schism. An old sports jacket, also unfastenable, and a pair of carpet slippers completed the robing and it was time to descend.

Downstairs no sounds offered him a clue to the location of the hot drinks, but after three false starts he at last opened a door into an inhabited room.

"Who the devil are you?" demanded the old man, glaring at him through the steam rising from a mug held at his thin bluish lips.

"Andrew Dalziel. I was given a lift. My car broke down. Can I have some of that?"

He advanced to the broad kitchen table on whose scrubbed wooden top stood a steaming jug.

"No. That's mine. You'll find some on the hob through there."

There was the adjacent back kitchen where on a gas stove coeval almost with the house Dalziel found a pan of what his mother would have called "nourishing broth."

He plucked a large mug from a hook on the wall, filled it and tasted. It was good.

He returned to the other room. Probably nowadays an estate agent would call it a breakfast-room, but the plain wooden furniture pre-dated the studied pseudo-simplicities of modern Scandinavian pine. These chairs threatened real painful splinters to the unwary. Dalziel sat down cautiously.

"Those are my son's clothes you're wearing!" exclaimed the old man. "I recognize them. Even the slippers. Ye gods, ye gods, how little time it takes!"

"My clothes were wet," explained Dalziel, thinking that someone ought to have persuaded the old man also to a change of clothing. The raincoat and umbrella had not been able to protect the bottom of his trousers and his shoes from a soaking.

"I'm sorry about your son," he said.

"Why? Did you know him?"

"No. How could I? I'm here by accident."

"So you say. So you say. Men come, men go, and it's all put down to accident. Have you known Bonnie long?"

"Your daughter-in-law? I don't know her at all, Mr. Fielding," averred Dalziel. "I don't know anyone here."

"No?" The emphasis of Dalziel's answer seemed almost to convince the old man. But only for a moment.

"You're not from Gumbelows, are you?" he suddenly demanded. "Or television? I have positively interdicted television."

Dalziel's patience was wearing thin, but now the door opened and the stout youth who must be Bertie

Fielding came in. He ignored the inmates and passed straight through into the back kitchen, returning a moment later to stare accusingly at Dalziel.

"That's my mug. You've taken my mug."

Dalziel blew on his soup till he set the little globules of fat into a panicky motion.

"Sorry," he said.

Bertie turned once more and went back to the stove.

"My grandson is an ill-mannered lout," said Mr. Fielding sadly.

"Can't think where he gets it from," answered Dalziel.

Bertie returned, drinking soup from what appeared to be an identical mug.

"I hear Charley sank your case," he said, more amicably now. Like a baby who doesn't really mind what teat gets stuck in his mouth, thought Dalziel.

"Mr. Tillotson? Aye, there was a spot of bother," he answered.

"There would be," said Bertie maliciously. "Evidence of divine whimsy is Charley. Looks like a Greek god but things happen to him like Monsieur Hulot."

"You haven't quite got the balance right," mocked Mr. Fielding, explaining to Dalziel, "Bertie likes to rehearse his witty abuse till he's got the lines off pat."

Bertie smiled angrily.

"Still can't bear a rival near the throne, Grandpa?"

"Rival?" exclaimed the old man, pushing himself upright. "When has the eagle considered the boiling fowl a rival? Or the antelope the hog? Good day to you, Mr. Dalziel. If you are as uninvolved in our affairs as you claim to be, it seems unlikely that we shall meet again. On the other hand . . ."

He walked stiffly from the room, his shoes squelching gently on the stone-flagged floor.

"Your grandfather seems a bit upset," probed Dalziel, sucking in a noisy mouthful of broth.

"Yes, he usually does, these days. It's not surprising, I suppose, when you've lost your last surviving child. Especially as he thinks I killed him."

The door opened again at this point and the arrival of Tillotson, Louisa Fielding, Uniff and the Indian Maid masked Dalziel's surprise and prevented him from following up Bertie's statement.

"Hello," said Tillotson. "I say, are your things all right? I hope there's no permanent damage."

"If there is," said Dalziel, "I'll send you a bill."

"That's right, captain," said Uniff. "Don't let him polite talk you out of your legal rights. I'm a witness. Hey, Mavis!"

The Indian Maid came over to them with two mugs of soup. She was really a striking girl with much of Uniff's prominence of feature, but regularized into something approaching beauty. The likeness was confirmed when Uniff said, "Mave, meet the captain. Assumed command in our hour of need. Captain, may I present my sister?"

"How do you do, Mr. Dalziel," said the girl. Her voice confirmed his assessment of Uniff's origins. It was unrepentantly Liverpudlian.

"Pleased to meet you," said Dalziel.

"It was you we saw on the bridge, wasn't it? You looked as if you were going to walk into the water."

"Or on it," said Uniff. "The second coming, nineteen-seventy style."

"He hasn't had much luck stilling the waters this time," said Bertie, peering out of the chintz-curtained window.

The door opened once more and Mrs. Fielding came in.

"Everyone here? Good. Is there plenty of soup to go round? I can't see Herrie. Or Nigel."

"Grandpa was here. But Nigel hasn't been down, has he?"

Bertie looked enquiringly at Dalziel who shook his head.

"I hope he's not mooning around in his damp clothes," said Mrs. Fielding. "Lou, darling, run upstairs and find him. Make him come down."

"But I've not had my soup yet," protested the blonde girl. "Bertie can go. He's nearly finished."

"He'll take no notice of Bertie," her mother answered firmly. "Or worse, even if he was on the point of coming, Bertie would make him change his mind. You go.'"

"Oh bugger," said Louisa. But she went.

Mrs. Fielding came over to the table now and smiled down at Dalziel.

"I just rang the garage," she said.

"I'm sorry, you shouldn't have bothered, I was just going to," answered Dalziel.

"No, it struck me you wouldn't know which was nearest, or best for that matter. Anyway they were a bit worried when I told them where the car was. There's a great deal of water all along that road now and they aren't sure their breakdown truck can get along. Once it stops raining the water will go down pretty quickly, of course."

"So I'm stuck," said Dalziel. "Well, that's life. Well, if I can use your phone, I'll try to find myself a hotel and a taxi. How close can a taxi get?"

"He's worried about another trip with Charley," said Bertie Fielding. "Be comforted, it's just on the south side that the water lies, Mr. Dalziel. The road to the north is a bit damp, but passable. I'd say the Lady Hamilton in Orburn would be your best bet, wouldn't you, Mother?"

Dalziel groaned inwardly, visualizing the under-manager's mixture of dismay and triumph at his return.

"Nonsense, Bertie," she replied. "It's expensive, unhygienic, and nearly ten miles away. Mr. Dalziel will stay with us until he can pick up his car. Please do, Mr. Dalziel. We would all be delighted to have you."

Dalziel looked slowly round the room and saw delight manifest itself in a variety of strange ways. It masqueraded as indifference on Mavis's face, amused knowingness on her brother's, vague uncertainty on Tillotson's and downright dislike of the idea on

Bertie's. Only on Bonnie Fielding's did delight appear in anything approaching full frontal nudity.

"I'd be delighted to stay," said Dalziel.

"Mother," said Louisa from the door.

"Hello, darling. Did you find Nigel?"

"No, but I found this in his bedroom." She held up a piece of paper.

"The little sod's taken off again."

CHAPTER IV

Premises, premises

The general atmosphere of resigned annoyance told Dalziel he was in the middle of a routine upset rather than a major disaster. Nigel, it seemed, had left home to seek his fortune on several previous occasions. Looking at the flaking paint and faded wallpaper around him, Dalziel felt that perhaps the boy had a point. It would take a fool or a clairvoyant to seek a fortune here.

The current weather, however, added a new dimension of concern to this latest escapade, for his mother at least. His brother and sister seemed completely unworried, though the Uniffs whether out of sympathy or politeness were much more helpful.

"He can't have gotten far," said Hank. "Poor kid. He'll soon have his bellyful of this rain."

It was not the most diplomatic use of the idiom. Quickly Mavis stepped in.

"Hank, take a look outside. He might be sheltering quite close. If not, we'll take a run down the road in the car."

Hank left, and Mrs. Fielding sat down at the table. She appeared quite composed now.

"Lou, darling," she said. "How's the soup? Nigel will be freezing when he gets back."

"There's oodles left," said Bertie. "We're hardly down below yesterday's tide mark."

44

"I like it best when we reach that ox-tail we had at New Year," said Louisa. "That was my favourite."

Indifferent to this family humour, Dalziel picked up the note which Mrs. Fielding had dropped on the table.

I am leaving home because (1) my plans for the future don't coincide with yours (2) I have no desire to live off money coined by my father's death and (3) there are some people I don't care to have near me. Nigel. P.S. I don't mean you. I'll write when I'm settled.

He turned it over. It was addressed to the boy's mother.

Hank returned.

"Any sign?" asked Mavis.

"No. But the rowing-boat's gone."

"He always threatened to run away to sea," said Louisa.

"Lou, shut up, will you?" said Mrs. Fielding. "Oh damn. I wish he hadn't taken the boat. I don't like the thought of him on the water."

"Shall I go after him in the punt?" volunteered Tillotson, a suggestion which drew derisive groans from everyone except Mrs. Fielding and Mavis. And Dalziel too, though he groaned internally.

"Thank you, Charles, but no," said Mrs. Fielding. "Hank, did you see Pappy out there?"

"Not a sign," said Uniff.

"See if you can find him and tell him Nigel's loose again. Then perhaps you'll join us in the study. It's time to talk."

Uniff left and the other young people drifted out after him. When Mrs. Fielding spoke, Dalziel noted approvingly, the others jumped. He liked a strong leader.

"I'm sorry to leave you alone, Mr. Dalziel," she said. "But we have to have a business conference. Make yourself at home."

"Thanks," he said. "I'll keep the soup hot for Nigel."

"That boy. You must think us very odd."

Dalziel did not deny it.

"He sounds a sensible lad," he said, indicating the note.

"You think that's sensible?" she asked, surprised.

"Well, it's neatly laid out. One, two, three. I like that," he said with the authority of one whose own official reports were infamous for their brevity. *I came, I saw, I arrested* was the Dalziel ideal according to Pascoe.

"It's possible to be methodical and still find trouble," she answered. "There's probably a cold joint in the pantry if you're hungry. We usually eat on our feet during the day and sit down for a meal about six-thirty."

She left and Dalziel glanced at his watch. It was one o'clock. Five hours.

He went into the kitchen in search of food. There was a small deep freeze into which he peered hopefully. It contained very little and nothing of particular appeal. He shuffled the contents around in the hope of coming across one of his favourite frozen dinners-for-two, but there was no sign of such delights. One foil-wrapped package caught his eyes. The remnants of a cold joint perhaps. He unwrapped it.

"Well bugger me!" said Dalziel.

Inside the foil, sealed in a transparent plastic bag, was a dead rat.

These sods might be hard up but there were limits, he told himself. Gingerly he re-interred the corpse in its icy tomb and closed the lid.

His appetite had left him for the moment so he lit a cigarette and sat down once more to muse upon this odd household.

Just how odd was it? he asked himself. Well, the atmosphere for a start. It didn't feel very funereal. Not that that signified much. He'd been at funerals where by the time the poor sod was planted, half the mourners were paralytic and the rest were lining up for the return to the loved one's house like homesteaders at the start of a land-race.

Anyway atmosphere was too vague. You could breakfast on atmosphere, but you'd better make your dinner out of facts.

Fact one was the age of the non-Fieldings. Coeval with Bertie and Louisa, they were hardly the mourners one would expect at the funeral of a man of Fielding's assumed age.

Fact two was this business conference going on. What were they doing—reading the will? Not likely these days. Then what?

Fact three was the lad, Nigel. His farewell note hinted at household relationships more turbulent than the usual teenage antipathies.

Fact four was the enigmatic remarks people kept dropping about Fielding's death.

And fact five was a freezer with a dead rat in it.

He stood up and dropped his fag end into Bertie's mug. When it came down to it, he distrusted facts almost as much as atmosphere. He knew at least three innocent men who would be bashing their bishops in Her Majesty's prisons for many years to come because of so-called *facts*. On the other hand, on other occasions other *facts* had saved all three from well-deserved sentences. We are in God's hands.

So he abandoned facts and set off on a walkabout of the house hoping to encounter truth.

He strolled along the brown horror of the entrance hall opening doors at random. One room contained a full-size billiard table, presumably the one on which the coffin had rested. There were two or three balls on the table and a cue leaned up against a pocket. Someone had not waited long to resume playing.

Dalziel moved on and reached the next door just as a telephone rang inside.

"Hello!" said old Fielding's reedy but still imperious voice. "Yes. This is Hereward Fielding speaking."

So that's what "Herrie" was short for. Jesus wept!

He remained at the door. He was firmly of the conviction that if you didn't have enough sense to lower your voice, then you either wanted or deserved to be overheard.

"No, I will not change my mind," said Fielding. "And I am too old to be bribed, persuaded or flattered into doing so. Now please, leave me alone. I have just buried my son today, yes, my son. Spare me your sympathy. You may come tomorrow if you wish, but I make no promises about my availability. Good day."

The phone was replaced with a loud click. Dalziel pushed open the door and entered.

The room was large and ugly, its furnishings and decoration old enough to be tatty without getting anywhere near the ever-shifting bourne of the antique. Fielding had turned from the telephone to a wall cabinet, the door of which seemed to be jammed. He glanced up at Dalziel.

"Oh, it's you," he said, heaving. The door flew open and a glass unbalanced and fell to the threadbare carpet. He ignored it, but plucked another from inside and with it a bottle. Dalziel fixed his gaze on this. It took a strong man to stand with a bottle in one hand, a glass in the other, and not offer him a drink.

"Can I help you?" asked Fielding.

"No. The others seem to be in conference and I was just having a look around," said Dalziel.

"Were you? Well, this room, by general consensus the coldest and draughtiest in this cold and draughty house, is sometimes regarded as my sitting-room. Though naturally should anyone else wish to eat, drink, sleep, play records, make love or merely take a walk in it, my selfish demands for privacy are not allowed to get in the way."

"That's good of you," said Dalziel heartily, closing the door behind him. "Terrible, this weather. I pity all the poor sods on holiday."

"I understood *you* were on holiday," said Fielding, filling his glass.

"So I am," said Dalziel, mildly surprised at the idea. "Pity me then. Yes, it's still chucking it down. I hope your grandson's all right."

"What?"

"Your grandson. He's run away, I believe. I'm sorry, didn't you know?"

The old man took a long swallow from his glass. What was it? wondered Dalziel. He couldn't see the label which was obscured by Fielding's long bony fingers, but the liquid was an attractive pale amber.

"It would be too optimistic to hope you might mean Bertie?" said Fielding.

"No. The lad. Nigel."

"I feared so. It was ever thus. Wilde was wrong. You don't have to kill the things you love. Just wait long enough and they'll go away."

"Who?" said Dalziel, pouncing on this further reference to killing and wanting to get its provenance right.

"Who? You mean, who . . . Oscar Wilde. *The Ballad of Reading Gaol.*"

"Oh, the poof," said Dalziel, his interest evaporating.

Unexpectedly Fielding laughed.

"That's the one," he said. "Will you have a drink, Mr. . . .?"

"Dalziel. Yes, I will." Here's another one who thinks he's summed me up and can start patronizing me, thought Dalziel as his huge hand held the glass he had retrieved from the floor steadfastly under the bottle till the meniscus touched the rim and Fielding said ironically, "Say when."

It was brandy, a cheap brand Dalziel suspected, not from any connoisseurship of the liquor but by simple taste-bud comparison with the smoothness of his own favourite malt whisky. Something of his reaction must have shown and he realized he had inadvertently got back at Fielding for his suspected condescension when the old man said, "I'm sorry, it's not terribly good, but these days we all have to make sacrifices."

"It's fine. Just the job for this weather," said Dalziel, emptying his glass and proffering it for a refill.

"The weather. Yes. That foolish boy. I hope he

will be all right. He never goes far, at least he didn't when Conrad—that's his father, my son—was alive."

"Fond of his dad, was he?"

"Very," said the old man firmly.

"But he still ran away, even then?"

"Certainly. It's in the family. Conrad was always taking off when he was a boy. I myself ran off to join the Army in 1914. I was sixteen at the time."

"Did they take you?" asked Dalziel.

"Not then. I looked very young. We *were* younger then, you know. Balls dropping, menstruation, it all happened later in my generation. But now they seem to need jockstraps and brassieres in the cradle."

Fielding laughed harshly.

"Anyway, it was a blessing I see now. I went legally and forcibly in 1916 and within six months I was ready to run away again, home this time."

"It must have been terrible," said Dalziel with spurious sympathy. "All that mud."

"Mud? Oh no. I don't mean the trenches. I never really saw the trenches. It was just the sheer boredom of the whole thing that made me want to run away. Very unfashionable. I wrote a book about my experiences a few years after the war. A light, comic thing, it went down well enough with your general reader, but it put me in bad with the intelligentsia for the next decade. But then I did a bit of Eliot-bashing and that was a help. Even so, I still got the cold shoulder, more or less, until the fifties. After that it was just a question of survival. Hang on long enough and you're bound to become a Grand Old Man. Like the essays Paul Pennyfeather set in *Decline and Fall*. The reward is for length, regardless of merit."

He laughed again, a series of glottally stopped cracks, like a night-stick rattling along metal railings. Dalziel contemplated making him laboriously explain what he had just said, sentence by sentence, but decided against it on the grounds that the poor old sod probably couldn't help himself.

"So you're not too worried about the boy?"

"In the sense that he is too sensible to contribute willingly to his own harm, no. But as you say, the weather is appalling and in addition, we live in troubled times, Mr. Dalziel. The post-war period is an age of unbalance, of violence. Women and children cannot wander around with impunity as in my boyhood. Even the police seem more likely to be a source of molestation than a protection against it."

"They've a hard job," said Dalziel mildly.

"I dare say. They certainly make hard work of finding an answer to the crime wave."

"Oh, the answer's simple," said Dalziel. "Charge two guineas a pint for petrol, have a dusk to dawn curfew, and deport regular offenders to Manchester."

It was a Yorkshire joke. Fielding was not very amused.

"It's in man's mind, not his motorways that the answer lies," he said reprovingly. "Has Bonnie organized a search for Nigel? No, you said they were in conference, didn't you? Conference! You see how this house is run, Mr. Dalziel!"

Dalziel felt impelled to defend Bonnie Fielding.

"The man, Pappy, has been warned to keep a lookout. The lad took the boat, it seems."

"Worse and worse," said the old man angrily. "That fool Papworth is totally unreliable. Let's go and find him and you'll see."

He drained his glass and led the way out at a pace which had Dalziel's borrowed carpet slippers flip-flopping on the uncarpeted floor.

Dalziel paused in the hallway as he heard the sound of raised voices drifting down the stairs. Someone, it sounded like Bertie, was shouting angrily and other voices mingled in the background.

"Come on!" commanded Fielding, irritated by the delay and obediently Dalziel followed him through a door which led into a new complex of meaner corridors running through what presumably had once been the servants' quarters.

Fielding strode on ahead till he reached a door on which he rapped imperiously. Then without waiting for a reply, he flung it open with an aplomb which won Dalziel's professional admiration.

The room looked as if it had been furnished from an army surplus sale. The metal bed was made up with a neatness that invited inspection and the objects on the bedside locker—ashtray, alarm clock and a box of matches—were placed at the corners of an isosceles triangle.

Pappy was not there and in an almost unconscious reflex Dalziel stepped into the room and opened the metal wardrobe. It contained a couple of jackets and an old but well preserved black suit.

Glancing round, he realized that Fielding was regarding him strangely. Bursting into a servant's room was evidently OK, but searching it was something else.

"He's not here then," said Dalziel.

"No. I doubt if he spends a great deal of time in the wardrobe."

"Perhaps he's out looking."

"Hah!" snorted Fielding, setting off again. Dalziel followed after glancing out of the window. It was still raining and the cobbled yard which lay outside was inches deep in water so that it looked like a sea of semolina. For the second time since coming into this house, Dalziel felt a sense of physical belittlement.

Fielding was knocking on another door now, more gently this time and without trying the handle. A woman's voice answered from within.

"Who is it?"

"Mr. Fielding. Sorry to trouble you, Mrs. Greave, but I'm looking for Papworth. Do you know where he is?"

After a short interval, the door was opened by a bright-eyed woman of about forty, whose magenta-tinted hair and green dressing-gown wound tight around her body gave her the look of a cornfield poppy. She was not unattractive in a bold and brassy kind of way.

"I was having a nap," she said with more of accusation than explanation in her voice.

"I'm sorry," said Fielding. "Do you know where Papworth is?"

"No," said the woman yawning, showing good teeth in a moist pink mouth. Her glance flickered towards Dalziel who looked her up and down from her bare feet to the untidy brightness of her hair and leered grotesquely at her. Dalziel's leer was so unambiguous that it was like a lesser man exposing himself. Mrs. Greave screwed up her mouth in distaste and said, "Sorry, I've no idea. I'd better start thinking about dinner, I suppose, so if you'll excuse me."

She began to close the door but Dalziel leaned forward so that his belly curved into the doorway. It was more subtle than putting your foot in the jamb.

Sniffing noisily, he said, "Is something burning?"

The woman half turned, then swung back again to prevent Dalziel from entering the room.

"No," she said, and swung the door to so violently that he had to skip back to avoid a collision. But he smiled to himself as they moved on. He had penetrated far enough to see a man's suede shoe lying on the floor. It looked wet.

"So she's the cook, is she?" he asked.

"So rumour has it," said Fielding drily. "It was probably the dinner you smelt burning."

Dalziel laughed. It was turning out to be a very interesting household, this. It had to be Papworth who was in the woman's room. Perhaps he was just taking evasive action. With this old fusspot on the prowl, who could blame him? Though, of course, you didn't need to take your shoes off to hide.

"Papworth's knocking her off, is he?" he said, voicing his thought.

"Who?"

"Mrs. Greave. The cook."

Fielding laughed again.

"I hope not," he said. "She's his daughter!"

"His daughter?" echoed Dalziel. "You're sure?"

"No one can ever be sure of their father," said

Fielding. "We believe what we're told, don't we? Come on. We might find him in the Hall."

It seemed that this hunt for Papworth was becoming an obsession with the old man. Dalziel's own enthusiasm had waned, partly because he still had not discarded his theory about Papworth's whereabouts (a man could visit his daughter in her bedroom, couldn't he?) but mainly because Fielding now proposed that they should go out into the rain-filled yard.

"Hold on," he said at the door. "Where are we going?"

"Just over there," said Fielding, pointing to a long high-roofed building which ran out from the main house. It looked as if it might once have been a stables, but surprisingly in this neglected house, this particular block looked as if someone had been working on it fairly recently, an impression confirmed by the wording on a sign propped against the wall. *Gibb and Fowler, Building Contractors, Orburn.*

"It joins up with the house," said Dalziel reasonably. "Can't we get into it without going outside?"

"If you must," said the old man crossly, shutting the door.

Their route this time took them through a new world in the form of a large room (or perhaps two or three rooms knocked into one) where the old stone walls had been plastered and painted a brilliant blue. On one side were a pair of large freezers and on the other, gleaming in silver and white, a row of microwave ovens. It was like stepping out of a bus shelter into a space ship.

"What's all this?" asked Dalziel in bewilderment.

"We drink a lot of soup," said Fielding, not stopping to offer further explanation but pressing on through the room with unflagging speed.

Dalziel followed down another short corridor, then into the building which was the object of Fielding's forced march.

Here he halted and let his eyes get used to the dim light filtering through the narrow arched windows. If the microwave ovens had been a step forward out of the nineteenth century, what was going on here was just as determined a step back.

The building had been a stables he reckoned with an upper floor used perhaps as a hay-loft. This floor had now been removed with the exception of a small section at the far end which had been transformed into a kind of minstrels' gallery. The joists supporting the arched roof had clearly lacked something in antiquity and they were being supplemented by a new fishbone pattern of age-blackened beams, standing out starkly against the white-washed interstices. Dalziel rapped his knuckles against one of these beams which was leaning against the wall, prior to elevation. It rang hollowly and felt smooth and cold to the touch. Dalziel was not repelled. He had nothing against plastic. He would as lief eat off colourful Formica as polished mahogany. Nor did it seem distasteful to him that the panes of stained "glass" which were being fitted into the windows were plastic also. His reaction was one of simple puzzlement.

To what end would the Fieldings be transforming an old stables into something that looked like a set for a remake of *Robin Hood*?

Old Fielding, having peered into various recesses and through various doors, now abandoned his search for Papworth and returned to enjoy Dalziel's bewilderment.

"What do you think of this?" he asked, gesturing with a flamboyance more in keeping with his surroundings than his person. "Is it not a fit monument for our times? What would Pope have had to say?"

"Monument?" said Dalziel, wondering momentarily if the old man was being literal and this place was indeed intended to be some sort of mausoleum, a kind of bourgeois Taj Mahal. But what about the ovens?

The answer was obvious.

"It's a café," said Dalziel.

This solution sent the old man into paroxysms of laughter which modulated into a coughing bout from which it seemed unlikely he would recover. Dalziel watched for a moment coldly, then administered a slap between his shoulder-blades which brought the dust up out of the old man's jacket and sent him staggering against a section of stone reproduction wall which gave visibly.

"Thank you," said Fielding. "Though I fear the cure was more dangerous than the disease. Well now. A café. Yes, that's the word. Not the word that will be used, of course, should this sad enterprise ever come to fruition. No. Then this place will be called a *Banqueting Hall*. My daughter-in-law is too careful, I think, to risk the penalties prescribed under the Trades Descriptions Act by calling it a Medieval Banqueting Hall, but the word 'medieval' will certainly appear somewhere on the prospectus."

"People will eat here," said Dalziel.

The prospect did not displease him. Eating was one of the Four Deadly Pleasures. Though he could not see the necessity for all these trappings. A meal was a meal.

"That's right. A dagger and a wooden platter. At a given signal, chicken legs will be thrown over the right shoulder. It's a pastime very popular I believe in the North-East where the past is still close and tribal memories are long. My foolish family believe the inhabitants of Orburn and district will be equally gullible. The dreadful thing is, they may be right."

"There's still a bit of work to be done," observed Dalziel. "Where are the builders today?"

"They would not come today," said the old man significantly.

"No? Oh, of course. Sorry. The funeral."

Fielding laughed again, but this time, with a wary eye on Dalziel's hand, he kept it to a controlled barking.

"Builders are not noted for their delicacy, Mr. Dalziel, not here, anyway."

Dalziel ran his mind's eye down a list of building contractors working in his area and had to agree.

"What then? The weather?"

"Money, Mr. Dalziel. When the head goose has been killed, you make damn sure someone else is going to start dropping the golden eggs."

"Ah," said Dalziel. "Then this business conference . . .?"

But his cross-examination was interrupted.

"You looking for me, Mr. Fielding?" said a voice from above.

They looked up. Leaning over the rail of the minstrels' gallery was Papworth.

"There you are," said Fielding. "About time too. Have you seen anything of my grandson yet? Young Nigel?"

"No," said Papworth. "Should I have done?"

"Don't you know he's missing? Hasn't anyone told you?" demanded Fielding.

"No," said Papworth. "I've been busy. What's the fuss?"

"The boy's run off again. It seems he's taken the rowing-boat and naturally we are all very worried."

"The rowing-boat," said Papworth thoughtfully.

"That's right, man. Aren't you going to do anything? You can take the punt out and scout around, if you are not too busy, that is."

You didn't have to be a detective to spot the dislike the old man felt for Papworth, thought Dalziel. If only all relationships were so clear!

"No. That's just what I was going to do when I heard you wanted me," said Papworth.

"But you said you didn't know the boy was missing," interjected Dalziel.

"No. But the boat is. Or was."

"Was?"

"Yes. I can see it drifting out beyond the island. But one thing's certain. There's no one in it."

CHAPTER V

A Pleasant Surprise

For the second time that day, the three men got soaking wet. Papworth seemed impervious to the rain as he propelled the gun-punt over the water with strong economical strokes, but Dalziel was concerned about the old man who had rejected all attempts to make him stay ashore. His clothes were clinging to his body, accentuating its frailty, and the skin of his face seemed to have shrunk in the downpour and be clinging almost transparently to his patrician skull.

Dalziel himself drew comfort from the thought that this time at least it was not his own clothes that were getting wet. There was a philosophy in there somewhere if he had the time or energy to winkle it out. Or a rule of life at least. He was dimly aware that his blacker moments were often survived only because he had certain usually unspecified and often arbitrary rules of life to cling on to, though whether these added up to the weight and dignity of something called a *philosophy* he did not know. Duty was one of them, or at least the notion that a man got out of bed and went to his work no matter what he felt like, and saw the job through if he could manage it without collapsing. It had proved a useful and necessary rule in recent weeks.

The rowing-boat was drifting with one oar missing

and the other trailing from the rowlock. The island referred to by Papworth was, Dalziel realized, a real island in the real lake, with water lapping shallowly at the roots of the trees growing there. It would be possible to land here still at the expense only of getting your feet wet, and he scanned the trees closely. They were willows mainly, packed tight together as though drawing back from the threatening waters, but the total area of the island couldn't have been more than a quarter-acre and he felt pretty certain that Nigel was not lurking there, watching them pass.

Nor was the boy in the boat. Papworth had asserted it was empty from the start, but Dalziel had not been so positive. You could lie in the bottom of a boat and not be seen from the shore, he suspected. But the boy was not in it and suddenly the dimensions of the problem had changed.

Papworth jumped lightly into the boat and pulled the trailing oar inboard. From the punt Dalziel examined the rowing-bench closely, looking for he did not know what.

"Where's it come from?" he demanded.

"God knows," said Papworth with a shrug.

"Can't you tell?" said Dalziel.

"They don't leave tracks," said Papworth. "And there's no regular currents, tides, that sort of thing here. No, the wind'd move it most, and *you* tell *me* which quarter that's in."

He was right. What wind there was gusted fitfully from no constant direction.

Old Fielding who had been uncharacteristically quiet ever since they had left the shore now said, "There's an oar missing. Surely if we can find that, it will give us a clue."

"Mebbe," said Papworth laconically. "But to what?"

"Listen," said Dalziel, glowering at the impassive boatman. "There's three things. The boat could have drifted back from wherever Nigel got off; or it could just have drifted away from the landing-stage in the first place and the boy's on the road; or if he did

have a spot of trouble he could be stranded on a tree
or on top of a hedge or something. He can swim,
can't he?"

"Like a fish," said Fielding.

"Right then," said Dalziel, standing so that the
punt rocked dangerously. He ignored the movement
and scanned the waters. It was pretty obvious where
the lake proper ended and the floods began. A line
of trees and half-submerged undergrowth delineated
the sweep of the farther bank and beyond this, the
geometric outlines of fields were marked where their
hedges broke the surface of the water.

"OK," said Dalziel. "Shout."

"What?"

"Shout," he said. "If he is stuck somewhere, he'll
answer."

They started to shout, sometimes separately and
sometimes with Fielding's reedy tenor, Papworth's
strong baritone and Dalziel's totally unmusical bel-
low blending into a single dreadful cry. The damp
air absorbed all their effort with indifferent ease and
returned nothing.

"Let's try a bit farther out," said Dalziel finally,
reaching for the punt pole. But as he did so, he
realized their yellings had not gone entirely unheard.
Standing in the garden near the flooded landing-
stage were the rest of the Fieldings and Tillotson. He
guessed what anxieties were swarming through Bonnie's mind and spoke to Papworth.

"We'd best let Mrs. Fielding know what's on," he
said. "Can you scout a bit farther in that thing while
I take the punt back?"

"If you like," said Papworth. He removed the oar
from the thole-pin and using it as a rather cumber-
some paddle began to move away.

"Where's that fellow going?" demanded Fielding.
He looked to be in the extremities of distress, both
physical and mental. Even without his daughter-in-
law's right to an explanation, it would have been
necessary to get him back to the house soon.

"He's going to search," said Dalziel, wielding the

pole inexpertly and for the first time feeling some sympathy for Tillotson. "We'd better get back to the house and organize things there."

Mrs. Fielding remained controlled when she heard what Dalziel had to say, but he sensed a strong underlying concern.

"Let's get inside," she said. "Herrie, you're soaking! What possessed you to go out in only your jacket?"

She gave a half-accusing glance at Dalziel. She had the kind of solid, bold-eyed face much admired by the Edwardians and which had still stared provocatively at an adolescent Dalziel from Scarborough What-the-Butler-Saw machines a couple of decades later. He felt an in the circumstances incongruous urge to wink invitingly.

Surprisingly in the light of her earlier indifference, Louisa was outwardly the most agitated.

"We can't just hang about, doing nothing," she cried. "Let's get something organized."

Her urgency seemed to infect the others and her mother and brother began to move back to the house at an accelerated pace almost beyond the means of the old man who hung on to his daughter-in-law with the stoic look of one who is ready at a moment's notice to make his final exit.

Dalziel followed, eager to get out of the rain but without any feeling of urgency. He doubted whether speed was going to contribute much to Nigel Fielding's safety now. Either the lad was safe or his body was waiting to be grappled from the water by a boat-hook. But the illusion of great activity was a useful anodyne.

The Uniffs who had had enough sense to stay out of the wet met them at the door and received explanations in the hall.

Mavis displayed the same calm competence as before and even Hank made conventional soothing noises, putting his arm around Louisa's thin shoulders and pressing his *University of Love* T-shirt (the same one? or did he have duplicates?) against her soaking sweater whose new skin-clinging properties managed the merest hint of a female figure.

"We must ring the police," she said. Dalziel sighed and prepared to step forward to reveal himself. It would be unprofessional to let this short-tempered girl give her unstructured and semi-hysterical account of the situation to the local bobby when he could get things moving in half the time.

"Perhaps," he began. And the telephone rang. For a moment they all froze. It was Bonnie Fielding who was quickest off the mark, heading for the room which old Fielding claimed as his own.

They heard her pick up the phone.

"Nigel!" she exclaimed.

"Yes," she said, as the rest of them crowded into the room. "Yes. Look, Nigel, where are . . . no . . . oh, damn!"

It was clear from her face that the boy had rung off.

"Where is he?" demanded Fielding.

"I'm sorry, Herrie," said the woman. "But he didn't say. Just that he wanted us to know he was OK. He saw the boat go adrift after he'd abandoned it and thought I'd be worried. Anyway, thank God he's safe. Now, Herrie, let's see about you before you get pneumonia."

She ushered the old man out of the room, and though the news of his grandson's safety revived him enough to snap a token protest at this unwanted solicitude, he let himself be led upstairs with no physical demur.

"End of crisis," said Uniff cheerfully. "All's well, etcetera."

The telephone rang again and the bearded man picked it up.

"Hi," he said. "Yeah. Look, man, you take that up with the Post Office, OK? No, she's not available right now. I mean, we just had the funeral so she may not want to talk insurance. OK. I'll tell her."

He replaced the phone.

"Sphincter?" said Bertie.

"That's it. Seems to think we're trying to avoid him. The usual moans. He's a pain. I should have asked if we were insured against Nig's taking off!"

Louisa's sibling solicitude, recently overflowing, was now completely spilt.

"Little bastard," she said. "He should have been drowned at birth."

"That's a bit strong," protested Tillotson, but she ignored him and followed Uniff out of the room.

Tillotson caught Dalziel's eye and grinned sheepishly.

"Someone ought to tell Pappy," said Bertie suddenly. He was right, thought Dalziel, but he obviously had no intention of doing anything about it himself.

"Yes, they should," said Tillotson. "I'll take the punt."

He left, whistling cheerfully.

"Go with him," said Dalziel.

"Do you mean *me*?" said Bertie incredulously.

"I'm not so old I see bloody spectres," said Dalziel. "Who else? You really want a drowning on your hands, then let that lad go punting by himself. Hurry up."

"Why can't you go?" demanded Bertie.

"I'm older than you," said Dalziel, patience draining away. "And I'm colder than you, and I'm wetter than you, and I'm a guest in your fucking house, and I don't care a toss if yon silly bugger ends up in the South Pacific. But he's *your* friend. So get a bloody move on!"

Bertie moved, looking rather dazed. At the door he paused, opened his mouth goldfish-like, but left without speaking.

"You've had practice," said Mavis admiringly. "What was it? Army?"

Dalziel had lost sight of her presence and looked at her assessingly, working out if an apology were in order. He decided not.

"Not really," he said. "Natural leadership qualities. That one needs a bit of stirring."

"Mebbe so," said the girl. "But don't be too certain about Bertie. Some people develop that kind of complacency as a cover. The world's ruled by calm, smug, self-righteous pigs, and they've all been clever enough to get to the top of the dungheap."

"Cocks," said Dalziel.

"Eh?" said the girl warily.

"It's cocks on dunghills, not pigs," he explained. "I don't expect there's a lot of nature study in Liverpool."

"You'd be surprised. Hank's right. You *are* wet. Better get into something dry or you might find yourself spending more time here than you plan."

"I don't *plan* to spend any time here," said Dalziel. "What about you? Just down for the funeral, are you?"

She shook her head, her straight black hair moving with it and stopping when the negative movement stopped. It was heavy and wiry, perfectly natural and with none of the gloss and bounce the TV commercials projected as the most desirable qualities of the female—and male—coiffure.

"No," she said. "Business, mainly."

Dalziel sneezed.

"Business," he echoed invitingly, but all she answered was, "You're mad to hang around like that."

"I suppose I am," he said. "I'd best go and see if I can borrow any more clothes from the late lamented. Hey, he didn't die of anything catching, I hope?"

"Not unless having a hole drilled through your chest's catching."

"What?"

"He fell off a ladder in the Banqueting Hall," said Mavis. "You've seen the Banqueting Hall, have you? Well, when the builders stopped coming, Conrad decided to have a go at the do-it-yourself. He was up the ladder with an electric drill trying to fix one of the beams. The ladder slipped. Down he came. Unfortunately he fell on to the drill and it was locked on. Straight through his ribs into the heart. Goodbye, Conrad."

"That's nasty," commented Dalziel, more because he felt it was expected of him than because he felt any distress. But it was certainly an interesting way to go.

"Was he by himself?"

"Yes."

"So no one saw it happen?"

"What do you want? Colour pictures?"

"No. I don't think so. Well, I'd best get dried. It's been nice talking to you, Miss Uniff."

"Mavis will do. It makes me feel younger."

"You want to feel younger?" he said, surprised.

"Oh yes," she answered. "When I see what age does to you, I want to feel as young as I can possibly get, Mr. Dalziel."

"And what does age do to you?"

"It makes you crazy for money, I think," she said slowly. "Like, in the end perhaps that's the only way left to keep on pretending you're young."

"I've stopped pretending," grinned Dalziel.

"That's what they all think. But you'll see. You're not rich are you, Mr. Dalziel?"

"Does it matter?"

"It might do. If you've got money and you stay in this house much longer, you'll be offered a deal. You might not even notice but you will. Go and get dry now."

Dalziel lay naked in the dead man's bed under half a dozen blankets. After stripping off his wet clothes and towelling himself down till his flabby and fat-corrugated skin glowed, suddenly a warm nap had seemed best of all things.

He had pondered a long time on the events of the day and decided that though there was enough in this household to make him curious, so far it was curiosity at a personal rather than professional level. There must have been an inquest on Fielding and the usual investigations. It wouldn't require much effort on his part to get an unofficial look at the finding. But he had no intention of doing so. Oh no.

This was an interesting interlude, a bit damper but probably a bit more lively than following a guide round some mouldy cathedral or making conversation with some poofy hotel barman. But tomorrow he'd be on his way. If they couldn't do anything about his car, then sod it. He'd hire another and collect his own later.

Relaxed by his resolve, he fell asleep.

When he awoke it was quarter to six and he was starving. He rubbed his eyes, yawned, scratched his groin sensuously and headed for the bathroom.

What kind of nosh did they dish up here? he wondered as he pushed open the door. Old Fielding had made some nasty crack about Mrs. Greave, the cook. But it'd have to be very bad to blunt Dalziel's appetite tonight.

The bathroom was full of steam. He paused in the doorway. Someone moved among the wraith of vapour and he had no difficulty in recognizing Mrs. Fielding though her head was half covered by a towel and the rest of her body was not covered by anything but a healthy post-hot-bath glow.

"Beg pardon," he said, stepping back and closing the door. But he couldn't close out the mental picture of what he had seen and when he sat down on the bed, he realized he had the beginnings of an erection.

He whistled softly as he considered the phenomenon. He was far from being a sexual obsessive. Indeed, since his wife had left him, his sex life had been minimal. Not that opportunity was short. Like any society dedicated to money and male chauvinism, Yorkshire provided the kinds of relief strong men need from the pressures of the day. But a police officer had to be very careful. It was on the surface a very conventional society and scandals were easily kindled. As for paying for it, Dalziel refused on a point of pride rather than principle.

So generally he went without. It wasn't too difficult. With age, lust became an aesthetic tingle rather than a physical shock. It was a long time since desire had manifested itself to him so uncompromisingly as this!

He felt absurdly pleased with himself, as though something valuable had been proven. She was a fine-looking woman, mature, well-fleshed, without the flabbiness which his own once well-muscled body had declined to. He looked down at himself with distaste and his pleasure drained away at the thought that this ton of lard was all that she had had to look at in return. Not many women reacted to the pleasure of visual stimuli in the same way as men, but revulsion at ugliness must be a shared reaction.

There was a tap at the bathroom door and he jumped up, and dragged a blanket off the bed and wound it round him.

"May I come in?" she called.

"Yes," he answered.

She entered, wearing a dressing-gown and carrying with her a coathanger festooned with his clothes.

"This lot's dry," she said. "I've been over them with an iron, so they should be fit to wear."

"That's kind," he said stiltedly.

"I brought them an hour ago, but the bedroom door was locked. You must be a distrustful soul, Mr. Dalziel. Whereas me, I don't even remember to lock the bathroom."

She laughed as she spoke, but he took it as a rebuke.

"I'm sorry, Mrs. Fielding," he began.

"For what?" she said. "I'd be sorry if you were altogether sorry. We'll be eating soon. First come, first served, so I shouldn't hang about."

She went back through the bathroom and Dalziel followed her a few moments later, making sure the door into the farther bedroom was locked before setting about his ablutions.

She was a kind woman, he thought, and she didn't shock easily. But that was hardly a basis to build erotic fantasies on. She didn't sleep with her husband, that was an interesting point. Could be good. Could be bad. He'd guessed at first it was because the poor sod was sick. But now it seemed he'd died from an accident.

Dalziel opened the cabinet again. One shelf was now entirely clear and all the pill bottles had gone. The process of clearing out in the wake of the departed had begun.

Or perhaps, some ridiculous and hitherto unsuspected romantic area of his imagination suggested, perhaps she had cleared the space for him, anticipating a longer than overnight stay . . .

These were mere hunger-fantasies, he told himself. He shook them out of his head and began to dress.

CHAPTER VI

A Step into Summer

Dinner was served in the room in which they had taken their nourshing broth. The only alteration was the covering of the big kitchen table with a white cloth liberally spotted with the stains of previous meals and with one corner unravelling. Mrs. Greave was present to start with, emerging from the back kitchen with a series of covered serving dishes which she deployed over the table with more panache than strategy. Dressed now in a pair of tight-fitting yellow slacks and a flowered blouse, with her red hair piled high in a precarious beehive, she looked less like a flower of the field and more like some exotically gaudy insect. Dalziel made no attempt to make contact with her, but he felt her eyes examining him from time to time as she came in and out.

"You all right now, Mrs. Fielding?" she asked finally.

"Yes, thank you, Mrs. Greave," said Bonnie from the head of the table.

"Good night then."

She left and there was a general uncovering of serving dishes as though no one had cared to delve beneath the china surface while the cook was still in the room.

"I can't believe it," said Louisa.

"What?"

"Sausages. And some of them look only mildly burnt. First or second degree."

"It must be because we've got a visitor."

Pleased to be thought the cause of such a treat though unable to comprehend its particular nature, Dalziel seated at Bonnie's right hand in the place of honour piled bangers and mash on to his plate.

"Mr. Fielding not coming down?" he asked, glancing round the table.

"No. He's a bit under the weather, I fear. He's well over seventy you know and today's been a great strain," said Bonnie.

"I hope he doesn't snuff it before Gumbelow's cough up," said Louisa.

"Would it make any difference? The award has been announced," mumbled a fast-chewing Bertie whom Dalziel had picked out as his only serious rival in the race for a second dip into the depleted sausage dish.

"Children!" reproved Bonnie. "This is no way to talk!"

She smiled apologetically at Dalziel. She was wearing a white sleeveless blouse, semi-transparent. Her right bra strap had slipped and was visible at her shoulder. Dalziel concentrated on his plate.

"What's Gumbelow's?" he asked.

"Oh, haven't you heard?" said Tillotson, "Herrie's got an award."

"What for?" asked Dalziel, meaning to be polite. But they all laughed.

"That would please him!" said Uniff. "Where've you been, man? Herrie's a great poet. At least that's what Gumbelow's have decided. Yes, sir. Sixty years, but they get there in the end!"

"It's an American thing called the Gumbelow Foundation," explained Bonnie seeing Dalziel's puzzlement. "They have various artistic prizes they dish out every so often. Herrie's will, of course, be for his poetry. He gets a silver plaque, I believe."

"It should be a silver loo seat for the stuff he writes," said Bertie viciously. "Ouch!"

He started to rub his leg, glancing round the table as he did so. Plainly someone had kicked him beneath the table, but it was impossible to tell who. Dalziel put away two sausages and a substantial portion of mash while his rival was recovering and sent grateful vibrations out to the assailant.

"Of course there's the money too," said Bonnie. "Fifteen thousand."

"Pounds?" asked Dalziel, amazed.

"Oh no. Dollars."

But even *dollars*, he thought. Fifteen thousand. For *poetry*.

Uniff was grinning at him, openly amused.

"Are we getting to you now, Mr. Dalziel? That old silvery, tinkly sound?"

"I'm a plain, poor man," responded Dalziel. "I know nowt about poetry, and I wouldn't recognize fifteen thousand dollars if it got into bed with me."

"Well, you may have the chance to see it," said Bonnie. "These people want to have a little award ceremony. Herrie's too old to go wandering across the Atlantic so he's told them that if they want to give him anything, they have to come here. It's a marvellous bit of cheek really, but, as he says, he didn't ask them to make the award."

"He also says he doubts he'll live long enough to enjoy the money," said Uniff.

"What's that mean?" said Bonnie, staring across the table at the bearded man.

"It means he's old, and he's sick, and what the hell is there down here you can spend fifteen grand on," answered Uniff slowly and coldly.

There was a pause of complete silence, even Dalziel stilling his champing jaws for a moment.

"There's the restaurant," said Louisa brightly.

Uniff roared with laughter.

"You know what your grandfather thinks of the restaurant, Lou," said Bonnie reprovingly. "We've been through all this before."

"Now that'd be the place out back," said Dalziel. "The one that's being done up."

"You've seen it?" said Bonnie, surprised.

"Mr. Dalziel gets around quite a lot," said Uniff with a malicious inflection Dalziel found it hard to understand.

"Your father-in-law took me in there this afternoon," explained Dalziel. "Looking for Papworth."

"Ah. And what did you think?"

"It looked—" he searched for a word which would combine admiration and reservation—"all right."

Uniff and the young Fieldings laughed. Dalziel glared at them. They didn't know how lucky they were that he chose to pick his words carefully. Their amusement stung him to go on.

"Me," he said, "I don't much care where I eat. If the food's good and there's lots of it, the surroundings don't matter."

He dug out a spoonful of sausages from under Bertie's questing hand.

"You're missing the point, Mr. Dalziel, baby," said Uniff.

"Oh aye?" grunted Dalziel.

"The thing with this medieval banquet kick is the food doesn't matter. Serve up this—" he held up an impaled sausage—"and call it King Henry's Banger and they'll shovel them down. What we're talking about is the cafeteria system with five-star prices. You dig?"

"I know nowt about the catering trade," said Dalziel heavily, "but that sounds fraudulent to me."

"Hank's exaggerating as usual," said Bonnie quickly. "This is a simple business enterprise, Mr. Dalziel. We've all got money in it."

"Though whether we'll get anything out of it's a different matter," said Louisa.

Tillotson spoke for the first time, with a reproving look at Louisa.

"I'm sure we'll all get a good return on our investment. The Hall's nearly finished and the kitchens are ready. With a bit of luck we could still open on time."

He looked defiantly round the table.

Bertie shook his head.

"You don't listen, Charley. You *were* at the meeting, weren't you? Confucius he say, no pay, no play."

"Everyone done? Right, pass your plates," said Bonnie firmly. "Mr. Dalziel, how do you feel about apple crumble and custard?"

"Keen," said Dalziel.

"You look like a crispy edge man to me," said Bonnie, piling a substantial portion on to his plate. "That do you for now? Good. Now, no more shop till we've finished. Understood? Hank, how's your film coming on?"

"Fine, man, fine. I showed Herrie some clips yesterday and he made a couple of suggestions."

"Painful, no doubt," said Bertie.

"No, no. Pertinent. Words are his scene. You should learn to give credit, Bertie boy. Bend a little."

"You're making a film, Mr. Uniff?" said Dalziel.

"That's right. Don't be surprised. I mean, do I look like a tycoon? I mean, do any of us look like tycoons? Bertie there, perhaps. Yeah, Bertie's got some of the distinguishing marks of your lesser duck-billed tycoon. No, we've all been sweet-talked into this business in the hope and expectation of much bread, by which, verily, man might not live alone, but without which, verily, he surely can't live with anyone else."

"We agreed, no shop," said Bonnie warningly.

"Did we? You need to watch yourself in this house, Mr. Dalziel. You can be lying in bed minding your own business and wham! you find you've made an argument!"

He subsided behind his apple crumble and the rest of the meal passed in meteorological chitter-chatter, though Dalziel had to field a couple of invitations to reveal his own line of business. Never before could he recall himself concealing his profession—except for professional reasons. There were none that he could formulate, so why was he doing something which, when admitted by his colleagues, had always filled him with contempt?

After dinner they drank coffee whose bitterness resisted the addition of four teaspoons of sugar. The dinner dishes were then piled on a trolley to be wheeled down to the new kitchen where a huge dishwasher was the one positive benefit so far derived from the restaurant scheme.

"You know, it's stopped raining, for the moment at least," said Bonnie, looking out of the window. "I think I'll stroll out and post some letters. Anyone fancy a walk?"

"I'd like some fresh air," said Tillotson, but Bonnie shook her head.

"Sorry, but I told Herrie you'd go up and read to him. There's nothing wrong with his eyesight," she explained to Dalziel, "but there are many things he prefers to hear read aloud. And Charley's got the best voice for it."

"It's those upper class vowels," said Bertie. "Basically the old man's a simple snob."

"Hush. So you run along, Charley. Mr. Dalziel, what about you?"

"It'd be a pleasure," said Dalziel. He thought he saw an ironic smile flicker across Mavis's face, but it was hard to be sure.

"Right. Gum-boots and wet kit, I think. Your stuff should all be dry now. I'll see you outside in five minutes."

The rain had indeed stopped, but the atmosphere was damp to the point of saturation. What light there was seemed to glint dully from the surface of the water rather than come from above. There was at first an illusory silence which after a while fragmented into a myriad soft lapping, splashing, dripping noises and the gentle night wind was like a damp breath on Dalziel's face.

They walked without speaking along what he took to be the main drive of the house. It ran downhill but only reached the level of the floods at the gateway to the road and the light from Bonnie's torch showed that the water though extensive was easily fordable here. They splashed through it, turned away from the lake, and were soon back on dry tarmac as the road began to climb.

"It's a pity the drive didn't dip lower," said Bonnie. "It would have been rather nice to be quite cut off."

"Why's that?" asked Dalziel.

"I don't know. Isolation. An interlude before the outside pressures started up again. As it is, well, everything's been going on at the same time. Business troubles, legalities, funeral arrangements."

"It can't have been easy," said Dalziel.

"No. You've heard how my husband died, have you, Mr. Dalziel?"

Dalziel's professional instinct was to say no and get it from her own lips, but he had no difficulty in subjugating it.

"Yes," he answered. "Terrible."

"Yes. And it couldn't have happened at a worse time."

"Money?" asked Dalziel.

"That's right." For a moment she sounded like Uniff in her inflection. "We were scraping the bottom of the barrel. Conrad—my husband—was more enthusiastic than expert in business matters. He spent ten years in the Army—REME, nothing heroic—and came out convinced his gratuity was going to be the basis of a financial empire. Well, I always added fifty per cent on to his estimate of the cost of anything, but I think he must have started taking that into account! Anyway, we were well short and the contractor stopped work. That's why Conrad was trying the do-it-yourself thing."

"Tragic," said Dalziel. He felt he was doing well. Single words, the odd phrase here and there, a man could make quite a good impression if he watched his tongue. But when you hadn't cared to watch it for twenty years, it needed maximum alertness.

"Yes, it was tragic, I suppose. The inquest helped in an odd way. It made things official, gave us a bit of red tape to get tangled up with. In the end we were glad to get Conrad out of the house. Well, you saw yourself what a fetch we got up to. But I'm sorry. I must be boring you to tears. Your holiday's gone wrong enough without having other people's woes to contend with!"

"No, I'm interested," said Dalziel. "Well, you'll be all right now, are you? There must be some insurance."

Everyone had insurance in Yorkshire. Even Dalziel had insurance though he did not know why as there was no sod living he particularly wanted to benefit from his death.

"Conrad wasn't a very provident man," said Bonnie. "The only insurance he had was the cover the finance company insisted he should take out when he got the loan to start the business moving. Naturally it would be fine to have that paid off, it's a lot of money. But the insurance company doesn't seem to be in a hurry to settle up."

"Oh?" said Dalziel. His use of the monosyllable filled him with pride.

"Yes. I don't know what the trouble is. It's straightforward enough, I should have thought. But they sent this man round. He asked a lot of questions. The police asked a lot of questions. *Everyone* asked a lot of questions. And the only question I wanted to ask was, how the hell are we going to be able to open a week on Saturday?"

You'll be bloody lucky! was the brutal answer that rose in Dalziel's mind but he held it back and said instead, "You'll have to postpone, that's all."

"Not quite," said the woman. They had reached a railway bridge the arch of which curved so sharply it was almost a humpback. Bonnie stopped and leaned on the parapet staring down the line which, as far as the darkness permitted Dalziel to see, ran arrow-straight through a deep cutting. Dalziel presumed that there must have been a natural valley there, perhaps containing a stream diverted by the engineers, for even his untutored eye could tell that the stone work they leaned against pre-dated the railway age. Bonnie spoke into the dark hollow.

"Conrad at his high moments was pretty much of an optimist. We decided on a provisional opening date when we started the scheme, just something to aim at. When I went through his desk after the accident, I discovered what I might have guessed. Nothing was provisional to Conrad. He'd been taking advance bookings for the opening night!"

"*Had* he? How many?"

"One hundred and twenty. Our full capacity."

"Jesus wept!" said Dalziel. "But you must have known he was doing it! I mean, advertising, that kind of thing?"

"Oh, that I would have noticed, but Conrad didn't work that way. No, he told all his cronies in the local pubs and down at the Conservative Club in Orburn. People approached him, I suppose. I don't mean for a couple of tickets for a quiet anniversary dinner. Oh no. This is a togetherness thing, haunch to haunch on a hard bench. These are group bookings. A dozen from the Bowls Club, twenty Young Wives looking for Fellowship, forty Rotarians, six Pigeon Fanciers, the Townswomen's Guild. That's the way it went. None of them bodies that any of the rest of us were likely to have dealings with. I think Conrad realized he'd gone too far when the contractor refused to go on with the work. Hence his eagerness to do it himself. He just didn't dare tell us about the bookings."

"It's a bad way to start," agreed Dalziel. "But not disastrous. Nice apology, a bit of creeping, special circumstances and all that, money back, first refusal next time."

She turned round, leaned backwards against the parapet, and laughed. It was a good laugh, very infectious, so that Dalziel found himself beginning to smile even though his detective's mind had hopped ahead to the cause of the laughter.

"There's no money to give back," he said.

"You're very sharp, Mr. Dalziel. Conrad had no machinery for retaining money. I used to tell him to get his suits made without pockets. What did he need them for? I kept quiet about it till today, hoping that the insurance people might cough up enough to pay off the Young Wives at least. But they're still dragging their feet. My business partners were far from pleased when I told them."

"I heard something," said Dalziel. "It sounded like Bertie, mainly."

"Yes. The others are less committed," she said. "Or rather, he's the only one who understands enough about finance, to know just how close to bankruptcy we really are. If Conrad had let Bertie look after the business side . . . but you know what fathers are like with their sons."

"No," said Dalziel. "You're an odd lot though."

"What?"

"For a board of directors. I mean."

She laughed again.

"I suppose we are. We just happened, really. Bertie started it. He did a business studies course at Liverpool, then got a job up there with a big combine, Provincial Traders. They have a lot of interests and he sampled them all, including catering. But he didn't like company politics and wanted his own business. The house is mine, or rather mine and Lou's. It belonged to her father, my first husband. The boys are just her step-brothers, you must have spotted that, of course. When he died he left it to me, but entailed so that it couldn't be sold and would become hers when I died. Well, as you've seen, it's a white elephant. We tried letting it, but for what? We couldn't get anyone to pay enough to keep us somewhere else. There's no fish worth speaking of in the lake and the big marshes to the east where there used to be some good duck-shooting were drained over ten years ago. Now we've got to stop Charley Tillotson going out and blowing up the few poor survivors!

"Anyway Bertie suggested a restaurant, one of these medieval junket places. A licence to mint your own money, he said it was. The catering was done on a production line, no skill needed. And the discomforts were part of what the customer was paying for. So, the innocents abroad, we launched ourselves into it. It was either that or board up the house and apply for a council flat somewhere."

"What about money?" asked Dalziel.

"Money?"

"You need cash. Nowt gets done without some cash."

"You're right there," Bonnie said. She turned once more and peered down at the railway line. Her movement brought her within a few inches of Dalziel who contemplated a brotherly arm around her shoulders but dismissed the idea on the grounds of indecency. A fraternal gesture would make what was happening beneath his mackintosh incestuous.

"We borrowed, mainly. Lou and myself raised a small mortgage on the house. They don't like lending money to women. Conrad was more successful. He didn't have much to offer as security, but he did have the gift of the gab. Bertie had no cash, but it was his idea and he knew something about the catering trade. Also he brought along Hank Uniff and his sister from Liverpool. Hank had just had a bit of a disaster. His studio had just been gutted by a fire, so he was desperate for somewhere to work. He's making a film and was delighted at the chance of being somewhere nice and quiet while the fire-insurance money worked for him in the business. He says he despises cash, really. Well, when we go bankrupt it'll be a test of his principles! His sister, Mave's, very artistic too, terrific with clothes. She's in charge of costumes."

"What costumes?" interrupted Dalziel.

"Your retainers, court jesters, minstrels, serving

wenches. Don't ask me what serving wenches. We're
all serving wenches. Lou sings a lovely 'Greensleeves.'
I can manage anything that stays within a four-note
range. Hank plays the guitar—don't they *all*, these
days? We were planning to hire *some* help, of course,
but all of us in the business were going to be very
actively involved."

"You haven't mentioned Tillotson," commented
Dalziel.

"You notice *everything*, don't you?"

He glanced at her sharply. She was grinning slyly—
there was no other word for it. It did not diminish
her attractiveness one jot.

"Charley; well, Charley came along with Lou one
weekend and he seems to have been around more or
less ever since. He had a few hundred which he
poured in almost uninvited and he'll make a lovely
Sir Philip Sidney or someone to direct traffic. So,
there it is. Not a bad setup. Money to be made. But
we'll probably have to sell up to pay off our debts.
We'll be lucky if we break even."

There it was, thought Dalziel. If Mavis had been
right, this was the gentle flick of the fly over the
trout stream. No. Wrong picture. He was no trout.
Carp, perhaps. Or shark. But even sharks could
flounder in unfamiliar waters.

"What kind of money were you looking to make,
Mrs. Fielding?" he asked.

"I can't really say. Finance isn't my line, I wouldn't
know which way up to hold the *Financial Times*. But
the gross income's easy enough to work out. Five
pounds a head; well that includes VAT, so we get
four-fifty. Five hundred and forty from a full night.
Bertie says other places like this in the north get six
full nights a week *and* booked up for months ahead.
So, six times five-forty."

"Three thousand two hundred and forty a week,"
Dalziel said, unimpressed. Income was nowt without
expenditure. He didn't read Dickens but he'd heard
of Mr. Micawber.

"What do they get for a fiver?" he asked.

"Soup," she said. "Half a chicken. Spare rib. Cold pudding. Rye bread. Salad. Half a litre of red wine. Coffee. And a night's entertainment."

"Uniff on guitar. Tillotson tripping over his codpiece," he said. He didn't mean to be sarcastic nor did she take offence.

"You can pay more and get less," she answered. "Try to walk out of the Lady Hamilton's restaurant with a full belly and change from a fiver. And that's without any drink or floor show. We've got a bar too, of course."

"Have you?" he said. That could double the profits. People came in groups, in a minibus, taxi, coach; someone else driving; one night when you could afford to let go without risking bother from the sodding police.

"Sounds a good proposition," he said.

"It was," she answered. "Conrad will be sorry to have missed it, wherever he is."

Dalziel glanced at her again. She was staring out into the night with a faintly puzzled look on her face.

"Or perhaps not," she went on. "You know, this is one of the straightest bits of track in the country. Look."

She pointed. Dalziel stared into the blackness for a few seconds before spotting the light.

"Train," she said. "One of our rare expresses. Conrad and I often used to stop on this bridge if we'd been up to the village. Just about this time it must have been, because we'd watch this train coming nearer."

The light was growing and now the sound of the wheels on the track was quite audible.

"It must touch a hundred or whatever it is that trains can travel at," Bonnie continued. "Conrad would stand here and watch it getting nearer. As if he couldn't take his eyes off it. And you know what he once said to me, one hard, frosty midwinter's night? 'Bonnie,' he said, 'Bonnie, you realize it's just a step into summer.' "

The diesel seemed to cover the last few hundred yards in a single leap, the horn blasted its three-note clarion call over the quiet countryside, and the upward blast of air as the train punched through the bridge made Dalziel take an involuntary pace backwards. Bonnie did not move.

"Some fucking step," said Dalziel.

CHAPTER VII

A Fried Egg Sandwich

Dalziel woke up early the following morning and lay in the darkness knowing it was full of menace. He forced himself to relax, and gradually the menace faded as the shapes and angles of the unfamiliar room began to emerge in gradations of grey, bringing with them something worse than fear, a sense of the grey hours, days, weeks, stretching ahead like a desert landscape of unrelieved, grinding, unsharable monotony.

Depression was a sickness, they told him. The previous year he had been worried enough by symptoms of physical illness to visit his doctor and had come away with a series of warnings and prohibitions concerning diet, alcohol, tobacco—the usual nonsense. But paradoxically his efforts to comply had led him inexorably to ask himself why he was bothering; what was so bloody marvellous about this life he was trying to preserve. Such metaphysical speculations were entirely foreign to his make-up and their formulation now was light years from being precise and intellectual. It was just a feeling of hollowness at the centre, a reluctance to awaken from the safe blackness of sleep, a sense of life like a hair floating on dirty bath water, sinking imperceptibly, moment by moment, till a final, spinning gurgling rush carried it away.

So he had taken a holiday. He had never cared much for holidays, but they were better than the happy-pills he knew many people took to preserve their truce with life. He was not one of those nuts who had to keep taking the tablets. A holiday would set *him* right. And this was it.

He forced himself to start thinking about this odd household he had fallen into. These people interested him. Professionally it might be a mistake to get involved, personally it might be a mistake not to. The previous evening had ended with no proposition of any kind from Bonnie. Most likely he had been entirely mistaken to expect one, but it had been a slight disappointment. Christ almighty, what did he expect? The bathroom door opening in the night and the shadowy figure in the diaphanous nightie stealing to his bedside? Kids' fantasies. No, he told himself grimly, if he had any attraction for the Fieldings it was what Mavis had hinted, as a potential investor, and they weren't going to start carving their roast beef for him till they knew what he was worth.

Not that he disapproved of this way of thinking, he told himself as he got out of bed. He liked people who trod carefully. And he liked people who took money seriously. That was what his job was about, mainly. The thought made him smile as he went into the bathroom and suddenly he realized that on this occasion at least his self-prescribed therapy was being successful.

He washed and shaved, making as little noise as possible, conscious of the sleeping woman behind the farther door. He wondered if it were locked, but did not feel able to try it.

He glanced at his watch as he got dressed and saw that it was six-thirty, later than he thought. The gloomy, overcast skies explained his error. Sunrise had been a secret ceremony that morning.

Guests should lie abed till they were certain the household was awake. This was a maxim he had learned long ago, but if he'd obeyed all the rules of polite behaviour he had ever known, he would still be a well-mannered constable. In any case, six-thirty was quite late enough.

He was not the only one stirring, he discovered. His nose told him there was someone in the kitchen making coffee. Uniff, he guessed. He looked a restless sod.

It was Mrs. Greave.

"Morning," he said.

She was wearing her green dressing-gown again and had obviously gone to bed without making any special provision for adjustment to her hair. The beehive now hung askew, giving her head a curiously bent appearance as though seen through a funfair mirror.

She didn't reply. Dalziel helped himself to a mug (Bertie's again, he suspected) and poured coffee from the jug she had placed on a tray.

"You're an early bird," he said after a scalding mouthful. "And it's a long walk. What's wrong with them shiny new kitchens down there?"

"They're for cooking chickens, hunks of meat, a hundred portions at a time," she said. "Want a piece of toast?"

"Thanks," he said, interested by this sudden thawing. Her dressing-gown was loosely belted and as she bent forward to butter the toast for him, he saw she was wearing nothing underneath.

He took another more careful sip of coffee and said, "Careful you don't spill something."

"You needn't look," she said indifferently passing him the toast.

"Why not? There's no charge, is there?" he said.

"What the hell do you mean?" she snapped angrily.

"Nothing. Nothing. How long have you been here with your father, Mrs. Greave?"

She sat down opposite and watched him chew on his toast.

"Six months, maybe seven," she said.

"Six, maybe seven. I see. This marmalade's good. Do you make it yourself, Mrs. Greave?"

"No."

"Pity. I like home-made stuff. But you've done a bit of cooking in your time. Those sausages last night. Grand! I bet you kept Mr. Greave happy."

"Pardon?"

"Mr. Greave. Your husband," said Dalziel. "What happened? Died, did he?"

"Yes," she said.

"I'm sorry. Poor fellow. What was it? Road accident? Coronary? Now Mrs. Fielding did mention it last night, but I can't quite recall."

He looked at her expectantly, his expression sympathetic but hopeful like a parson's at a funeral.

"I'd rather not talk about it."

"Of course not. Then after the unhappy event, Mr. Papworth, your dad, found you a place here."

"They needed a cook-housekeeper. And they'll need help when the restaurant opens."

"True," said Dalziel. "Then you'll be able to use all that lovely shiny equipment. Mind you, things look a bit dicey just now."

"I don't know anything of that," she said, rising. "I'm just the paid help. Excuse me. I'd better go and get dressed."

She made for the door.

"Don't forget your tray," called Dalziel.

She stopped, then slowly returned, picked up the tray and left. Someone spoke to her outside the door and a second later Louisa came into the room. She was wearing a short flowered tunic from which her thin white legs forked with, for Dalziel, all the provocative power of a couple of pipe-cleaners. But tastes differed, he was willing to concede, and he suspected she thought she was the sexiest thing since co-education.

"That was pretty nosy," she said as she headed for the stove.

"You were listening," he accused.

"I didn't like to butt in," she said. "All that about the way she was widowed. It was embarrassing."

Dalziel laughed derisively.

"What's that mean?" she asked.

"It means I don't think either of you were embarrassed," he answered.

She left the stove, came to the other side of the table, put her hands on it and leaned towards him.

She'd have to stand on her head and waggle her legs in the air to be interesting, thought Dalziel.

"Who the hell do you think you are to talk to me like that?" she demanded.

"I'm a man you punched on the nose without explanation or apology," he retorted. "That gives me rights."

She decided to postpone confrontation and grinned.

"You want me to say I'm sorry? Well, I suppose I was later. Hitting a stranger's not like hitting someone you know. But since I've met you again, I'm not certain whether I'm sorry or not. And if you talk to me like you talked to Mrs. Greave, I might just punch you again."

"Mrs. Greave didn't punch me," said Dalziel. "And your kettle's boiling."

"It's easy to intimidate servants," she called from the back kitchen. "If she tells Pappy, you watch out. He's no respecter of persons."

"Aye. I doubt if he respects Mrs. Greave's person much," grunted Dalziel.

"What do you mean?" said Louisa, returning with a mug of coffee.

"Come on, love," said Dalziel. "You're not *all* blind innocents here, are you? There were two cups on that tray. And a couple of doughnuts as well as toast."

"So she's got a sweet tooth and she's giving her old dad his breakfast in bed. I like that," said Louisa.

"It's not all she's giving him," said Dalziel. "It's plain as the nose on your face. I know a scrubber when I see one."

"Clearly I haven't had your educational advantages," said the girl. "But if what you say is right, and she's Pappy's fancy bit, what's it matter? He's old enough and conventional enough to feel he needs

a cover story, that's all. Your generation's made quite
an art of hypocrisy."

"What *are* you, Miss Fielding?" asked Dalziel suddenly. She was taken aback and looked at him in
puzzlement.

"I mean, all the others seem to be something, to
have done something. *You*, though. How old are
you? Eighteen? Nineteen? Twenty? What do *you* do?"

"Haven't you heard?" she said, recovered. "I've
got shares in a restaurant. You might say, I own it.
Or will do."

"What? Oh, the house. You're hoping to live off
your inheritance, are you? It's always the way. What
one generation makes, the next spends."

"No one asks to be born, Mr. Dalziel," she said.

"Not many return the gift," Dalziel said. He was
trying to remember what it was like when he was
nineteen. The girls he knew hadn't been like this,
but was that just a difference of class rather than of
time? A bit of both. Time marched on, but you could
always make allowances. The class thing was different. Dalziel liked a fairly rigid class structure. A
sense of social level made people easier to deal
with—to manipulate, if you spelled it out. That was
also what his job was about. But more importantly it
gave a man a sense of what he was, whereas these
young sods didn't seem to worry about being anything in particular. And it was catching if you weren't
careful. You could wake up and feel the numbness
of self-doubt spreading to the heart.

He rose and went into the back kitchen to boil the
kettle once more.

The girl sat still, inhaling the steam from her cup.
She might have been twelve or thirteen, he thought,
glancing at her narrow shoulders from behind.

Suddenly something about her age struck him,
something so obvious he couldn't understand how
he'd missed it before.

"How old's Bertie?" he asked, putting a spoonful
of instant coffee into his mug.

"Twenty-four. Why?"

"And Nigel's fifteen. And they're your step-brothers?"

He made a business of pouring out the water and looking for the milk. From the outer room came a laugh.

"Oh, I see. You've just noticed. Yes, Bonnie had Bertie shortly after meeting Conrad for the first time. I think she fell for his Army uniform. She likes men in uniform, you know. She was bringing Bertie up herself when she met my father. They got married. Later I appeared. Then Daddy died and who should turn up again but Conrad. This time she was wise enough, or stupid enough, to get him to the altar. And after fifteen years of intermittent marriage, here we all are. Happy Family."

"I see," said Dalziel.

"It took you long enough," she said, raising her voice. "I thought everyone could see at a glance that Bertie was a bastard."

When he rejoined her, he saw the reason for the change in tone. Bertie was standing in the doorway. Dalziel looked at his watch. It was still only seven o'clock. They really were early risers here; Bertie was fully clothed and from the look of his shoes, he had been outside.

"Don't let me interrupt," said the fat youth, walking through the kitchen. He shot a malignant glance at Dalziel's mug as he passed but said nothing.

"Morning," said Dalziel. "What's it like out? Cold?"

"Why don't you try it?" said Bertie from the other room.

"Later. This restaurant was your idea, your mam says."

Bertie returned with some coffee and looked insolently at Dalziel.

"What's it to you?" he asked.

"Nothing much," said Dalziel. "I was just hearing about your financial troubles. Wondering if it was worth pouring good money after bad, that's all."

He was quite proud of that. The statement went no further than a general comment but obviously from the glance the other two exchanged it was the particular application that had been made.

Bertie's voice was definitely politer when he replied.

"I don't know what my mother's been saying, Mr. Dalziel, but you mustn't get hold of the wrong end of the stick. The work's nearly finished as you can see. A token payment of a couple of thousand would get the contractors back in twenty-four hours. There's no question of long-term difficulty. Any finance house would be keen to advance money once they saw the state of the project. It's just a matter of time."

"Oh. If that's all . . . well, I'm glad to hear it," said Dalziel. "I must have mistaken Mrs. Fielding. Would anyone mind if I fried myself an egg?"

He didn't wait for an answer but set about the business with the expertise of a man long used to living alone. There was some bacon in the fridge, nice thick-cut rashers which looked as if the pig had seen the light of day in the recent past. He kept his mind off the contents of the foil-wrapped package which he had found here yesterday.

"Anyone else?" he called.

"I'll try one," Louisa said, joining him at the stove. "I can't cook for toffee."

"I bet your mam can," said Dalziel.

"When she wants," said the girl. She lowered her voice. "Don't take any notice of Bertie. He thinks all big businessmen talk like that."

"Tell lies, you mean?" said Dalziel, cracking another egg one-handed and draining it through his fingers into the pan.

"Don't worry, love," he went on. "I know you can't even refund the Bowls Club their money. God knows what else I don't know about! No. If I was a finance house, I wouldn't lend you your bus-fare home."

"Up you, then," said Louisa angrily.

"But I'm not a finance house. You know what? I'm going to have mine in a sandwich. It can be messy, but what's life without risks?"

There was no need for him to be talking like this.

The first hint that he might be interested in the project had been just about justifiable. Even then you had to pretend there was some kind of case and he was investigating it. But this was just economic prick-teasing. He tried to retrieve his position.

"If a couple of thousand's all that's needed, I can't see your problem," he said, carefully organizing his montage of egg and bacon on a slice of thick-cut bread. "Your grandfather's got this Gumboot thing coming; how much? Fifteen thousand dollars? Won't he chip in?"

"Not bloody likely," said Louisa, eating her egg more conventionally, albeit straight from the pan. "He's been against the project right from the start. He's got a little bit of money from his writing, enough to pay his way in the house, and there's not much he can do with the Gumbelow money at his age. But he'd rather flush it down the loo than let Bertie get his hands on it. That's how he sees the business, you see. Always has. Bertie's balls-up. They don't get on, you may have noticed. And now Herrie thinks Conrad would still be alive if it weren't for the business."

"Is that right?" said Dalziel.

"So any knight in shining armour willing to take a small risk for a short time would be gratefully received and bounteously recompensed."

She looked seriously at him and ran her tongue along the prongs of her fork.

"Is that right?" said Dalziel again. "Short time."

He bit into his sandwich. The egg burst, spread, overflowed faster than his mouth could take it in and ran down his chin.

"I said it could be messy," said Dalziel.

CHAPTER VIII

Family History

As soon as it was a reasonable working hour, Dalziel rang the garage.

Yes, they remembered talking to Mrs. Fielding. Yes, they hoped to send someone out for the car that day. No, they didn't think it would take long to put it right, just a drying-out job. In fact if they'd realized it was so urgent, they'd have brought it in yesterday afternoon. Of course (full of rural indignation) their breakdown truck could get through the floods if it had to.

Dalziel arranged to ring them later in the day and replaced the phone thoughtfully. At that rate, he could be on his way by tea-time. In fact it sounded as if he could have been on his way the previous day.

He was in Hereward Fielding's room and as he left the old man met him at the door.

"I was just using the phone," Dalziel felt constrained to explain.

"There are other phones in the house," snapped the old man. "But feel free. Feel free. It's Liberty Hall here."

"Are you better?" asked Dalziel.

"Better than what? I was never unwell, if that's what you mean. I've been wet before, I'll be wet again before I go. You'll see."

"There you are, Herrie. Why on earth have you got out of bed? You are being very silly."

It was Bonnie, looking very stern and disciplinarian.

"You must allow me to judge what is best," said Fielding. "I am perfectly well. In any case those Gumbelow people are likely to turn up today and I've no intention of letting a lot of damned Americans find me in bed."

"They may not come," said Bonnie. "Even if they do, you could have waited till they'd rung and said definitely."

"The phones in this house are in such constant use that it may prove impossible for them to get through," said Fielding, glowering at Dalziel.

"Well, sit down in here, I'll put the electric fire on and get Mrs. Greave to bring you some breakfast."

"Coffee only and a slice of toast," said Fielding. "That woman's not to be trusted with anything else. That meal last night. Vile!"

"The sausages weren't bad," said Dalziel.

"You had sausages? I was given some nauseating stew of a kind hitherto undescribed in prose or poetry, unless on the occasion that Dr. Henry Spooner recited the opening lines of 'The Burial of Sir John Moore.' "

"It was chicken fricassée and it came out of a tin," said Bonnie. "Now go and sit down."

She spoke in a stern schoolmistressy tone and Fielding obeyed. Dalziel felt he too might have obeyed if addressed in such a way, but her voice when she spoke to him after closing the door behind her father-in-law was humorously long-suffering.

"No wonder Herrie and Nigel got on so well! They're both at the awkward age."

"Don't you think you ought to try to find where the boy went?" suggested Dalziel diffidently.

"I'll make some discreet enquiries round his friends," she answered with an unworried smile. "Boys of that age are very contrary. Any hint of a search would just make him burrow deeper. Did Herrie say you'd been telephoning?"

Dalziel considered.

"No. No, he didn't," he said. "But I have. I rang the garage."

"What do they think?" she asked.

"They're not certain. I'm to ring again later." The lie came easily.

"Well, you're welcome to stay as long as you need to," said Bonnie. "If you can stick us, that is."

"I'll bear it," said Dalziel. "Tell you what. I'd like to go into Orburn if anyone's going that way. One or two things I'd like to get."

"There's a shop in the village," said the woman.

"Do they make up prescriptions?" asked Dalziel.

"No."

"Well then. Perhaps I can phone a taxi if no one's going that way."

"Don't be silly. I'll drive you myself. There's always some shopping to get."

Any hopes Dalziel had of another solitary excursion with Bonnie disappeared when he met the car outside the house at the prearranged time of nine-thirty. It was an old Rover with what looked like the remnants of a nest in the radiator grille. In the front passenger seat was Tillotson and when Dalziel opened the rear door he found himself looking at Mavis Uniff.

Bonnie drove with considerable panache, passing through the flooded bottom end of the drive with an angel's wing of water arcing away on either side. Dalziel hoped the undercarriage was in better repair than the bodywork, but no harm seemed to be done. The suspension felt as if it had given its best and was now in decline, a state understandable if corners were always taken like this. The humped railway bridge where they had stood the previous night provided another interesting obstacle, but the Rover took it like a thoroughbred 'chaser which was more than Dalziel's stomach did.

They slowed to a sedate fifty to pass through Low Fold village, which was a cluster of cottages, a Post

Office, a pub and a church. A thought occurred to Dalziel as they passed this last building.

"Why didn't they bury him there?" he asked Mavis *sotto voce*.

"I don't know," she replied and, leaning forward to tap Bonnie on the shoulder, asked, "He wants to know why you didn't bury Conrad in Low Fold?"

Dalziel shook his head reprovingly at the girl but Bonnie seemed happy to answer.

"Lake House dead have always been buried in High Fold churchyard. You see, Low Fold's high and High Fold's low, if you follow me. Mike, my first husband's, there as well, so it's convenient for all the family."

Dalziel glanced surreptitiously at his companions but no one seemed to find the comment either amusing or odd. He scratched his left armpit thoughtfully and the rest of the journey was completed in silence.

Orburn appeared to him as a town he'd visited many years ago in his youth rather than one he had left just the previous morning. The main street widened into a kind of square, or rather an ovoid, as if someone had pressed his thumb on the narrow thoroughfares which ran out of it and the street had blebbed to four times its normal width. At one end of the bleb was the Lady Hamilton. Bonnie parked a little farther along, next to a marble statue which age or modesty seemed to have rendered anonymous.

"There's a chemist's over there," said Bonnie. "I'll make for the supermarket first, I think. What are you two going to do? Labour for me or your own thing?"

Tillotson and Mavis seemed uncertain of their respective plans and in the end Bonnie said to Dalziel, "See that baker's over the road? There's a little café behind it. We'll have a coffee there in about forty-five minutes. All right?"

She strode away, long firm strides stretching her simple denim skirt taut against her thighs. Tillotson hesitated a moment before following. One thing about your posh upbringing, thought Dalziel. Properly done, it instilled good manners. Their fatal weakness.

"What about you?" he said to Mavis.

"I never go into shops if I can help it," she replied. "Especially supermarkets. I'll show you the sights if you like."

"That's kind," said Dalziel, which it was. It was also a bloody nuisance. Time was short and he didn't want the girl hanging around.

"But it's shopping I'm after, too," he went on. "Just bits and pieces, but the sights'll have to wait till another time."

"You *are* staying long enough for another time then?" she asked. "Should I welcome you to the club?"

"We'll see. Thanks for your offer anyway."

"That's all right. I'll go and brood on nature."

She smiled at him and walked slowly away. He crossed the road and went into the chemist's where he watched Mavis out of sight while the assistant wrapped a bottle of aspirin.

"Anything else, sir?" asked the girl.

"Yes," said Dalziel. "Where's the police station?"

Fortunately it turned out to be in the direction opposite to that taken by Mavis and with the other two trapped in the canyons of the supermarket, Dalziel was able to enter the single-storied building which was the local station with minimum furtiveness.

"Yes, sir?" said the uniformed constable seated at a typewriter resting on a paper-littered desk.

"Always stand up for the public, son," said Dalziel, producing his warrant card. "Who's the boss here?"

"Inspector Grantley, but he's not in just now, sir," said the constable standing at a curious semi-attention occasioned by the fact that he had eased one foot out of its boot and was unable to fully re-insert it.

"CID?"

"That's Detective-Sergeant Cross. He's in his office. Shall I ring him?"

"No, it can't be far in a place this size. Which one?

Second on the left. Thanks. You haven't got a rupture, have you, son?"

"No, sir!"

"If you stand like that much longer, you'll likely get one."

Dalziel rapped sharply on the indicated door and entered.

The sole occupant of the room was not a pretty sight. He looked as if in the best of circumstances he would have been unprepossessing; unshaven, haggard from fatigue, his shirt collar open, feet on his desk, a still steaming mug of coffee propped perilously on his belly, he was quite revolting. Dalziel regarded him with vast approval. This was how a hard-working Detective Sergeant ought to look at least once a day.

"Who the hell are you?" said the man with semi-somnolent irritation.

Dalziel reached forward and plucked the threatening mug from his lap.

"Embarrassing that," he said. "Scalded cock. Makes the nurses wonder about you. I'm Dalziel."

His fame clearly had not penetrated to these dim recesses of the land and though the production of his warrant card set Cross struggling to his feet, it was a Pavlovian reaction to the rank rather than a spontaneous tribute to the reputation.

"Sit down," ordered Dalziel, "before you fall down. Hard night?"

"A bit," said Cross, running his fingers through black spiky hair which might have been petrified for all the effect this had on it. "Eight hours in a hen battery. God, the stink!"

"I thought there was something," said Dalziel, sniffing. "Anything to show for it?"

"No, sir," said Cross gloomily. "A waste of time. I've got my report here if you're interested."

He proffered a sheaf of typewritten papers which Dalziel waved aside.

"No, thanks, Sergeant. I see enough of those on my own patch. This is unofficial. I'm on holiday in the district, so I thought I'd drop in and pay my respects."

Cross looked at him with the utter disbelief of one who had seen enough of detective superintendents to know that courtesy calls on sergeants belonged with Father Christmas and the fairies.

"Thank you, sir," he said. "Nice to see you. Can I show you round?"

"I don't think so," said Dalziel. "Seen one, you've seen 'em all as the actress said. But you might be able to help me on another matter."

He pulled up a chair and sat opposite Cross who smiled slightly. Dalziel decided this wasn't insurbordinate and grinned back.

"Family by the name of Fielding," he said. "They live about ten miles out of town near a village called Low Fold."

"I know them," said Cross. "A big house; Lake House it's called. They're converting part of it to a restaurant. Mr. Fielding died recently. That the one?"

"That's it," said Dalziel.

"Ah," said Cross.

Dalziel watched and waited for a moment scratching his left buttock vigorously, a luxury he had been consciously eschewing in the company of Bonnie Fielding.

"I'm a stranger here," he said after a while. "I don't understand all the dialect. *Ah.* What does that mean? *Nice weather we've been having?* Or *hello cheeky, give us a kiss?* It's important I know."

"Sorry, sir," said Cross. "I was just wondering; I mean, are you a friend, or what?"

"It makes a difference? That's a start. I never knew these people existed till yesterday when they helped me after my car broke down. Now I'm curious. That help you?"

"Thank you, sir," said Cross, rising and going to a filing cabinet. "They're well known in the locality, the Fieldings. They've been around for about eight years now and, of course, Mrs. Fielding was here before that when her first husband was alive. Here we are."

He extracted a file and returned to the desk.

"The house belonged to Mr. Percival, of course."

"Who?"

"The first husband. The Percivals were very well known. Been around a long time. Not your aristocracy though they made some claims, but comfortably off. Their money came from trade, I believe."

He said the word as though it still had a definite pejorative meaning in these parts.

"Trade?" echoed Dalziel.

"That's right, but distant enough to be all right. Too distant, perhaps. It was cotton mainly and the Percivals were worse hit than most during the slump. I don't know the ins-and-outs but by the end of the war, I get the impression they were pretty well finished financially. And as a family too. The war saw three of 'em off, two in action, one in the blitz. The older survivors dropped off pretty rapidly afterwards, and Michael Percival, your Mrs. Fielding's first, got what little survived of the family fortune all concentrated in his own bank balance. It seems to have been enough for him to live modestly on—by his standards—and his wife too, when they got married in 1954. The girl, Louisa, was born the following year and a couple of years later, Percival died. Six months after that, Mrs. Percival married Mr. Fielding."

"The father of her eldest son, you knew that?" said Dalziel.

"Oh yes. She made no secret of it. The local gentry didn't like it. They prefer to hide their bastards. But she didn't care. They weren't around much for a few years in any case. The house was let and the Fieldings, according to best report, were living it up in swinging London. But money doesn't last forever and they'd spent so little of it on maintaining the house that it became unlettable. Also the marshlands where the tenants used to go shooting were drained and reclaimed in the mid-sixties and no one was interested in the place any more. So they came back to live in it. By this time, they had had the youngest boy, of course, and they brought Mr. Fielding's father along, to help pay the rates, I suppose. He's some kind of writer, they tell me."

He spoke, Dalziel noted approvingly, as if to be some kind of writer was the equivalent of being physically handicapped.

"You know a lot about these people, Sergeant," he said.

"I did a bit of research when this last business occurred," said Cross. "You heard about it?"

"You tell me," said Dalziel.

Cross opened his file.

"The deceased, Conrad Fielding, was discovered by his wife in what they're calling the Banqueting Hall at Lake House. Unfortunately by the time we became involved the body had been moved, but according to Mrs. Fielding's statement the man was lying on the floor there"—he passed over a glossy half-plate print of the Hall floor on which an outline of a body had been chalked—"with his chest pierced by the bit of an electric drill. The drill was still switched on. There was a ladder lying alongside the body, and there were drill marks in the wall about twenty feet up. It seems that the building contractors had packed up work till they got paid and Mr. Fielding had been trying to do it himself. The coroner decided that the ladder had slipped, he'd fallen down with the drill in his hand with the switch locked on, and unfortunately had fallen right on to the bit. Three-eighths doing two thousand four hundred revs. It makes a hole like that."

"I'd have expected it neater," said Dalziel, looking at the close-up of the naked chest on a mortuary slab.

"The bit stayed in the wound after death," said Cross. "The weight of the drill would force the bit sideways through the flesh till an equilibrium was reached. That's what the doctor said. Here's the p.m. report."

Dalziel scanned it quickly, expertly. He usually left it to his subordinates to extract what was important from technical reports and relay it to him succinctly and accurately. But Cross had not been moulded on the master potter's wheel.

"So," he said. "Accident. What's your interest?"

"We've a duty to investigate all sudden deaths, sir," said Cross blandly.

"Get knotted," said Dalziel amiably. "If I fell off this chair and broke my neck, you wouldn't dig into my family history for the past thirty years. So?"

"There were a couple of things," said Cross slowly. "First, the way they all behaved. They're an odd lot up at Lake House, you may have noticed, but you'd have expected a bit of, well, respect. Instead they all chattered away, ten to the dozen, and seemed bent on carrying on just as normal, except that they were a bit annoyed at the disturbance. Mark you, I didn't see any of them till some time after the death, so I can't report on immediate reactions. Mrs. Fielding seemed a bit distressed, but very much in control, and the boy, Nigel, seemed genuinely upset. But the others . . . well!"

"Even the old man?"

"Old Hereward? He was the oddest of all. No sign of grief but he said, 'I told him no good would come of it. I told him,' and that was all. Not another word."

Dalziel glanced at his watch. He was running out of time.

"There was a phone call," said Cross. "Not to us, but to the insurance company carrying Fielding's policies. One of their investigators, Spinx they called him, came round to tell us. Co-operation, he called it. What he was after was for us to tell him they needn't pay up! Evidently someone rang up their office the day after the death and said they should look very closely at the circumstances before handing out any money. Well, we have to take notice."

"Male or female?" demanded Dalziel.

"A woman, they think, though it could have been a male falsetto. Look, sir, can I ask if you're on to something? I mean, I don't want to sound as if I'm telling you your job, but it is *my* case."

Cross stared at him defiantly. He's quite right, thought Dalziel. Being his superior gives me no right to act in a bullying, arrogant way.

"Just curiosity, lad," he said with a disarming grin, showing teeth which were as perfect and as reassuring as a shark's. "I might be spending a couple of days with these people and I wanted to know what I was getting into. From what you tell me, there's nothing to worry about. There's always someone ready to make nasty phone calls. And as for their reactions, well, we're all entitled to be different, aren't we? It'd be a grey place if all folks were the same."

With these tolerant, liberal colours tacked to his masthead, Dalziel prepared to set sail through the door.

Cross reassembled his file and said casually, "You don't happen to know if they are still going to open the restaurant a week on Saturday, sir?"

"No. I'm sure they'll do their best," said Dalziel, never less sure of anything in a life of certainties.

"I hope so. I'm in the local Bowls Club and we've got a booking. There's ten quid of my hard-earned cash in that concern."

"There's better things to do with your money," said Dalziel reprovingly. "But I'm sure Mrs. Fielding will try to honour all commitments."

He must have sounded a little defensive. Cross looked at him and said neutrally, "She's a fine-looking woman, Mrs. Fielding."

Dalziel felt his tolerant, liberal colours slipping.

"What's that got to do with anything?" he said.

"Nothing at all, sir. Just think it's a pity her life should have been so full of tragedy. Two husbands, both lost in such nasty circumstances."

It was a question he should have asked. Had he

been in Cross's position investigating the business from scratch, it was one of the first things he would have looked to discover.

"How did Percival die?" he asked.

"An accident on the lake, sir," said Cross. "He fell out of a punt and was drowned."

CHAPTER IX

The Setting of Riddles

Dalziel moved swiftly once he had left the police station. There was one more call he had to make and he was short of time. Fortunately his destination was only round the corner from the station as he had ascertained in the chemist's.

He glanced quickly around when he reached the entrance to Gibb and Fowler's builders yard. The street was deserted except for a man entering a telephone-box about thirty yards behind him, and he pushed open the rickety wooden gates and went in.

It would have been simpler and more professional to get Sergeant Cross to do this, but for reasons he was still keeping obscure from himself, he did not wish to alert the local force more than he had done. Basically, he assured himself, it was just his own curiosity that was driving him on.

He was lucky to find the small, lop-sided and halitotic Mr. Gibb in, or so the small, lop-sided and halitotic Mr. Gibb assured him. Dalziel expressed his joy at such good fortune and tried to arrange Mr. Gibb and himself in one of these curiously oblique conversational tableaux so favoured of television drama directors. Mr. Gibb, however, would be satisfied with nothing less than confrontation so Dalziel produced his warrant card and came quickly to the point.

"Mr. Gibb, why did your firm stop work on the job at Lake House?"

"It's no secret," said Gibb. "They'd got no money. We're not a charity, Superintendent. When I found out they couldn't pay for what we'd done so far (which was nearly the whole job, I might add), I saw no reason to chuck good money after bad."

"I see that," said Dalziel. "But you were so near finished, why not complete the job and give them a chance to make some money? You must have known they were short of capital for a long while."

"You're right, we did. And that's the way we *were* thinking until, well, we got information suggesting that even if the place was finished, they didn't have a cat in hell's chance of getting the business under way. It would just mean they had a better-looking concern to sell off when the official receiver got to them, and I saw no reason why I should spend more time and materials just so other creditors could get a better dividend! So I said, if you don't pay now, that's it."

"I see," said Dalziel, releasing his held breath. "You say you got information. How did you get it?"

Gibb looked uncomfortable, then said aggressively, "It was a phone call. Some woman, anonymous. I wouldn't take notice of such a thing normally, but we'd been worried about that Fielding fellow for some time. You know the type, good talker, very convincing, gets you full of confidence till you go away and think things out a bit later. Know what I mean? So I thought I'll put him to the test, ask for a payment on account. Well, he started his usual patter. Mind you, it wasn't up to his usual standard. I mean, normally he could have talked the pants off a nun, but this time he seemed stuck for words. Perhaps it was his conscience."

"Perhaps," said Dalziel thoughtfully. "So you stopped work. Would you start again if there was some money forthcoming?"

"Yes," said Gibb without hesitation. "Like a shot. We're short of work just now. It's general. Six weeks ago, I was never in the office. Now, I'm never out of it."

"You said I was lucky to catch you," said Dalziel slyly.

"I thought you might be a customer then," grinned Gibb through his ruined teeth. "What's this all about anyway? Is there something up?"

"Not really," assured Dalziel. "Do me a favour, Mr. Gibb, and don't let on I've been asking questions. You never know, you might be back on the Lake House job sooner than you think."

That should keep him quiet, thought Dalziel as he left. The poor devil was probably down to his last Rolls-Royce. He strode back along the street, moving quickly for a man of his bulk.

I'm far too fat, he thought. I've let myself go. This belly's obscene. They'll need a domed lid on my coffin, like a casserole.

But it did have its uses sometimes. Like now, for instance, he thought, as he opened the door of the telephone-box and stepped inside, pinning the slightly built middle-aged man in the ill-fitting suit against the coin box.

"Right now," said Dalziel. "Who the hell are you?"

Even as he spoke he recognized the man. On the night he had been assaulted by Louisa in the Lady Hamilton it was this fellow who had come into the bar, asking about the disturbance. He had placed him then as a journalist. Whatever he was, it was probably this brief encounter which had made him familiar enough to stick out when Dalziel had got out of Bonnie's car in the square. Dalziel did not believe in coincidences and when the same man had been hanging around near the police station and subsequently near the builders yard, it bore investigation.

"What the blazes are you doing?" demanded the man. "Let me out at once, or I'll call the police."

"I *am* the police," said Dalziel. "So you needn't

call too loud. Why're you following me? Come on, quick as you can!"

"The police? So it's you. I didn't realize. My name's Spinx. Hold on."

Spinx tried to reach into his top pocket but Dalziel never took chances and his great paw closed firmly on the man's wrist.

"What've you got in there?"

"Just a card," said Spinx, very frightened now.

Dalziel reached into the pocket, took out a business card and sighed. It was a sad business, this suspicion. But it might have been a razor.

Alfred Spinx said the card. *Claims Department. Anchor Insurance.*

"Come on, Alfred," said Dalziel, stepping out of the box. "Let's walk and talk."

The open air seemed to make Spinx garrulous. He spoke in a strange not-quite-right accent and idiom as though he had learned English through a correspondence course with some minor public school in the thirties.

"I'm an insurance investigator," he said. "I used to be freelance, doing general work, you know. But the bottom's falling out of divorce now. Who needs evidence? Like a lot of dratted gypsies, break a pot and shout *I divorce thee* thrice, and that's it. I've thought seriously of emigrating, you know. By George, I have. To somewhere where they still have standards."

"Flags, you mean?" said Dalziel wondering whether to take this sodding little twerp for real. "Try Russia. They like flags there, so they tell me. But before you buy your ticket, why were you following me, Alfred?"

Spinx stopped and stared with nervous resolution at Dalziel.

"Excuse me, Mr . . . er . . .?"

"Dalziel. Superintendent."

"Superintendent. I'd rather you didn't use my Christian name. I've studied a bit of criminology and I know it helps to establish a proper subordinate and familiar relationship with a suspect, but you know

who I am now and I'd prefer to talk at the level of
equals. We're colleagues in a sense after all, don't
you know, you in the public, me in the private
sector."

The words came at a rush and Dalziel's first impulse was to laugh. But the man's attempt at dignity
was not merely comic. In any case Dalziel wanted
information and wanted it fast. He should be in the
coffee shop now.

"I'm sorry, Mr. Spinx. It is *Mister*? Good. But just
a few questions if you'd be so kind. What precisely
is the case you're working on at this moment."

"The same as you, I imagine, Superintendent,"
said Spinx. "Mr. Conrad Fielding's death."

"Why should that interest you?"

"Any insurance company looks closely at any large
claim on it, you must know that. We're probably
even more suspicious than the police." He spoke
with pride.

"And there was the phone call," prompted Dalziel.

"Yes. You'd know about that, of course. Such
things cannot be ignored, you understand."

"Tell me about it again," commanded Dalziel.

"Certainly. Wait a moment. Here we are. My book
of words."

He produced a plastic-covered notebook from his
inside pocket, thumbed through it, his lips pattering
together in time to the riffled pages, finally pursing
in a reluctantly proffered kiss as he found his place.

"Here we are. It was a woman who phoned. Or so
the oral evidence suggests. *Hello*."

"What?" said Dalziel.

"That's me," explained Spinx. "I've got the whole
conversation. *Hello!* Then she said, *You thinking of
paying any insurance money on Conrad Fielding? Well, I
wouldn't.* Then I said, *Hello!* I was playing for time,
you understand. *Who's that speaking?* She said, *Never
mind that. Just ask yourself what a man like that would be
doing up a ladder in his condition.* I said, *Hello!* and she
rang off."

He shut the book and looked hopefully at Dalziel

like a dog waiting to be patted. The fat man reached forward and plucked the book from his hands.

"Let's have a look," he said opening it. "Christ! What's this? Egyptian?"

"No," said Spinx with pride, peering at the lines of minute matchstick men which marched over the paper. "My own shorthand code. A method I devised to preserve confidentiality, you understand."

"It does that, right enough," said Dalziel returning the book. "So you told the police like a good citizen and did a bit of looking round yourself. That's what you were doing at the Lady Hamilton, was it? Keeping tabs on the family?"

"It was a last fling. I thought a little close observation might lead me to something," admitted Spinx. "It didn't and I'm having terrible trouble with my expenses. I only had an omelette, but the prices there are really shocking."

"So you found nowt," said Dalziel, impatiently glancing at his watch again. He was late. They were at the corner of the square in which the car was parked and he halted there, restraining Spinx with one brutish paw. "The inquest said accident. So now you pay?"

"Well, we would have done," said Spinx. "Indeed the letter had been written and was ready for dispatch yesterday. Then I heard about you."

"About me?" said Dalziel in surprise. He recalled Spinx's reaction in the phone-box. *So it's you* he had said when Dalziel identified himself. Which must mean . . .

"She phoned again, yesterday afternoon."

The book was opened once more.

"*Hello!*" said Spinx.

"Just the gist," growled Dalziel. "Forget the witty interchange."

"She said that if we were thinking of paying the money, we ought to know that the police were still looking into the business. There was one actually staying in the house at present. That was all. So we decided to bide our time again, you understand."

"Well bloody well," said Dalziel. "It was the same woman?"

"I believe so."

"Right," said Dalziel. "Listen, Mr. Spinx, I've got to go now but I may want to talk to you again."

"If you ring the number on my card, they'll find me," said Spinx. "Before you go, Superintendent, without breaching professional ethics, can you give me any hint of how your investigations are going?"

Dalziel examined the eager face before him. He didn't like small men and he didn't like private investigation and he didn't like the assumption that he had anything in common with this pathetic shadow. On the other hand Spinx wouldn't believe the truth and there was no point in antagonizing him by the rude rejoinder which was ever ready to leap from his tongue.

"Can't say," said Dalziel. "You understand?"

"Yes, of course."

"Good. Now we mustn't be seen together. Cheerio!"

He stepped smartly into the square and strode towards the baker's shop. As he approached Bonnie emerged from the doorway with Tillotson and Mavis close behind.

"Hello," said Bonnie. "We thought you must have got lost, though God knows how in this place!"

"No, I just went a bit farther than I thought," said Dalziel. "Got your shopping?"

"Yes. We're ready for off, if you don't mind missing your coffee."

They moved towards the car.

"Look," said Tillotson. "There's Sphincter."

They followed his gaze. Standing at the corner of the street from which Dalziel hoped they had not seen him emerge was Spinx who stepped back furtively when he realized they were looking at him.

"Who?" he said.

"His name's Spinx," said Bonnie. "He works for the insurance company that's being so bloody about coughing up for Conrad. The children call him Sphincter. Very apt."

"He's just doing his job," protested Mavis.

"He shouldn't have chosen such a nauseating job," said Bonnie calmly. "Strange, isn't it, Mr. Dalziel, how little bankruptcy means to those with nothing to lose?"

It was hard to tell if she were getting at Spinx or at Mavis.

The drive home was silent, but when they reached the house they found plenty to talk about. The representatives of the Gumbelow Foundation had rung and confirmed they would be coming that afternoon bringing with them a photographer, a freelance feature-writer whom Dalziel had never heard of, and a couple of men from the BBC with sound-recording equipment. For a while it was touch and go whether Hereward Fielding would include this under the interdict he had placed upon television, but recollection of an unnamed kindness offered to him by a Third Programme producer in 1952 swayed the balance.

"But I will not recite for them," Fielding averred fiercely. "I never have done. Have you heard Eliot? Like an old man straining on a bedpan."

Dalziel left them to their excitements and, pausing only to pick up a meat pie and a bottle of stout from the do-it-yourself lunch offering in the kitchen, he made his way towards the Banqueting Hall. When the investigatory mood was upon him he regarded open doors as invitations and closed doors as affronts and he peered into everywhere that wasn't locked. He found nothing of interest except a couple of rooms which looked as if some large and short-sighted squirrel had decided to use them as store houses. They were piled high with junk, old furniture, planks, tree branches even, and festooned with moth-eaten curtains and old clothes which would have been rejected by even the most desperate jumble sale.

The Banqueting Hall promised even less in the way of stimulation. He peered down at the patch of floor on which his memory of Cross's photograph told him Conrad Fielding had lain with an electric drill burrowing through his rib cage. A bit of gristly pork had got stuck in his teeth and he picked it out with a fingernail and burped. The floor had obviously been well scrubbed. Who by? he wondered as he placed his bottle and the remnants of the pie carefully on a wooden trestle and dragged a ladder from the shadows under the gallery. He was a careful man and after he had placed it against the wall, he wedged the trestle against the bottom rungs for extra stability before beginning his ascent. By the time he reached the level of the gallery he was wishing he hadn't bothered. The rungs felt far from secure under his bulk and the floor seemed a long way away. He reached across to the balustrade running across the gallery and felt somewhat reassured by the extra support.

The unfaced stone wall gave little away. There were a variety of scratch marks on it, some of which might have been made by a ladder scraping along the stone as it tumbled to one side.

About fifteen feet up the wall, the stone ended and was replaced by a band of white roughcast about three feet thick which reached the angle of the roof. There were signs of drilling here and Dalziel wondered if Conrad Fielding had intended to fit another beam in here, though it would have spoilt the symmetry of those already erected.

He climbed a little higher and craned his head sideways in an attempt to see how the next beam along was fixed. It was nearly three feet away and he had to lean out at a dangerous angle to get a decent view. The position suddenly made him feel very giddy, so much so that as he leaned forward and clung closely to the ladder it seemed as if it moved quite violently from side to side. He held on tight for a moment, then began to descend. Halfway down he felt able to look to the ground and he stopped abruptly when he saw a figure below, grasping the ladder and peering up at him. It was Papworth.

Quickly now Dalziel almost slid down the remaining few feet.

"You want to be careful," observed Papworth. "I thought you were going over just now."

Dalziel did not reply at once but retrieved his beer bottle and emptied what remained in a single draught.

"Lucky you were here," he said.

Papworth shrugged, an ambiguous gesture.

"I heard you," he said. "What were you doing?"

It was a blunt question, bluntly put, but justifiable from an employee of the house to a comparative stranger, thought Dalziel charitably.

"Morbid curiosity," he answered. "I just wanted to see where it happened. Was he much good at do-it-yourself?"

"Fielding?" said Papworth. "I suppose so."

"He didn't ask you to give him a hand in here then?"

"No," said Papworth turning away. "I'm not paid to work at this."

He began to walk towards the door.

"Just what are you paid to work at, Mr. Papworth?" said Dalziel to his back.

"Maintenance," said the man, pausing and glancing over his shoulder. "House and garden. Not this."

"I see," said Dalziel. "And Mrs. Greave? She's in charge of cooking and cleaning. That right?"

"Right," said Papworth.

"So neither of you would have much occasion to come in here," continued Dalziel. "Strange, I've found you in here twice."

"Wrong," said Papworth, turning. "I've found you in here twice. I don't know what right you think you've got questioning me, mister. You stick to the family. Do what you want there. You can get your leg across each of 'em in turn, and see if it bothers me. But don't try leaning on me."

"Sorry," said Dalziel with a smile. "Like I said, just morbid curiosity."

Papworth set off for the door once more but a man more acquainted with the sunshine of Dalziel's smile would have known matters were not at an end.

"What about Mrs. Greave?" mused Dalziel.

"What about her?" demanded Papworth, halting.

"You still here? I'm sorry. I was just wondering if it was all right to get my leg across Mrs. Greave. Or is she taken?"

"What do you mean?" said Papworth, his brown leathery face set in a mask of suspicion.

"I mean, what about you and Mrs. Greave? Have you got full-time rights there?"

"She's my daughter," said Papworth in a low voice. Dalziel laughed.

"And I'm your long lost sister Annie," he mocked. "Come on, Papworth. There's nothing to be ashamed of. We all need it now and then! It won't stay in the mind for ever."

"With a gut like yours, it's got to be in the mind," snapped Papworth. He looked for a moment as if he were going to say a great deal more, but his control was good and he left without another word.

Dalziel watched him go, then resumed his inspection of the hall and his ingestion of the meat pie. Afterwards he collected his raincoat without meeting any of the others and set off at a gentle walk along the road which led to the village. The pub was still open when he got there and it seemed silly to miss the chance. The landlord proved to be an amiable and forthcoming drinking companion, ready to talk knowledgeably and scandalously about everything in the neighbourhood. Fortified with drink and information, Dalziel next retired to the telephone-box outside the little post office. He spent an interesting half-hour in there too.

As he strode vigorously back towards Lake House he was passed by a total of three cars, each containing two men. None offered him a lift though one did

slow down. Thirty minutes later, when with somewhat diminished vigour he finally splashed through
the water by the gate and climbed up the drive, he
saw the trio parked outside the house.

The Gumbelow deputation had arrived.

CHAPTER X

The Presentation of Awards

The house was full of noise, most of it emanating from Hereward Fielding's sitting-room. Dalziel met Bonnie in the hall. She looked exasperated but her face lit up when she saw him. He did not know what he had done to cause this reaction but felt himself basking in the glow.

"There you are!" she said.

"I went for a walk," he explained.

"We'll have to do something about that surplus energy," she said. "These people have arrived; you know, the award people. But Herrie's throwing another tantrum. I used to think Conrad was the world champion, but he was minor county stuff compared with this. Do you think you could speak to him?"

"Me?" said Dalziel. "You must be joking! I'm not even good with animals. Besides I don't know what the old bugg—fellow is talking about half the time."

"That's part of your charm," said Bonnie. "He mentioned you at lunch today, said it was nice to have someone safe and ordinary about the place for a change. I know it's a liberty, but if you could just let him know you think it's daft to turn down good money, he might take some notice."

Dalziel let himself be led into the sitting-room, the whiles considering *safe* and *ordinary*. They were not adjectives many of his acquaintance would have applied to him, he thought. But *safe* in particular was an interesting choice for the old man to make.

The room seemed crowded with people, all gathered round the bay window in which, looking both defiant and trepid, stood Fielding. Dalziel's expert eye categorized the onlookers in a trice. The family and the other residents were there, of course. In addition there were two men in athletic middle age and well cut grey suits, wearing such similarly cast serious expressions that differences of feature were eliminated and they might have been brothers. They also might have been gang leaders, astronauts, presidential aides or Mormon PR men, but they were unmistakably American. Alongside them preserving the symmetry of the tableau were two equally unmistakably Englishmen (it's something about the eyes, decided Dalziel) who had had the misfortune to turn up, presumably without premeditation, in identical off-white corduroy suits. They looked as if they were part of an advertising campaign for spaghetti, thought Dalziel. One was balding rapidly but wore his hair so long at the back that it seemed as if the weight of it had merely pulled his forehead up over his crown. Associated with him was a pop-eyed girl, festooned with the impedimenta of photography and wearing a light green tunic which matched her chosen make-up. The other spaghetti man was presumably the radio interviewer for no one else could so impassively have ignored the comments and questions of a small negro with hornrimmed spectacles who was fiddling apparently haphazardly with a large tape-recorder.

"Let's all have a drink, shall we?" said Bonnie in her best no-nonsense voice. No one, Dalziel noted with approval, attempted to breach Herrie's well fortified drink cupboard, but Tillotson disappeared and returned almost immediately with a laden tray, which must have been prepared for just such an emergency. Pausing only to seize two large glasses of scotch, Dalziel joined the old man.

"You drinking?" he asked, glancing at the almost empty brandy balloon which stood on the window sill. "Well, sup up and try this."

"You're *still* here," stated Fielding with scornful surprise. But he took the drink.

"Aye," said Dalziel. "I only start enjoying parties when I've outstayed my welcome."

"I'm sorry. I had no right to be rude," said Fielding, suddenly contrite.

"Don't apologize for Christ's sake," said Dalziel. "Once you start that game, you never can stop. I've no right to tell you to take this sodding money, but I'm going to. Why don't you want it?"

"It's not the money, it's the principle of the thing," protested Fielding, raising his voice so that the others could hear him. "All these people can talk about is *Westminster Bridge* which I published in 1938. They seem to imagine I've written nothing since then."

"Keep your voice down," said Dalziel grimly. "All you want to worry about writing now is cheques. Don't give me this point of principle crap. What's the matter with the money?"

Hereward Fielding glared at him with an air of indignation approaching the apoplectic. Dalziel began to feel that his excursion into diplomacy was going to be as unsuccessful as it had been uncharacteristic. But now the old man's face paled to a less hectic hue and he said in a low conversational tone, "Money's not everything."

Dalziel sensed that this banal assertion was not a mere continuation of the hurt pride debate.

"A thousand quid's two hundred bottles of good brandy," he said reasonably. "That's a lot of drinking."

"Which needs a lot of time," mused Fielding. "It's your considered opinion, is it, Dalziel, that I would have this time?"

It was an odd question, but Dalziel took it in his stride.

"I can't guarantee it," he said. "But it's worth a try."

"Mr. Fielding, sir," murmured a low, flat, American voice.

One of the Americans had approached with an expression of deferential determination, like an undertaker who is not going to let you buy pine.

"Sir," he said, "let me assure you that the Gumbelow Foundation is aware of and wishes to honour the totality of your achievement. My colleague, Mr. Flower, mentioned *Westminster Bridge* merely as a volume of radical interest to the student of your mature work. Volumes such as *Victory Again, Indian Summer* and *A Kiss on the Other Cheek* are, of course, equally well known to us and equally admired also. It would be a grave disappointment . . ."

"Oh come on," snapped Fielding impatiently. "Let's get on with it."

Long-winded the American may have been, but he could move at great speed when the circumstances demanded. Fielding was led to an armchair by a low table on which copies of what Dalziel presumed to be his books were strewn. There were five or six, about the size and thickness of police promotion manuals. The photographer, who answered to Nikki (the spelling formed itself unbidden in Dalziel's mind), took a stream of pictures not seeming to care much who she got in the frame. Her camera appeared to require as little reloading as one of those guns the good cowboys used to have in the pre-psychological westerns. The tape-recorder was switched on and the Negro placed a microphone on the table and invited Fielding to say a few words.

"Must we have this sodding thing cluttering up the place?" he demanded. He referred to the microphone, but each of the visitors looked perturbed for a moment.

"We'd like to get the moment permanently recorded for posterity," said the second spaghetti man.

"Who are you?"

"I'm Alex Penitent, BBC. I shall be interviewing you after the presentation."

"Shall you? We'll see."

"Gentlemen, gentlemen, may we commence?" said the American. "Mr. Flower."

"Thank you, Mr. Bergmann."

Flower sat on a hard chair opposite Fielding while Bergmann stood alongside his colleague and put one hand inside his jacket. They looked as if they were about to make the old man an offer he couldn't refuse.

"Gentlemen, gentlemen," said Bergmann. "Right, Mr. Flower."

Flower began to speak in the deep vibrant tones of the travelogue commentator.

"For fifty years and more the Gumbelow Foundation of America has been seeking out and acknowledging rare examples of merit in the Arts. The Gumbelow Foundation does not make annual awards, for so high is the standard set that in some years no work attains this standard. Past recipients of awards have included . . ."

Here followed a list which might have been an extract from a telephone directory to Dalziel except that it contained the name of a British artist whose talents had burgeoned during a gaol sentence for armed robbery. Dalziel did not know him through his paintings but through the more personal contact of having kneed him in the crutch when he resisted arrest. As far as he could make out, the Gumbelow Foundation had not given any money to a policeman.

Flower proceeded with his potted history of the Foundation and after a while Dalziel was pleased to note most of the others were beginning to look as impatient as he felt. Someone squeezed his arm. It was Bonnie who smiled at him and mouthed "Thanks."

Fielding brought matters to a head by turning away from the table and waving his empty glass at Tillotson who nodded understandingly, came forward with a bottle and tripped over the microphone wire.

When the confusion had been sorted out, Flower

looked enquiringly at the tape-recorder man and said, "Shall I start again?"

"Oh no, oh no," cried the Negro. "We can tidy it up. Oh yes."

Flower seemed to sense the mood of the gathering for the first time and when he resumed his speech, his voice rose half an octave and accelerated by about fifty words a minute.

"In conclusion," he concluded, "may I say that few occasions have given me personally greater pleasure than this meeting with you, Hereward Fielding. On behalf of the Gumbelow Foundation of America, I ask you to accept this award for services to literature. It comes with the admiration, awe and sincere respect of lovers of beauty the whole world over."

He held up his left hand. Bergmann withdrew his right from inside his jacket and slapped a large white envelope into Flower's palm. The envelope was then thrust aggressively towards Fielding and Nikki's camera began clicking like a Gieger-counter in a uranium mine.

"Keep it there, keep it there, good, good, super, super," she said. Flower held the pose, smiling fixedly at Fielding who, it gradually began to dawn on the spectators, was staring at the outstretched hand as if it were holding a dead rat. Even Nikki eventually became aware that all was not quite right and the clickings became intermittent, finally dying away into a silence which for a moment was complete.

"Oh Herrie!" breathed Bonnie.

The old man spoke. His voice was light, meditative.

"It is interesting to me that you only make your awards in those years which see the production of work of rare merit, particularly as I have published nothing for more than five years now. Still, better late than never, they say. Though I am not sure I agree with that either. I have been writing for over fifty years now and half a century is very late indeed. I am, of course—I *have* to be I suppose—grateful for your offer. But fifty years . . . !"

He shook his head and sighed.

"If you'd given me this when I was twenty, I might have bought myself a big meal, a floppy hat like Roy Campbell's and one of those delicious little tarts who use to hang around the Café Royal.

"If you'd given it to me when I was thirty, I might have bought my kids some new clothes and my wife a sunnier disposition.

"Even if you had given it to me when I was forty or fifty, I'd have found a use for it. A more comfortable car, for instance. Or a cruise round the Greek islands to see the cradle of civilization.

"But now I am old and I am ill. I have little appetite for food or women. My children have grown up and gone their ways. Or died. I no longer care to travel by car. And civilization is dying where it began.

"So you might say that in a fashion not untypically American you have come too bloody late."

He paused. No one spoke. The envelope remained in Flower's outstretched hand. The American's expression never deviated from respectful admiration, and the expressions of the others varied from amusement via distaste and indifference to Bonnie's evident anxiety.

"Bravo."

It was Bertie who broke thhe silence, uttering the word with overstressed irony.

"Shut it, Bertie," said Mavis warningly.

Bergmann shrugged, a massive Central European bewildered shrug, which crumbled his streamlined New York façade as an earth tremor might destroy a skyscraper. Flower seemed to take a cue and relaxed in his chair dropping his hand to the table. The old man's arm shot out as the envelope moved and he plucked it rudely from Flower's grasp.

"However," he said, very Churchillian, "I will not refuse your gift, late though it is. For I recall that I never did get a hat like Roy Campbell's. But now I shall. And I shall wear it slightly askew as I walk through the village in the hope that the tedious inmates will shun me as a man unbalanced and in

the even vainer hope that this reputation might somehow distress my neglectful friends and ungrateful
descendants. Bonnie, my glass is empty."

After that somehow a party began. The BBC man
tried for a while to get his intimate interview but in
the end recognized that his efforts were losing him
ground in the drinks race and set about catching up.
The feature writer, aptly named Butt, was well in
the lead, though Bergmann would have been neck
and neck if his new flamboyancy of gesture had not
been joined by a matching volubility of speech. Flower
on the other hand was a recidivist and his speech
got lower and slower and more and more slurred till
he sounded like a second-rate English mimic doing
James Stewart. Nikki had stopped clicking and was
gurgling merrily through glass after nauseating glass
of port and brandy. Even Arkwright, the tape-recorder
man, found time from his task of preventing others
resting their glasses and persons on his equipment
to down mouthfuls from a half-pint glass of gin.

Nor were the residents of Lake House far behind
and Dalziel, ever a pragmatist, put all care for the
past or the future out of his mind and set to with a
will.

After a while for a relatively small gathering the
noise became deafening. He found himself next to
Fielding who was still holding the envelope tight to
his chest as though fearing it would be taken from
him. His words to Dalziel seemed to confirm this
impression.

"It will be all right, you assure me of that?" he
cried in what was relatively a whisper.

Dalziel nodded wisely, winked and turned away
in search of Bonnie. Behind him the conversation
between Fielding and the Americans resumed.

"I don't care for Updike. Overwrought, overblown
and overpraised," cried Bergmann.

"Yeah," drawled Flower. "Updike's a shit."

Bonnie was in the window bay being leaned over
confidentially by Butt who seemed to fancy himself
as the great poke as well as the great soak, but

Dalziel's rescue mission was hindered by Penitent who grasped him by the arm, peered closely into his face and said something like, "What are you doing after the show?"

"What?" bellowed Dalziel.

"Haven't we met somewhere before?"

His voice had the controlled flatness with which ambitious public school men in the BBC attempt to conceal their origins.

"I doubt it," said Dalziel.

Someone grasped his other arm and he felt a surge of panic as if at any moment blows might be hurled at his unprotected gut.

It was Bertie. There was no physical danger but he was bent on being nasty.

"Enjoying yourself, Dalziel?" he asked. "Enjoying your free booze, are you? And your bed and breakfast? Pity you'll have to be leaving us."

"What's up, sonny?" snarled Dalziel. "You putting me out?"

"No, no. It's just that once your car's ready, you'll be on your way, won't you? Well, I rang the garage after lunch and they say they've got it and it'll be ready for you in the morning. At a pinch, you could go tonight. Not that we want to lose you, of course."

"Mensa!" said Penitent.

"What?"

"That's where we met, I think. Mensa."

Ensa, thought Dalziel. He thinks I'm sort of performer. Which I am.

"Not likely," he bellowed. "Nearest I got was seeing Tommy Handley at Catterick when I was in the MPs."

"I'll say cheerio now in case we miss each other in the morning," said Bertie. Dalziel shook his arm free and succeeded in slopping some of his drink over the youth's shirt which was some consolation for not being able to punch his fat, smiling mouth.

"MPs," said Penitent, puzzled. "Did Handley have something in the Eden administration?"

Dalziel smiled at him uncomprehendingly.

"You work at it, lad," he said in a sympathetic voice. "You can end up having as many 'O' levels as Jimmy Young."

"Charley!" He heard Bonnie's voice cut clearly through the din. "We need some more booze. Pop along to the store and bring up a couple of bottles of everything, there's a love. Oh, and while you're down there, tell Mrs. Greave I'd like a word. I suppose everyone will want to be fed eventually."

She seemed quite unperturbed by the prospect. Dalziel recalled that his own wife had required five days' notice if he was bringing a mate round for a glass of beer.

There was a click in his ear and he thought that Nikki must have started up again but when he looked it was Uniff.

"One not enough?" he asked, nodding towards the green tunic which he now spotted alongside Louisa by the door.

"Her?" said Uniff scornfully. "She's one of the creative accident mob. You shoot enough film, something's bound to be OK."

"While you use your genius?"

"Right," grinned Uniff. "Besides I'm not so rich. Like big John Wayne says, you gotta make every shot count."

"How's your picture going?" asked Dalziel.

"Up and down, you know how it is, man. You want to see it some time?"

"If you want to show it," said Dalziel.

"Why not? Hell, there's got to come a time for every artist when he exposes himself to the average bum in the street."

"You try exposing yourself to me," said Dalziel, "you'll make a pretty picture yourself."

Uniff laughed heartily.

"I like you, Andy baby," he said. "Christ, man, how do you stick it in here with this load of phoneys?"

His gesture seemed pretty well all-inclusive.

"Are they phoneys?" asked Dalziel.

"Can't you tell?"

"I don't know what the real thing looks like, so it's a bit hard," said Dalziel.

Nor could he see any reason why anyone should want to *pretend* to be what he saw around him. In particular, you'd have to be bloody revolting to make it worthwhile *pretending* to be a conceited, blubber-lipped, purple-cheeked, perfumed ponce in a corru-gated suit.

"Andrew," said Bonnie. "Have you met Eric Butt?"

His pleasure at hearing her use his Christian name almost overcame his distaste for Butt. The journalist smiled briefly at him and returned his attention to Bonnie.

"Next time you're in town," he said, "give me a ring. We can lunch together. Fellow I know has just taken over a little French place in Hampstead. Not for the *hoi polloi*, you know, but you'd love it."

"How sweet," said Bonnie. "I was thinking of taking all the children up next week. Perhaps we could meet there. Would Tuesday suit you?"

Butt emptied his glass and came up smiling.

"Sorry," he said. "Better to ring. I'm off to Brazil tomorrow and I'll be there over a week. It's a great thing, did you read about it? There was a bit in the *Observer* supplement last week. I'm doing a piece on the Brazilian football team and they've agreed for me to stay and train with them. It's a bit unique, actu-ally. The Brazilian Ambassador fixed it, likes my stuff, felt I would do a good job. I wouldn't miss it for worlds. Ever been to Brazil, darling?"

"No," said Bonnie. "Andrew though has been around a lot, perhaps he could give you a few travel-ler's tips."

She turned away to greet Tillotson who had re-turned with an armful of bottles.

Dalziel moved close to Butt and sniffed.

"The trouble with corduroy," he said, "is that it doesn't half smell if you piss on it."

"Oh damn the woman," said Bonnie crossly. "It's not her night off. I'd better go and look in the larder myself. Andrew, see that everyone's got plenty to drink, will you?"

"What's up?" asked Dalziel.

"I couldn't find Mrs. Greave anywhere," said Tillotson. "Her door was locked."

"Did you look in Pappy's room?"

"No. Why should I?" said Tillotson.

Dalziel smiled and plucked a couple of spirit bottles out of the box. The smile died on his face and was replaced by an exasperated grimace. One of the bottles was quite empty. Was there nothing Charley could do without making a balls-up? He checked through the box and found three other empties. That still left eight which was plenty to be going on with, even for this lot.

He looked around the room. Arkwright was asleep on his tape-recorder. Nikki was trying to take a self-portrait with her camera, at the same time as, unawares, she was being photographed by Uniff. Bertie and Mavis were in close confabulation in a corner. They looked at him as he stared towards them, then hastily looked away. Penitent was talking to Louisa, probably offering to make her a star on *The Archers*. And the trio of Hereward and the two Americans still held the centre of the stage. Bergmann was gabbling away at a pace just short of incomprehensibility while Flower nodded his head sagely and drawled, "Melville's a shit. Mailer's a shit. Hawthorne's a shit. Longfellow . . . well, Longfellow . . . well, Longfellow's a shit also."

Seizing one of the full bottles of scotch, Dalziel went to help Bonnie.

He found her in the kitchen looking in disgust at a table covered with sausages.

"That's all there is," she said. "I thought we ate enough sausages last night to deplete local stocks for fifty miles around."

"Perhaps she got them in a sale," said Dalziel. "Have a drink."

He poured a tumberful which she sipped like cold tea.

"What shall I do?" she asked.

It was a comfort to be consulted. A woman could be too competent.

"Stick 'em between two slices of bread and call 'em frankfurters," said Dalziel. "These Americans eat nothing else."

"Fine," said Bonnie. "What about cooking them? It'll take hours."

"Not," said Dalziel, "if you use one of those nice new ovens you've got out back."

"You're a genius," said Bonnie seriously. "And we might even unearth Mrs. Greave while we're out there."

They had another large scotch apiece to celebrate the decision. Then the sausages were swept off the table into a large round basket and they set off for the Banqueting Hall kitchens like Red Riding Hood and the Wolf. The image put Dalziel in mind of Butt.

"That fellow Butt," he said. "You handled him nicely."

"Thank you kindly," she said. "Though I reckon I lacked your finesse."

"What? Oh you heard that," said Dalziel sheepishly. She laughed.

"You don't exactly whisper, Andy. May I call you Andy? No, I've met your Butts before. Always off to Brazil, meeting exciting people, but usually ready to fit you in for a quick roll between jets."

"I hope he gets a football up his . . . nose," said Dalziel.

"Poor man! How's he harmed you?" she asked, then added thoughtfully, "But if he really trains with them, it could be chancy. He looked a bit hearty to me."

Dalziel mused upon this as they reached the kitchens where the ovens proved a complete failure. Dalziel seated on an old wooden chair watched with amusement as Bonnie, festooned with sausages, moved around trying to get them to work.

"Useless things!" she exploded.

"Is the power switched through?" asked Dalziel.

"Yes. I think so. At least, Bertie said it was. The dishwasher certainly works."

"Shall I take a look?" asked Dalziel, heaving himself upright.

"No. Never bother. I'll tell Bertie. He's the only one who understands these things. God, I'm whacked!"

She slumped into the chair vacated by Dalziel who turned from his examination of the first oven with a comment on his lips which died when he saw her. Her head was bowed forward and her arms rested slackly over her knees as though they had been carelessly deposited there for collection later. One leg was crooked under the chair, the other stretched straight out. The whole composition was ugly, awkward, a study in defeat. When Dalziel approached and she looked up, the pores of her face seemed to have opened; the fine Edwardian strength he had admired before was eroded by an admission of age and weariness into a puffy substanceless outline. She was, Dalziel realized, more his contemporary than he had imagined.

And at the same time he realized she was letting him see her like this out of choice. There was strength enough there still to have taken her back to the party and set wildly coursing whatever passes for blood beneath a corduroy suit.

"I don't think these sausages are going to get cooked," he said.

"No, I don't think they are," she said.

It had been the beginning of an explanation but he let it rest as the oblique comment she obviously took it for.

"Why don't you lie down?" he said.

"I should like that," she answered. "Will you lie down with me?"

"Aye, will I," he said.

They lay together fully dressed for nearly an hour while Bonnie dozed and Dalziel counted the chrysanthemums on her William Morris wallpaper, wondering if this was going to be one of those queer Platonic relationships he heartily disbelieved in. Finally he gave her a bit of a shake and set about confirming his disbelief.

Bonnie was agreeable enough, her body and mind soft and yielding in a half sleep. But Dalziel was no subtle wooer with diplomas in the arts of pleasure. The only prelude to penetration he had ever bothered with in his married life was four or five pints of bitter and now the brutal directness of his approach shocked Bonnie wide awake.

"Why not take a run to get up a bit of speed?" she demanded.

"What's the matter?" asked Dalziel.

"Well, for a start, get your clothes off. All your clothes."

Grimly he undressed at one side of the bed while Bonnie stripped at the other.

"Now let's begin at the beginning," said Bonnie.

Five minutes later she pinched his flabby left buttock viciously and said "For God's sake, don't be so impatient. There's two of us to consider."

"We'll have to take turn about," gasped Dalziel.

Bonnie shook with laughter and the movement removed any chance of restraint on Dalziel's part. When he'd done and recognized that there was no mockery in her laughter he joined in.

"I've never laughed on the job before," he said finally.

"Why not? It's a funny business," said Bonnie. "What was that you said about turn about?"

Evening was well advanced when they rose and the house was quiet.

"Perhaps they've all gone," said Dalziel.

"They're more likely to be too drunk to speak," said Bonnie. "Or they're in the kitchen guzzling sausages."

Dalziel felt guilty. After the welter of confused emotion which had immersed him during the past couple of hours, it was almost a relief to isolate and recognize a simple reaction. It was a conditioned reflex rather than an emotion; policemen were bred to put the investigation of crime before their personal pleasure and he had been false to his breeding.

"I doubt they'll have cooked those sausages," he said.

"Why's that?" she asked, tugging a comb through her thick brown hair which, unfastened, had tumbled in surprising profusion over her shoulders.

"Come downstairs and I'll show you," he said grimly.

Puzzled, Bonnie finished her tidying up and let herself be led to the kitchen once more. They met no one en route and the basket of sausages remained untouched where they had left it.

"It's a bit like the *Mary Celeste*," said Bonnie.

"No mystery," grunted Dalziel. "They'll all be stoned out of their minds."

He took a coin from his pocket and rapidly unscrewed the control panel of one of the ovens.

"Take a look in here," he invited. "What do you see?"

Bonnie peered in cautiously.

"Nothing much," she admitted.

"Right," said Dalziel. "Now what you should see is what makes these things work. Magnetrons, they're called. Don't ask me how I know."

"Where are they?" wondered Bonnie making her way round the kitchen inspecting every oven. "What a stupid thing! You'd think Bertie would have checked when they installed them."

"He probably did," said Dalziel. "I think you've been robbed."

"Robbed?" She laughed. "Don't be silly. Why should anyone steal whatever you said?"

"Some people'd steal owt for a bob or two," said Dalziel. "Don't mistake. Everything's sellable. But I'm feared this is just an extra."

"Extra?"

"Aye. Where's the drink store?"

"Oh Jesus!" she cried, catching his drift now. "There's a cellar . . . we've got all our opening stock in there. Conrad got it in just before our credit gave up the ghost completely."

They clattered down a narrow flight of stairs which led to an open door.

"Damn Charley!" snapped the woman. "He had strict instructions to lock up behind him."

"Don't blame the lad," said Dalziel. "I doubt if it's worth locking."

At first glance all looked well. The crates of spirits, apéritifs, wine and liqueurs were all stacked in militarily neat array. But a few moments' investigation revealed the worst. Only the nearest bottles were full. Behind the front rank, all the liquor had been decanted, and in the nether crates there were no bottles at all.

"Charley got some of the empties in his mixed dozens," said Dalziel. "I thought it was just another bit of daftness then."

Bonnie who after an explosion of blasphemous obscenity had got hold of herself very well demanded, "What made you think differently. The ovens?"

"Aye. And one other thing."

They went back up the stairs, Dalziel leading now. He strode belligerently to Mrs. Greave's room and without knocking, kicked the door open so that it rattled against the wall and went inside. When Bonnie caught up, he had opened every cupboard door and drawer in the place. They were uniformly empty.

"You mean you think that Mrs. Greave . . ." said Bonnie incredulously. "But why? She's Pappy's daughter."

Dalziel laughed, a short humourless bark very different from the deep guffaws he had emitted in the intimacy of the bedroom.

"If you believe that, you'll believe anything."

"But how do you know? How can you be sure it's her?"

"I know a slag when I see one," said Dalziel brutally. "When her type and your property go missing at the same time, then don't waste your time praying for guidance."

"If you worked this out before, you haven't exactly struck while the iron was hot," said Bonnie reprovingly.

"No. Well, something got in the way," muttered Dalziel. "I'm sorry."

"Don't be," she said smiling. "Well, what now? I suppose I'd better phone the police."

Dalziel scratched the back of his neck and looked at her assessingly. The thought had already occurred to him that she might know he was a policeman. If so, she was playing it very cool for reasons which were far from clear (and, his constabulary mind whispered to him, perhaps just as far from virtuous). Those same reasons, the brutal whisper continued, may have got him into her bed. He'd been a detective too long to be surprised by what some women would do in the cause of injustice. No, it wouldn't surprise him. But what *was* surprising him was the realization of just how much it would hurt him.

"That'd be best," he said. "Though I doubt you've had your booze. It's probably been long gone."

And someone had thought it worthwhile postponing the moment of discovery by first of all ringing the builders and telling them that Fielding was near on bankrupt, then ringing Spinx and telling him not to pay out the insurance money. And, he recalled, the anonymous caller had known there was a policeman in the house. That put it even more firmly at Mrs. Greave's door. This kind of sixth sense was two-way traffic.

By the time they re-entered the main entrance hall, he'd decided that it was worth trying to remain anonymous for as long as possible.

"I'll ring the cops," he said. "You go and see if you can find Papworth and see what light he can throw."

But his ruse to get a quiet word with Sergeant Cross was unsuccessful. A door opened and Bertie

appeared, flushed violet with drink. Surprisingly this
seemed to have made him more affable.

"Dalziel!" he said. "Come in and have a drink. On
me. You mustn't take my words to heart, mustn't
sulk. You're too big for sulking. Your *hulk* has too
much *bulk* for you to *sulk*. How's that? Herrie'd get
fifty dollars for that and you know how much the
old sod would give us? Bugger all. *That's* all. What's
your poison"

"I shouldn't bother," said Bonnie sharply. "There's
likely to be quite a drink shortage round here shortly."

"What do you mean?" demanded her son, swaying.

"I mean we've been robbed. Mrs. Greave, it ap-
pears, has been steadily removing all our drink stock
and anything else she could lay her hands on. Including the working part of your precious ovens.
And now she's taken off."

Bertie stood amazed. His colour remained the same,
perhaps deepened slightly, but affability drained visibly from his face.

"Oh, the cow, the stupid cow! I'll kill the bitch!"

He smashed the fist of his right hand into his left
palm. Dalziel caught Bonnie's eye and raised his
eyebrows. She did not respond but looked away.

"All right, Dalziel," said Bertie. "What now?"

"There's only one thing to do," interrupted his
mother firmly. "We must ring the police."

"We must ring the police," echoed Bertie mock-
ingly. "What's the matter, Mother dear? Have his
hidden charms enthralled you? I'll ring the police,
never fear."

He approached close enough for Dalziel to smell
the gin on his breath.

"Dring dring," he said. "Dring dring. Is anyone there? I'd like to speak to a big, fat, ugly Detective Superintendent, please. You recognize the des-
cription? Good. Well, what happens next, please sir,
Mr. Dalziel?"

Dalziel looked from the youth to his mother. She
made no effort to look surprised but shrugged her
shoulders minutely. He took in a deep breath and let

it out slowly, carefully, like a man decanting a rare wine against the light of a candle.

"What happens next?" he repeated stepping forward so that Bertie had to move back quickly to avoid being knocked over. "Well, first of all, sonny, you start talking polite to me or I might just level off your spotty ugly face so that it'd take emulsion. Then next after that, we'll start really digging into just what makes this place tick, shall we?"

CHAPTER XI

Hello Sailor

Dalziel sat in the old man's sitting-room and drank brandy. He had no authority to investigate crime on this patch, he assured Fielding. But the truth was he had been so discomfited and irritated by Sergeant Cross's reproachful expression that the choice had been between escape and expulsion. The sergeant had not openly said that Dalziel had withheld information, but his suspicions—clearly roused by the fat man's visit to Orburn that day—must have seemed confirmed when Dalziel told him that Annie Greave (or *Annie Grimshaw*, or *Open Annie*) was well known to Liverpool CID.

"I telephoned them just on the off-chance she was using her proper name," he explained. "Not much imagination, these pros."

"Ah," said Cross.

The only immediate potential source of information about Mrs. Greave was Papworth and he too had disappeared. His room, however, showed no signs of a hurried or permanent leave-taking and it seemed safe to assume he would return.

"You mustn't blame Bonnie," said Fielding suddenly. He occupied the same chair in which he had received the Gumbelow award and Dalziel wondered if he had moved out of it since then.

Apart from the debris of glasses and bottles which

littered the room, the only other sign of the afternoon's junketings was Arkwright, the sound engi-
neer, who slept with his head pillowed on and his
arms still clasped protectively around his recorder.
From time to time a bubbly and rather musical baritone snore emerged from his mouth.

Whether the others had gone or were also to be
found unconscious round the premises, Dalziel did
not know.

"Blame her for what?" he grunted.

"Going through your pockets," said Fielding. "It
is after all a sensible thing to do when hanging up a
suit to dry."

"What was she doing in my wallet?" demanded
Dalziel. "Ironing my money? And why didn't you
lot say you knew I was a policeman?"

Fielding shrugged.

"Why didn't you tell us?"

"Why should I?"

"Why indeed? But it doesn't create an atmosphere
of confidence having someone in your house under
false pretences."

Dalziel refilled his glass with a brusqueness which
in another man might have resulted in spillage.

"I pretended nowt."

"Come, come," said Fielding mildly. "This morning Bertie and Lou went to Bonnie with some story
about the possibility of your putting money into the
restaurant. They were very put out when she told
them who you were."

"Oh. They didn't know till then?" said Dalziel
thoughtfully.

"No."

"And you?"

"Bonnie told me this morning too. She's a very
discreet woman."

Dalziel considered the implications. It was a comfort to know there hadn't been a general conspiracy,
with everyone watching the big thick policeman blun-
dering around. It was also good to know that whatever asexual motives Bonnie might have had for

going to bed with him, the hope of more money for
the business wasn't one of them. But this still left
some disturbing possibilities. A detective grew accustomed to attempts to use sex either as a means of
buying him off or compromising him. It didn't happen every night or every week or even every month.
But it happened. Dalziel didn't want this to be the
truth, but his self-image argued against him. He had
never considered himself a lady's man, but he had
had his moments, and until a few months ago would
have been complacent enough to accept that a big,
burly, balding middle-aged detective superintendent
might set some female hearts astir. Now there was
too much darkness in his nights for the overspill not
to cloud all but the brightest day, and his diminished concept of what he was hardly admitted the
generation of love at first sight, or even enthusiastic
lust.

Which left one more question. Why? What was he
being bought off from, or more simply perhaps,
distracted from.

He leaned forward and peered at the old man.

"Got your envelope safe?" he asked.

Hereward winked and tapped his stomach indicating, Dalziel surmised, either that he had stuffed it
down his undervest or else eaten it.

"Why were you so bothered about taking it?" continued Dalziel.

Fielding looked at him cunningly.

"Pride," he said. "Literary pride."

"Piss off," said Dalziel easily. "You wouldn't let
pride get between you and all that brandy."

"All right," said Fielding. "Ambition then."

"Ambition?"

"Yes. This year I shall equal Browning. Another
three will take me up to Wordsworth. And if I can
hang on another three, I'll be past Tennyson."

Dalziel laughed.

"Good-living bastards these poets, were they? So
you want to be a hundred? Hey, you know what the
Queen's Telegram says?"

"No. What?"

"Drop dead you silly old bugger."

Fielding found this so amusing that he choked on his drink and for a moment Dalziel thought he was going to anticipate his sovereign's alleged command. But the cause of the upset also proved a remedy and after a moment he returned to his line of questioning.

"So what were the magic words I uttered that made you change your mind?"

"Nothing really," said Fielding. "I just wanted to be reassured that you would make your presence felt, which you have done with admirable timing. To be worth several thousand pounds in a household of relative paupers is no comfortable thing, Dalziel. You understand?"

"No," said Dalziel. "Not unless you're implying one of this lot'd try to knock you off. You're not saying that, are you?"

"Of course I'm saying that," snapped Fielding. "What do you want—a bibliography and index?"

"When people start talking about murder threats I want owt that'll stand up as evidence," retorted Dalziel. "Come on now. This is a serious allegation. What do you know?"

"I know that I am an old man," said Fielding slowly, "and in the eyes of many I have lived my life and run my race. I know that an old man is susceptible to heat and cold, to accidents, heart attacks, broken limbs, dizziness and dyspepsia. I shall not die, I think, from daggers or bullets or strange exotic poisonings. But die I shall and, as with many of the old, I suspect, I fear that a less than divine shoehorn will be used to ease me into my grave."

Dalziel drank his brandy, shaking his head and marvelling inwardly at this strange and loving submission to the monstrous tyranny of words.

"Well," he grunted, "no bugger in this house'll kill you now, not while I'm around."

"A champion!" said Bertie from the doorway. "Sound the trumpet three times and Dalziel will gallop to the rescue!"

"What's happening out there, Bertie!" demanded Fielding. "And spare us your tedious wit in the telling."

"Nothing much," said the stout youth, flopping into a chair. He seemed to have recovered both his sobriety and his temper. From the paleness round his eyes Dalziel judged that he had been sick.

"Sergeant Cross has been asking everyone questions," said Tillotson, who had followed Bertie into the room. "But he seems to have finished now. Is it true that you're a policeman too, Mr. Dalziel?"

Dalziel regarded him kindly. Here was the last person anyone ever told anything. Tillotson and his kind would be carrying on normally days after the Last Trump had summoned everyone else to the Judgement Throne.

"That's right," he said.

"Really? Sir George Cheesman who used to be Chief Constable of Worcester is my godfather. Do you know him?"

"No," said Dalziel. "But I used to have a budgie that whistled the 'Eton Boating Song.' What are you lot going to do now?"

"What do you mean?"

"I mean you were in bad enough trouble with this restaurant business before. Now with your booze gone and your ovens knackered, you are right up the creek."

"Which pleases you, does it?" asked Bertie.

"No. Not at all," said Dalziel.

"We're covered against theft by insurance, surely?" said Tillotson.

Dalziel and Bertie laughed in unison.

"What's so funny?" asked Tillotson.

"After you," said Bertie to Dalziel.

"Well, firstly no insurance company's going to rush to pay out on any claims coming from this household at the moment. Especially not if it's Anchor."

"And secondly," said Bertie. "I doubt if my late lamented father ever bothered to insure the new equipment and so on. I asked him about it once, but got told in no uncertain terms that financial arrangements were his pigeon."

"Oh," said Tillotson. He looked very taken aback.

"Worried about your investment?" asked Bertie. "Don't be, Charley. Just stiffen that upper lip and wave goodbye."

There was a tap on the door and Cross came in.

"I'm finished now," he said. "May I have a word, sir, before I go?"

Dalziel rose.

"What are the chances of getting the stuff back, Sergeant?" asked Tillotson.

"Pretty low, I'm afraid," said Cross. "Do you think you'll be able to sort things out for the opening night?"

Bertie to whom the question was addressed yawned rudely.

"Who knows, Sergeant? But don't you worry about our business, just work hard at yours, will you?"

Dalziel put his arm over Cross's shoulders and ushered him through the door. He himself turned just before he closed it and said, "Sergeant Cross has paid ten quid for two first night tickets. So think on; the customer is always right, eh?"

"Puffed up young git!" said Cross savagely in the hallway. "I'll sort the bugger before I'm through."

Inwardly Dalziel applauded the attitude but he put on his best impartial-guardian-of-the-law look and shook his head disapprovingly.

"That's no way to talk," he said. "You want to watch yourself, Sergeant."

"I'm too busy watching other people, sir," said Cross sulkily. "I've had three hours' sleep today, and when I leave here I'm going back to those bloody chickens again."

"It's a full life," agreed Dalziel. "What did you want to see me about?"

"Nothing really, sir. Just to ask, really, if there was any other way you could help me; I mean, you staying in the house, and everything . . ."

This was the closest he dared come to a spoken reproach, realized Dalziel.

"I don't think so," he answered.

"How long will you be staying here, sir?"

"Not long. Just till tomorrow probably. I don't know."

It was true. He didn't. Everything pointed the way to a quick exit. But there were questions still to be answered if he cared to, or dared to, go on asking them.

"I see. The man Papworth hasn't come back yet, sir. I wonder if you'd mind keeping an eye open and letting us know when he returns. I'd like a word with him as soon as possible and we don't really have the establishment to spare a man to hang around here half the night."

"A super in the house is worth a d.c. in the bush?" said Dalziel. "Aye, I'll watch out for him. Is anything known about him, by the way?"

"Not by us, officially. But he's well known in the district. He's been around for twenty or thirty years, most of them working for the Percivals. His reputation's not so good. A rough, tough character, keeps himself to himself, hard to beat in a deal or in a fight."

"Women?"

"What?"

"Is he known as a womanizer? I don't suppose he had Open Annie down here to cut his toenails."

Cross considered.

"No. I've never heard of anything out of the way in that line. But I'll ask around if you think it's important."

Dalziel shrugged indifferently.

"Your case, Sergeant. You ask what you want to know. Me, I'm just a tourist. Well, I won't keep you from your chickens. A tip-off, is it?"

Cross nodded.

"There's been a lot about and I've been told this battery's to be cleared out this week. I'll give it one more night."

"It'll be tomorrow," said Dalziel maliciously. "Good hunting."

He returned to the sitting-room. Louisa and Mavis had joined the others, but there was no sign of Bonnie. The two girls were looking down at Arkwright.

"Is he the sole survivor?" asked Dalziel.

Louisa nodded.

"The others left shortly before you and Bonnie reappeared," she said. "I think they got hungry. Also Herrie made it clear that he was fed up of listening to Abbot and Costello."

"It wasn't very kind of Penitent to abandon *him*," said Dalziel indicating the snoring Negro.

"What shall we do with him?" asked Tillotson. "We can't just let him lie there all night."

"Are you going to give him your bed then?" mocked Bertie.

"Stick him in Mrs. Greave's room," said Dalziel. "She won't be back."

"And of course the servants' quarters are the proper place for a black man," said Bertie. He looked healthier now and his nastiness was returning.

"A bed's a bed," said Dalziel, refusing to be drawn.

"A liberal policeman! But suppose it was your sister's bed, Dalziel. What then?"

"Personally," said Dalziel, "I wouldn't envy a randy billy goat getting into my sister's bed. Come on, sunshine. Charley boy, give us a hand."

Together he and Tillotson lifted Arkwright from his tape-recorder and carried him, feet trailing, down the corridor to Mrs. Greave's room where they dumped him on the bed, removed his tie and shoes and covered him with a patchwork quilt. Then at Tillotson's suggestion, they retired to the kitchen where the young man brewed a pot of coffee at the expense of only one cup and a few minor burns.

Dalziel glanced at his watch. It was still early, just a quarter past nine, but he found himself yawning.

"Tired?" said Tillotson sympathetically, pouring the coffee.

"A bit," said Dalziel. "It's been a hard day. Or a

day of surprises, and that's always hard. You don't care much for surprises when you're getting on."

"I don't like surprises either," said Tillotson sadly.

"No? Well, you're young enough to take things in your stride anyway. How much cash have you got in this business?"

"A few hundred," said Tillotson. "Not much, but all I possess."

"That's enough. All you possess is quite enough," said Dalziel. "What's your standing?"

"I'm sorry?"

"I mean, what's the deal? Is it shares? Or a partnership agreement? What kind of investment have you made?"

"Does it matter?" asked Tillotson.

Dalziel rolled his eyes and scratched the skin around his Adam's apple.

"Look," he said, "love's one thing but business is another. Of course it matters. One way you can just lose your investment if the thing folds. Another way, though, you can be held partly responsible if the thing goes bankrupt which might mean you having to find more cash. You follow? It depends what you signed."

"Oh, I didn't sign anything," said Tillotson. "I just made out a cheque to Conrad, Mr. Fielding that is."

"That was," said Dalziel. "Well, so much for the fatherly advice. If you're ever in the market for a used car, give us a ring."

Shaking his bull-like head, he drank his coffee. It was truly awful but something in Tillotson touched off a non-habitual response of kindness and he said nothing. They talked in a desultory fashion for nearly half an hour before Dalziel yawned again and said he would take a turn in the fresh air before heading for bed.

After checking that Papworth had still not returned he left the house and strolled down to the water's edge to smoke a cigarette and think. The flood level had perceptibly dropped, for the wooden slats of the landing-stage were now quite clear of the surface. He took a couple of tentative paces along the stage, then halted for the treads were not only still greasy from their long submersion, but in addition he felt them give under his considerable bulk. Indeed, at the end of the landing-stage there was a gap, just perceptible in the dim light, where the treads seemed to have fallen away altogether.

The waters of the swollen lake stretched away before him, stirred by a light wind so that small waves slapped against the recovered row-boat and the duck punt. They were moored together by the landing-stage, and occasionally in their rising and falling touched with a dull noise like distant artillery. Above, the cloud cover was broken now and the clustered stars shone through the uneven rents. Dalziel regarded them for a while, then looked away. There was something too much of the tribunal about the unblinking clarity of their regard to ease his mind. He had once promised a recalcitrant suspect justice if he cooperated. *Any cunt can get justice*, the man had answered. *Me. I want mercy.* He had got seven years. If, speculated Dalziel, instead of putting 'em away in prison, they could transfer the years from the criminal's life to the arresting officer's, I'd be nigh on bloody immortal!

All those years, his mind ran on. All those years for all those men. And for all those men guarding them. And for all those men chasing them and catching them and prosecuting them and condemning them. There were more stars, so they said, than could be counted. And in the end unless something strange and unbelievable happened to mankind, all those years too would add up beyond the reckoning of any human mind.

His mind was running on like a tuppeny novel. Such speculations were not for detective superintendents of the old school no matter how many sleepless nights they had had and no matter how many women proved to be as unreliable as the first. Eyes to the ground finds you sixpences. Cautiously but steadfastly he advanced along the landing-stage till he reached the gap left by the missing treads. In fact they weren't missing, but broken, their jagged edges sunk into the water.

Dalziel didn't move but stood quite still peering through the gap. There was just enough light to make out the surface of the water, dully shining and touched with little swirls of rainbow. The wind gusted, the small waves slapped, the boats came together. And rising to the surface as though drawn by a line from Dalziel's unblinking stare came a face.

Dalziel regarded it without surprise. Ever since he first looked on these floods he had been waiting for a body. The face began to sink again but he thrust his hands quickly into the chill water, grasped the sodden collar and hauled the upper part of the torso clear of the lake.

The features had not been long enough immersed for identification to be difficult. It was Spinx, the insurance investigator.

"Hello sailor," said Dalziel.

CHAPTER XII

A View in the Morning

"All right, so it's accidental death!" said Cross.

"I didn't say that," said Dalziel.

"Well, what do you say, sir?"

"You've had as good a look at the scene as I have. Those boards *were* rotten; there's a mark on his head where he *could* have banged it against the main support as he fell and there's traces of what *might* be blood on the edge of the support. You'll just have to wait for the p.m. and the lab reports."

"I know all that," said Cross. "But it's a question of what I do *now*. I mean, there's all these other features . . ."

"Such as?"

"Well, the Greave woman for instance. And Mr. Fielding's death so recently. Lots of odd things, sir. I'm asking for your advice."

"My advice," said Dalziel, "is to do what you would have done if I hadn't been here. Personally, and this isn't advice, just me thinking out loud, I'd put a tarpaulin over one end of that landing-stage and a copper at the other and bugger off back to my chickens."

Cross looked at him undecided, then the telephone rang inside the house. A moment later Bonnie appeared at the front door and said, "Sergeant Cross, it's for you."

Cross went inside. Dalziel lit a cigarette absently. It was about the twentieth he had lit absently in the past couple of hours. He was becoming quite adept at doing absently those things which he ought not be doing at all.

"It's been a hell of a day," said Bonnie wearily.

"Yes," he answered.

"We could stop the best bit being spoiled," she said after a pause.

"Oh. How's that?"

"I don't know, just by not letting it, I suppose. I saw your face earlier, Andy. You seem to think that for some reason I went to bed with you because you're a policeman. I mean, just think about it! What kind of reason would that be?"

"Not much of a reason," he agreed.

"Well then."

"Listen, love," he said brutally. "You put your husband in the earth yesterday. That's it, *yesterday.* And you met me yesterday. And you climbed into bed with me today. Now, whether you did it to keep yourself warm or whether you did it to stop me getting warm, I don't know. But I'm old enough, and I'm wise enough, and I'm fat enough to know you didn't do it for my bonny blue eyes and my fascinating conversation."

He hadn't meant to get angry but by the time he finished he felt anger creeping into his speech.

He threw his unfinished cigarette to the ground and screwed his heel viciously on the red cinder. When he looked at Bonnie again, to his surprise she was regarding him with a half smile on her face.

"I don't know why I did it," she said. "But one thing I do know. All my men have started by being able to make me laugh."

"Mebbe so," said Dalziel. "But none of 'em found much to laugh about at the finish, did they?"

The front door opened and Cross reappeared.

"Bugger it!" he said.

"*Sergeant,*" said Dalziel sternly in his best low church voice.

"Sorry, Mrs. Fielding," apologized Cross to Bonnie whose smile broadened. "Well, sir. I needn't worry about these chickens any longer. They've gone. The whole bloody lot! Sorry."

"I'll leave you to swear in peace," said Bonnie. "Herrie's gone to bed so if you want to use the sitting-room, you won't be assaulted."

She went inside.

"Nice woman," said Cross diffidently. "Pity about all this."

"Yes," said Dalziel. "Well, what's it to be?"

Cross shrugged.

"It looks like an accident and I hope it's an accident. Either way, it'll keep till morning." He yawned prodigiously. "One thing, with those chickens gone, I might get some sleep this night."

"I'll fix you up with something to give you sweet dreams," said Dalziel, ushering Cross into the house. "I could do with a nightcap myself."

It wasn't true. He had drunk enough that day and there was nothing more drink could do for him. But anything which put another activity between now and bed was welcome.

It was nearly two hours before Cross managed to drag himself away. After he had gone Dalziel sat alone in the half-lit room and whistled an idiosyncratic version of Sousa's "Washington Post" as, for the want of anything better to do, he thumbed through the books on Fielding's table. They were the old man's works.

Dalziel ignored the poetry but examined the fly-leaf and the prelims. First editions with autograph, they might be worth a few quid. He was as far from being a bibliophile as a man can get who has received the corrosive imprint of a Western European education, but it was his business to know what was worth stealing, what not. He weighed the books in his broad palm. Little enough for a life's work, he thought. Some uncharacteristic dramatic impulse made him hold out his other palm, empty.

Carefully he replaced the books. They held no attraction for him, either as objects or vehicles. Pascoe would care for them, he thought. Or Ellie. His new wife. With whom he was now cosily cocooned in some hotel bed. Inspector Peter Pascoe with a new wife by his side and all before him. Pascoe, who was as different from himself as chalk from cheese, who would go further than Dalziel's daftest dreams had even taken him, but who could also come to this, sitting alone in a darkling room full of drink and fear.

"Bugger this!" said Dalziel standing up. "I'm going weird!"

He switched off the reading lamp which dropped a cone of light on to the table and stood for a moment to let his eyes grow accustomed to the dark. As he opened the door into the hall he heard the noise of a car on the gravel drive outside and froze. A moment later the front door clicked open and someone entered. Dalziel retreated into the sitting-room and waited. The hall light went on and through the still open door Dalziel saw Uniff, wearing a belted suede jacket and carrying a black briefcase. His beard and his manner, controlled but stealthy, added to the overall impression he gave of a Balkan anarchist, up to no good. He closed and bolted the front door, looked round as though to get his bearings, switched off the light and began a careful ascent of the stairs.

Dalziel gave him five minutes, during which time he turned his formidably experienced detective's brain to the puzzles of this household and advanced not a jot. Then he too tiptoed cautiously up the stairs. As he opened his bedroom door with equal care, he suddenly realized that there existed in his mind a hitherto unformulated expectation that Bonnie would be waiting for him. But the room was empty and he was able to smile cynically at his own ambivalence. Quickly he undressed and went into the bathroom. He did not switch on the light but looked in some perplexity at the door to Bonnie's room. Was it open or locked? Which did he want, and either way what would he do?

Nothing, was the answer. He would of course do nothing. But still he wondered, and his hand was actually on the door knob when he heard the voices. They were speaking so low that even with an ear pressed hard against the woodwork, there was no chance of picking out words. But he could make out that there were two voices—a man's and a woman's.

As carefully as he had approached he retreated from the door. If he had prayed before sleeping he might have said, "Thank you, Lord, for changing nothing." But he didn't. He just climbed into bed and fell into the deepest, soundest sleep he had known for months.

At seven-thirty the following morning he was down at the lakeside examining the scene of Spinx's death by daylight. There had been no rain that night and the water-level had dropped another six inches. Having dispatched the constable left by Cross in search of breakfast, Dalziel peered at the gap left by the broken treads with considerable uninterest. His attitude to physical clues was rather like that of the modern Christian to miracles. They could happen, but probably not just at the moment. Nevertheless the possibility could not be ignored and he jumped down into the duck punt to get a duck's eye look at the landing-stage.

The three broken treads trailed in the water like old fishbones. Carefully Dalziel poked at them with the blade of an antique penknife whose possession by a long-haired youth at a football match would have got him three months. The outermost two treads were soft but reasonably solid; the third was rotten almost right through. This it must have been that triggered things off. If Spinx had come down on this with his full weight, it could well have snapped, sending him plunging forward so that his head cracked against the timber upright supporting the end of the stage and his body hit the other two treads with sufficient force to smash through them.

Unconscious from the blow, he would quickly have drowned and floated there, held between the submerged sections of the support baulks, till Dalziel found him.

That's how it could have happened, thought Dalziel, lighting a cigarette and relaxing in the gently jogging punt. If the post mortem showed death to be due to drowning and the head injury to be consistent with a crack against the upright, that would be that. Another Lake House inquest with a verdict of accidental death. And any journalistic interest thus engendered would mean merely so much free advertising for the restaurant. If it opened.

The odds against were now enormous. Dalziel was no businessman but it seemed fairly certain to him that unless they opened on time, the outcry from the disappointed (and uncompensated) customers would be so great that any remaining semblance of creditworthiness would be torn to shreds. His own discovery of the missing drink and the disembowelled ovens had probably been the scheme's death blow. Herrie's dollars might have made a difference but he was so obsessively against the venture that it would need another death to prise the money free. If it had been the old man's face that had peered up through the water the previous night, that would have been quite a different kettle of fish! Not all the rotten wood in the world would have bridged the doubts in Dalziel's mind.

Something clicked close by and he looked up to see Uniff towering above him with a smile on his face and a camera in his hand.

"What a shot!" he said. "The great detective at work! What were you thinking of, man? A single-handed trip round the world?"

"I thought you were short of film," said Dalziel, stepping up on the landing-stage.

"There are some things too good to miss," said Uniff. "Say, that could be dangerous."

He pointed to the broken treads and Dalziel recalled his late return the previous night. Presumably he had not yet met anyone who had told him about Spinx.

"It was," said Dalziel. "Oh shit!" He was looking at the sleeve of his jacket which was smeared with oil. He traced its source very quickly to the punt. Someone had been trying to clean up the duck gun.

"Tillotson!" he groaned. "I'll kill him!"

"If he tries to fire that antique, he'll kill himself," observed Uniff. "What were you doing down there, anyway, man?"

As they walked back to the house, Dalziel filled him in on the discovery of Spinx's body.

Uniff was incredulous.

"That little creep? I can't believe it! His kind live forever."

"You didn't like him?" said Dalziel.

"What? No, I didn't say that. Some of my best friends are insurance creeps. Anyway. I wasn't around last night, not after nine. So it's no use grilling me."

His Americanisms were sometimes venerably antique and in his initial surprise at Dalziel's news, he had sounded very like his sister. But the fat detective's mind had seized upon points of other than linguistic interest.

"I'm not grilling you, Mr. Uniff," he said. "But I'd be interested to know why you think I might be."

"Well, hell, sudden death, the fuzz start asking questions all round. I *know*; we've had some, remember?"

"I remember," said Dalziel. "Point two, why should nine strike you as being a significant time? There's nothing yet that says Spinx didn't take his bath earlier."

"It wasn't meant to be significant," said Uniff. "It was just the time I left, that's all."

The uniformed constable came out of the front door as they reached it. He had a half-eaten bacon sandwich in his saluting hand and treated Dalziel to a distant and fatty wave.

"Which brings us to where you were last night, Mr. Uniff," said Dalziel heavily.

Uniff laughed as he ushered Dalziel into the house ahead of him.

"Now you *are* grilling me," said Uniff.

The door which led to the kitchen opened at the other end of the hallway and Mavis appeared.

"OK," said Uniff. "If that's how it's gotta be, come on up to my pad. I got the equipment there."

He steered Dalziel up the stairs at a speed which left him short of breath by the time they reached the first landing. Looking back, he saw Mavis standing at the foot of the stairs watching their ascent with the impassive intensity of a totem mask.

The room Uniff led him to was huge. The design of the faded and torn wallpaper suggested it had once been a nursery, though no other evidence survived. There were no broken rocking-horses, no disfigured Teddy-bears, just a huge table littered with paper and film equipment, and at the farthermost end of the room surrounded by spot lamps a rostrum camera set-up.

"Here we are," said Uniff proudly. "What do you think, man?"

"They must have had bloody huge families in them days," said Dalziel.

"What? Oh, yeah. It was probably those long winter nights when the magic lantern broke down."

Uniff wandered across to the camera, turned one of the lamps so that it pointed full in his face and switched it on.

"OK, captain. But I tell you again, I don't know nothing."

"This your film then?" asked Dalziel peering without comprehension at a huge sheet of card pinned to the wall. On it were pasted a series of drawings, about fifty in all, like a strip cartoon except that the sequence of events escaped Dalziel.

"I thought you'd never ask," said Uniff, switching off his light. "Yeah, that's my story board. I've got some rushes here. You want to see them?"

Like all obsessives, he could not doubt the answer but quickly drew down the black-out blinds and set the projector rolling. On the screen appeared the letter O. It turned into a man's head. A stone age club appeared and hammered down on the skull. The mouth opened and out came a strip cartoon balloon containing the letter O which in its turn became a breast. A hand caressed it. The response again was O; and in sequence every part of the human body was represented by the letter, then assaulted or stimulated in some fashion more or less appropriate, always with the same response. The animation was clever, often wittily obscene, though Dalziel doubted if in these blatant days it was actionable.

"It's about language," explained Uniff. "Mave does the animations. Not bad, eh? No sound yet. That's a problem. What do you think? Do we need those O's vocalized?"

The film ran on. Eventually a stone age doctor presented his stone age patient with a bill. The mouth rounded to an O, the eyes to two more, then they all expanded and exploded into a torrent of letters.

"How'd you like that?" asked Uniff as the film ran to an end. "Commerce is the mother of language. Not love, hate, religion, sex. But money."

"Well," said Dalziel. "It's not very long is it?"

"Hell, man, that's just the opening sequence. Next we go on to a historical survey. The letters and words are the characters, you dig? All languages, all literatures. It's very funny, Mave's done marvels. All the time there's a struggle between the different functions of language. Finally figures start coming in until at the end we get nuclear physics formulae dominating, then the whole thing goes bang and we're back to O."

"Interesting," said Dalziel. "I like a good cartoon. Cheaper to make than a real film, I suppose?"

He was just fishing for some indication of where the finance for the project came from, but Uniff pulled up the blinds angrily, seized a large envelope from a shelf and spilled a dozen or more glossy half-plate prints into Dalziel's lap.

"Those more in your line, Superintendent?"

Dalziel studied them gravely. He was not one of those who found the vagina in close-up a particularly appealing sight, not even when its owner appeared to have a traffic no entry sign tattooed on the inner thigh.

"In a way," he said. "Professionally speaking."

Uniff retrieved the photographs hastily and returned them to their envelope. His anger had quickly vanished.

"They're harmless," he said. "I was just showing them to you, not asking you to buy them."

"No need to get legalistic, Mr. Uniff," said Dalziel. "Though you ought to know that under the Obscene Publication Acts, publication (that is, simply *showing* someone your dirty pictures) is an offence, whether done for gain or not. But you're in luck. I doubt if anything you've got here is liable to deprave or corrupt me. So let's forget I ever saw them, shall we, and try to remember where you went last night."

According to Uniff he had simply gone into Orburn for a drink and stayed on after hours as a guest of the landlord. He coyly refused to give the name of the pub on the grounds that he didn't want to risk spoiling a good drinking place. Dalziel found this quite reasonable and, in any case, he had no real authority for, or purpose in, questioning the man, so he didn't press matters.

He went downstairs again and as he reached the hallway, the door to the servants' quarters opened and Arkwright emerged. Dalziel had never seen a pale Negro before and the sight touched him.

"Morning, Mr. Arkwright," said Dalziel with the jovial sympathy of one hard-drinking man for another. "How are you feeling?"

"Terrible," said Arkwright. "Listen. I'm very sorry about all this. I don't know what happened."

"Something you ate I should think," said Dalziel, but observing that the man seemed genuinely distressed at what had passed he put on his avuncular air and added, "Think nowt of it. They're all silly buggers here, you wouldn't be noticed."

A little comforted by this, Arkwright let himself be led to coffee which comforted him even more.

"Penitent left, I suppose?"

"Yes, I think so."

"Shithead," said Arkwright. "I hate that bloody man. He always wants me on a job with him. I'm his liberal credential."

"I think he'll be after a divorce this morning," said Dalziel.

Arkwright laughed, regretted it, suddenly sat upright as though at a memory returned and said, "You put me to bed? Whose bed was I in?"

"Why?" asked Dalziel. "Have you spewed or something?"

"No. It's just, I remember now, some time in the night, I was woken up. Some guy was pulling at the blankets and saying, 'Annie, Annie.' So I sat up and said, 'Sir, you are mistaken,' and this guy shrieked like he was wetting his pants and ran."

Dalziel thought about it for a moment, then as the image of Arkwright's coal black face emerging from the blankets sharpened in his mind he began to laugh. After a while with great care, Arkwright began to laugh too.

"This man," said Dalziel finally, wiping his eyes with the khaki awning he used as a handkerchief. "Did you recognize him? Was he one of the men you met yesterday afternoon?"

"I can't say," said Arkwright. "Might be. But it was dark and I was still very drunk. It must have been pretty early. He sounded urgent. I suppose I was lucky he didn't just climb in and get on with it."

Dalziel smiled and nodded. The obvious interpretation of the intrusion would do for Arkwright, but he was by no means sure that the intruder's purpose had been sexual.

But the more interesting question was, who in this house had not heard last night of the discovered theft and Annie Greave's disappearance?

CHAPTER XIII

An Intimate Deodorant

Cross arrived shortly before ten bearing with him a preliminary autopsy report which indicated that Spinx had died from drowning and that the injury on his head was consistent with his having struck the wooden support as he fell. With grim amusement Dalziel recognized in Cross the mixture of relief and disappointment an overworked, middle-aged but still ambitious detective sergeant ought to feel.

"Never mind, lad," he said, "Perhaps there'll be an outbreak of double parking in the town square. No sign of Mrs. Greave?"

"No, sir. Nor of Papworth either. Do you reckon they might have gone off together?"

"Without his clothes?" said Dalziel. "I doubt it. And I can't see 'em as the great lovers somehow. Where'd they go anyway? He'd be as out of place in the middle of Liverpool as she was in the country."

"That's what I thought," said Cross. "Makes you wonder how they met."

"It does that," agreed Dalziel who had been wondering this same thing for two days.

"I wonder if Mrs. Fielding could help us there," said Cross diffidently. "She'd be the one who hired her, I suppose. What do you think, sir, knowing her as you do?"

Dalziel shot him a sharp glance. Christ! he thought.

Could the rustic tom-toms work this quick? What did they do round her? Hide seismographs in the mattress?

"Why not ask her, Sergeant," he said. "And less of the *us*. I'm on holiday, remember?"

"Yes, sir," said Cross.

Dalziel left him and strolled out of the room trying to look like a man whose only care in the world was whether to have one or two double scotches before lunch.

He met Bonnie in the hallway.

"Can we have a word together, Andy?" she asked. She looked very attractive in pea-green slacks and a tight silk blouse which would have gone seven times round Louisa and left enough to blow your nose on.

"Sergeant Cross is in there," said Dalziel with a jerk of his head. "I think his need's greater than mine."

Again his rudeness only seemed to amuse her.

"I didn't realize you were a once-a-month man," she said. "Later then. Say in an hour? In my room."

She brushed by him. The brief contact disturbed him more than he would have thought possible.

He wandered into the back of the house and looked in Papworth's room. Still empty, but now it bore signs of having been searched. Cross obviously didn't mind leaving traces of his passage.

Dalziel mused on Cross as he continued his stroll. He looked a good competent man, perhaps a bit long in the tooth for a sergeant but not yet hopeless of promotion. Perhaps he himself might put in a word . . .

Christalmighty! he suddenly laughed at himself. Lord sodding Dalziel dispensing bounty to the plebs! No. Cross could find another fairy godmother. Middle-aged superintendents needed belated christening gifts just as much as sergeants, though the one Dalziel wanted most of all just now had in fact been bountifully bestowed all those grey years ago and was only now beginning to run short.

Clarity of purpose.

Out in the yard he lit a cigarette and walked slowly

past the so-called Banqueting Hall. It felt derelict. A white elephant, a folly. Unless someone coughed up some cash. He thought of his own deposit account. Not insubstantial. He hardly gave it a thought till he wanted cash for something special. Like the set of crystal decanters and glasses he'd given Pascoe and Ellie. *Looking after your own interests* she'd mocked. But she'd been pleased. So she should have been too, it cost a bloody fortune even with the big discount his cash in hand and his bonny blue eyes got him. Still, there was plenty left. Last night as he lay on Bonnie's bed, he'd even thought about suggesting an investment, but had put it off. At that moment it might have looked a bit like tucking a fiver behind the clock. Besides there was still the business of the missing gear to resolve. Risking your money was one thing, chucking it away quite another. And after Bertie's revelation . . . no, she'd have to find another fool.

The sound of a vehicle approaching interrupted his thoughts. He reached the end of the hall, stepped out and was almost knocked down by a large truck which rattled past him into the cobbled yard. He turned to harangue the driver, and saw the legend on the opening door. *Gibb and Fowler, Builders.*

Little Mr. Gibb jumped out and the men on the back began to disembark.

"Hang around, lads. Have a smoke till I see what's what," commanded Gibb.

He looked around as if in search of somebody and showed his teeth in a gothic smile when he spotted Dalziel.

"Hello there," he said. "You were right then."

"Was I?" said Dalziel. "What about?"

"Me being back on this job sooner than I expected. You drop into my place before you go. There's a big bottle there for my friends."

He winked knowingly. Dalziel looked at him bewildered. Could he actually have *spoken* his thoughts about putting money into the venture last night?

And if he had, could Bonnie have taken him seriously after what happened?

He didn't believe it. Anyway, one thing was clear. Gibb wasn't going to start work just on a promise.

"Mr. Gibb!" a voice called imperiously.

They turned. Standing in the doorway of the main house was Hereward Fielding.

"Would you step inside for a moment, please."

"Right. See you around," said Gibb happily to Dalziel.

So, thought Dalziel. Mystery solved. But a bigger one put in its place. What had produced this complete turnabout by the old man?

He approached the men sitting on the tail-board of the truck who looked at him incuriously.

"What do you think of it then?" he asked jerking his head at the Banqueting Hall.

"Think?" said a venerable grey head wearing overalls overlaid with paint to the consistency of armour. "There'll be fancy prices, no doubt."

The others grunted with the sagacity of men who knew better than to be caught by fancy prices.

"Sad about the accident," said Dalziel.

Grey-head nodded agreement but another rounder, jollier man piped up, "Silly bugger shouldn't have been up there. Not his job."

"Whose job was it?" asked Dalziel.

This flummoxed them for a moment.

"Depends what he were doing," said grey-head cautiously.

"Come and have a look," invited Dalziel.

Ghoulish curiosity proved stronger than Gibb's command and they followed him into the Banqueting Hall, dropping their voices to the hushed murmurs of a stately-home-tours party.

"He was up a ladder, there," said Dalziel. "With a drill. They thought he was fixing a beam."

"Nothing to fix," said grey-head. "We put that beam up ourselves, last thing we did before knocking off. That won't come down in a hurry."

"So what could he have been fixing? Up there

along the wall a bit. You can see where he was drilling."

They peered into the shadowy arch of the high roof.

"Christ knows," said grey-head. "There's nothing there. I plastered right along this wall after they finished the wiring."

Suddenly everything was illuminated.

Gibb stood by the door with his hand on the light panel.

"So here you are then," he said. "Right, lads, let's get the gear in. We're in business."

The men streamed out of the hall with no signs of over-enthusiasm.

"So the old man's coughing up," pried Dalziel.

"Don't let on you didn't know," said Gibb. "I'll have cash in my hand before the day's out. That's the deal."

"And how long will it take you to finish the job?"

"Working hard at it? With lots of overtime, two or three days."

"That's not bad."

"No. Well, frankly, Mr. Dalziel, with things the way they are, I'd prefer to take it easy, give the lads a week, ten days even. But the old man's a tough nut. He's made it quite clear that he's no party to the original agreement. If I go to law, there's no way I can get my hands on his cash. So he's calling the tune. And that says, three days at the outside. So we're dancing the quickstep. Excuse me."

Dalziel followed him out, musing on what had been said, but especially on the flash of illumination which had come to him as Gibb switched on the lights.

Hereward Fielding was standing in the doorway of the main house once more. He beckoned imperiously.

"Come in, come in," he said impatiently. "I've great deal to do and it won't get done hanging around here, waiting for you."

"You're expecting me then," said Dalziel.

"Of course. When I saw you out in the yard with that man, I knew you'd be here in short time."

"Well," said Dalziel. "That saves me the bother of being subtle."

"Really," said Fielding. "A pity. *That* I should have liked to observe. To business then. I've changed my mind. I've decided after all to invest my newly acquired wealth in the family business. A foolish decision, you may think, but freely made. Blood after all is thicker than water."

"Your blood than lake water, mebbe," grunted Dalziel. "That's got shot of the crap. Now tell me what really changed your mind."

Fielding shook his head in reluctant admiration.

"If I could have written poetry of such simple directness," he said, "I would have been a set-book by now. No, Dalziel. That's all I have to say. Pry no further; or else."

"Or else what?"

"Or else I shall command my daughter-in-law to forbid you the house."

His eyes twinkled and an ironic smile tugged at his thin lips.

"You see, I am a man of influence now."

Dalziel was unimpressed.

"Think on," he said. "You might think it's bad having me here privately, but that's nowt to having me officially."

"I believe it," said Fielding. "But come now, there's no cause for us to quarrel. In your younger, greener days you must have been trained to help old gents across the street. Now you may drive me into Orburn if you would be so kind. I must visit my bank and make arrangements for the malodorous Gibb."

"And buy a big hat," added Dalziel.

"Perhaps not today," laughed Fielding. "But I shall certainly be laying in a stock of decent brandy. They can use the other stuff for flaming Christmas puddings. We could do a little sampling at the Lady Hamilton after lunch. On me, of course."

"I haven't got a car," said Dalziel.

"We'll take the Rover. I have the keys." He held them up as evidence.

"Five minutes then," said Dalziel, turning away.

Fielding's manner interested him. His speech style was normally what Dalziel designated as "clever poofy" but there was an element of strain behind it today which had nothing to do with intellectual affectation. Nor did he much care for the quick production of the Rover's keys. Fielding must have got them from Bonnie. And the house was full of young drivers. Indeed there was no apparent bar to the old man's driving himself.

Well, if they wanted him out of the way, he'd go. It suited him to go to Orburn anyway. But he'd go on his own terms.

He headed for the kitchen first. Tillotson and Louisa were drinking coffee together. They weren't speaking to each other but the atmosphere between them was manifestly more cordial than ever before in Dalziel's limited experience. When he had a moment, he must find out why she'd punched the poor sod on the nose that night.

"Morning," he said brightly.

"Hi," said Louisa. "Fancy a cup?"

This was real cordiality.

"No time, thanks all the same. I'm running Herrie to town. Like to come?"

They exchanged glances.

"No thanks," said Louisa.

"Things to do," said Tillotson.

"Great news about the restaurant," said Dalziel.

"Yes, isn't it," said Tillotson brightly. "With a bit of luck we can still open on time. I always knew it would be all right."

Unimpressed by this unlikely claim to clairvoyance, Louisa said nothing but pulled her lower lip forward so that the moist inner flesh showed. It was quite sexy, thought Dalziel. If you were as skinny as she was, he supposed you had to do your best with whatever protuberances you could lay your hands on.

"Grand," said Dalziel. "Excuse me."

He went into the back kitchen and returned a moment later with something in a plastic carrier bag.

"Taking a picnic?" asked Louisa.

"Just a nibble," said Dalziel. "Sure you won't come?"

"Sure. Any news about Mrs. Greave?" asked Louisa.

"No. You'll have to do your own dinner," said Dalziel. "Perhaps the great white hunter here will shoot a couple of flying fish. You owe me for a cleaning job, Charley."

Tillotson was full of apologies when he finally grasped Dalziel's meaning. Louisa was unsympathetic.

"Messing about in boats is messy," she said firmly.

"It seemed safer than the landing-stage," commented Dalziel.

"Poor old Sphincter," sighed Tillotson.

"Yes?" nodded Dalziel.

"Nothing," said Tillotson, puzzled. "Just poor old Sphincter."

"A sad loss," said Dalziel. "Especially to Anchor Insurance. They'll have to send someone else to investigate you."

He left on this good line. As he approached Herrie's sitting-room he thought he heard the noise of the door clicking to but when he peered in, the room was empty. Cross must have finished, which meant Bonnie would be ready for her talk.

On an impulse he pushed open the door of the next room in the corridor and stepped inside. It was the billiards-room, still heavily curtained, perhaps (though he doubted it) in recognition that Fielding's coffin had lain in here.

He found a light switch and clicked it on. A tent of light fell over the green baize, but enough spilled sideways to reveal a figure standing in the shadows of the old marble fireplace.

Another switch turned on the main light.

"Well, well," said Dalziel genially. "The wanderer returns."

Standing before him with an ancient rucksack slung over one shoulder was Nigel Fielding.

He looked very pale and in need of a good night's sleep.

"Just got back?" enquired Dalziel.

The boy nodded.

"And you thought you'd like a bit of peace and quiet before showing your face? Well, it always takes a bit of nerve to come home. Take the piss a bit, do they, Bertie and Lou?"

"A bit," said the boy.

"Pay no heed. Look, I'm just off upstairs to see your mam for a moment. I'll tell her you're here if you like. OK?"

"Thanks very much, Mr. Dalziel," said the boy.

A polite lad, thought Dalziel as he went up the stairs. But he didn't look well and it boded no good that he should shut himself up in the darkened billiards-room as soon as he got back.

Bonnie was sitting at her dressing-table applying with great care a rich damask lipstick to her lower lip. It must be sex zone of the day, thought Dalziel.

"Cross gone?" he asked.

"Yes. Did you want to see him?"

"No sweat. I can see him in town. I'm driving your father-in-law to the bank."

"That's kind of you. What about our talk?"

"It'll keep, won't it. Anyway there's someone more important than me for you to see."

"Who's that?"

"Nigel," he said. "He's just got back. He's in the billiards-room."

It is always good to see that one's exit lines are effective and before he left he allowed himself the indulgence of watching the surprise round her lips to a roseate O reminding him of Uniff's cartoon.

He thought of mentioning Nigel's return to the old man, but decided he would certainly have wanted to go straight in and see the boy. Bonnie was enti-tled to some time alone with him. He'd only been away a couple of days, true, but in Dalziel's estimation it wouldn't be long before he went away and didn't come back for much, much longer. So he drove the ancient Rover down the rutted and pot-holed drive without mentioning the boy.

Fielding was very quiet on the short journey and Dalziel made no attempt to break the silence. In Orburn he parked the car in the ovoid square once more and watched Herrie step smartly through the dignified portals of the bank. For a poet, he had a surprisingly stiff and military bearing, or perhaps it was just his contact with commerce which had effected the change.

Dalziel's first call was the same as on the previous day, the chemist's shop. The girl assistant smiled knowingly when he asked to see the chemist himself. She thinks I want a packet of rubbers, thought Dalziel, and he leered so grossly at her that the smile vanished and she retreated quickly into the dispensary.

"Yes, sir," said the chemist, a man with a Douglas Fairbanks profile and what looked like a duelling scar down his left cheek. He might have been Rupert of Hentzau in retirement.

Dalziel took him to one side and presented him with a piece of paper. On it he had written PRO-PANANNAL(?)

"What kind of condition would you take this for? I'm not sure of the spelling."

"Well," said the chemist dubiously. "May I ask why you want to know?"

Dalziel sighed. The less he had to use his police authority at this stage, the better he'd be pleased.

"My old mother," he said. "She's very independent but we're desperately worried. You understand?"

"I see," said the chemist, weakening.

"She's not local," urged Dalziel.

"In that case," said the chemist.

It turned out that the chemist was not a romantic hero in retirement but rather a physician manqué. Once he started, even Dalziel, famed throughout Yorkshire for his ability to halt the most garrulous of witnesses in mid-syllable, found it hard to drive home the plug. In the end he plucked a packet at random from the nearest shelf, pulled out his wallet and escaped in the caesura produced by the reckoning of change.

But it had been a profitable visit none the less, though he felt no very great sense of triumph as he made his way to the police station.

There was another man closeted with Sergeant Cross this morning. Something about the way in which Cross introduced him as Detective Chief Inspector Balderstone made Dalziel feel that they had just been talking about him prior to his arrival. He wasn't surprised. It would have been strange if Cross's report on the presence in Lake House of a senior police officer had not produced some reactions from above.

Balderstone's attitude was very correct but to start with at least very reserved. He can't make his mind up if I'm a biased witness, impartial observer, or fifth column, thought Dalziel. And he wasn't altogether sure he knew himself.

After ten minutes or so, the atmosphere had thawed considerably.

"Look," Dalziel had said. "I'm just there by accident. It's Sergeant Cross's case, for what it is. And what is it? Well, there's two accidental deaths. Curious, but not criminal as far as we can see. A woman and a man have disappeared. It happens all the time. Christ, I'm not where I was planning to be three days ago, so in a sense I've disappeared. And lastly there's been a theft. That's the only crime. Simple theft. And, I tell you straight, it wouldn't surprise me if that didn't get quietly brushed under the carpet soon."

"I don't understand," said Balderstone. He was about forty, with the squashed face of a bulldog.

"A mistake," said Dalziel. "The booze not ordered, or stored elsewhere. A misunderstanding about the kitchen equipment. Mrs. Greave exonerated."

"Why do you say this, sir?" asked Balderstone.

"It's just a theory," said Dalziel. "That's why I came here this morning. Like I said, it's the sergeant's case. Any information or ideas I've got, well, it's my duty to pass them on. So here I am."

He looked for a moment staunchly dutiful, like the centrepiece of a First World War music-hall tableau depicting patriotic pride.

A few moments later, after hearing what Dalziel had to say, Cross began to feel that it wasn't so much his rights as the officer in charge of the case that Dalziel was interested in as the facilities at his disposal. This was confirmed when Dalziel delved into his plastic carrier, produced a paper bag and handed it over with the instruction, "And get your labs to take a look at that."

Cross opened the bag and peered in.

"Any special instructions, sir?" he asked.

"What do you think?"

Out of the box in the paper bag, Cross lifted a large aerosol can of what was coyly described as an intimate deodorant.

"I don't know what to think, sir."

Angrily Dalziel snatched it back and put it on the desk top. From the carrier he produced another bag, took from it a cake box, opened it and showed its contents to Balderstone and Cross. It was a dead rat.

"I'd like to know how it died," said Dalziel.

"That's very interesting," said Balderstone after listening to Dalziel for some moments after Cross had left the office. "But what do we have if it all turns out to be true?"

"Bugger all," said Dalziel. He glanced at his watch. It was nearly eleven-thirty.

"Are you in a hurry, sir?" asked Balderstone.

"No. I've arranged to meet the old boy at twelve in the Lady Hamilton. He's buying me my dinner. I should think we'll be there till two or later. So if anything turns up by then, you know where to get in touch."

They talked a little more, exchanging gossip about mutual acquaintances till Cross returned with the news that Dalziel's enquiries had all been set in motion and the rat was on its way to the forensic laboratories.

"Grand," said Dalziel. "Well, I'd best be on my way. I'll hear from you later, I hope."

He got up to go.

"Oh sir," said Cross.

"Yes?"

"Don't forget . . . this."

He handed over the deodorant can.

Dalziel examined him carefully for signs of amusement, but the sergeant's face remained expressionless. He took the top off the can and pressed the button. A thin liquid haze filled the air for a moment then disappeared leaving behind a faint lemony scent. Dalziel sniffed.

"That's what the world's coming to," he said, tossing the can into Cross's waste-paper basket.

It was his third good exit line of the morning but he felt strangely hypocritical as he left the police station. He had withheld nothing which had any direct bearing on the case as it stood at present, he assured himself. Should the scope of Cross's investigations widen, then of course he would reveal *everything* he had surmised.

But his mind though not much given to symbolism told him that his reassurances smelt of lemon.

CHAPTER XIV

When We Dead Awake

Lunch at the Lady Hamilton was an expensive and alcoholic occasion. Only the best would do for Hereward Fielding and though the Lady Hamilton's best had won it no stars in the posher eating guides, the food was hot and plentiful and swam around very pleasantly in the three bottles of criminally costly claret that the old man insisted they drink with it. All this he regarded merely as a base for the brandy which followed and by two-thirty he was ready to tell the story of his life.

Dalziel whose caution and capacity had both proved larger was willing enough to listen to this personal history as long as it came fairly swiftly to the past twenty-four hours.

"My life has been tragic. Tragic," Hereward assured him.

"It's been very sad lately," agreed Dalziel.

"*Sad* is no fit word for it," reproved Fielding. "Sad is . . . sad. What I feel is despair. A despair all the stronger because I half believe in futurity. We may survive, Dalziel."

"That's hopeful," said Dalziel. Surprisingly, he realized he meant it. That bloody wine must have got to him after all.

"No. Oh no. Think of it. When we dead awake it

will be to each as if but a second ago he had felt the pangs of dying, the explosion in the head, the drowning of the lungs, the fingers tightening round the throat. What a noise of screaming and wailing there will be at that moment! Followed by what a moment of silence and amazement as we realize the pain is no more."

"Well, that *is* hopeful," asserted Dalziel. "These dead people, did you have anyone special in mind?"

But the old man was not listening to him.

"But this in turn will be followed by the onset of such a fear at the strangeness and uncertainty of this awakening that all we remember of that forever unattainable past—sunlight, sea-smells, the pleasures of mind and appetite, and even the pains of dying—will seem more desirable to us than all the fabled joys of immortality. Even *your* lonely, frightened and unhappy existence will beckon you backward with siren song, Dalziel. Even that. Even that."

He nodded emphatically, and set his brandy balloon like a specimen case over his nose as he sought the last few drops.

"I'll tell you what you are," said Dalziel, irritated by this unmannerly comment on his own state of being, "you're pissed. We'd best be on our way home."

Before I'm finished, he told himself grimly, I'll give these bastards something else to be sorry for.

The old man seemed to read his thoughts.

"Don't be offended, Dalziel. It's not pity I offer. Nor is it pity I ask for. It's merely an audience. And in return, I offer an audience. This is the best we can do for each other, be audiences. Shall we in good music-hall tradition exit with a song?"

He struck his brandy glass with a coffee spoon, took up the resultant note with remarkable accuracy and began to sing.

"Oh, the life of the spirit's a very fine thing
But you can't be a monk without flogging your ring

And strangely enough I believe you will find
You can't be a tart without flogging your mind."

The waiters gathered in a concerned but uncertain pose by the kitchen door. The large bill had already been paid with a lavish tip, but it wasn't just gratitude or hope of future largesse that immobilized them, Dalziel felt; it was disbelief that this patrician figure could be the source of the disturbance. Then they were joined by the shiny under-manager whose face set in horror and indignation as he recognized Dalziel.

"Come on, Herrie," said Dalziel grimly. "Let's go home."

He stood up, put his hand under the old man's arm and eased him up.

Outside he deposited the now almost comatose Fielding in the Rover and, puffing from the exertion, he closed the door with his buttocks, leaned against it and began to scratch himself against the handle. Chief Inspector Balderstone who turned up a few moments later was reminded of a brown bear he once saw up against a tree in a Disney nature film.

"Glad I've caught you, sir," he said.

"Hello, lad," said Dalziel genially. "You've been quick. What've you found out? Was I right?"

"Mainly, sir. But we'll come to that in a minute. More important is, they've found Mrs. Greave."

"And you think that's more important?" said Dalziel scornfully. "You've still a lot to learn, Inspector. Where'd they pick her up? Liverpool."

"Not quite," said Balderstone. "Epping Forest."

"Christ," said Dalziel. "She must have taken a wrong turning!"

"She did that all right," said Balderstone. "She'd been bashed over the head and then strangled."

Annie Greave's body had been discovered at nine o'clock that morning by a man riding through Epping Forest. His horse had been reluctant to pass close to a pile of loose branches and leaf mould which looked as if it had been heaped hastily into a shallow ditch. The man dismounted, pulled aside a branch and saw shining through in all its unnatural glory the red hair of Annie Greave.

With her in the ditch had been a suitcase and handbag, so identification had not been difficult. When the Liverpool police were contacted to be told of the woman's death and asked if anything were known, they recalled that Cross had rung them the previous evening asking for a watch to be kept for the woman.

"Time of death?" asked Dalziel, screwing up his face at the temperature of his beer.

After ensuring that Herrie was comfortable and not in any immediate danger of choking himself, he had escorted Balderstone back into the Lady Hamilton with the assurance that professional ethics forbade him to discuss so serious a matter in the street.

"Not known yet, but I doubt if it'll be much help. You rarely get better than give-or-take three hours. But they reckon she was dumped before three o'clock this morning."

"How's that?"

"There was a thunderstorm which started just about then. Very heavy rain for an hour. The body had obviously been out in it."

"Who've they got down there?" asked Dalziel. "Sherlock bloody Holmes? Anything else?"

"Well, she hadn't been robbed and she hadn't been raped. At least, not so you'd notice."

"What's that mean?"

"She'd had intercourse not all that long before death. But no signs of force. Also a meal."

"They're on the ball, these bloody cockneys," admitted Dalziel grudgingly. "Our police surgeon wants two weeks' notice to take a blood sample."

"Their pathologist just happened to be handy when they brought her in."

"What had she eaten?" asked Dalziel.

"Sausages."

"That figures," Dalziel laughed. "Sausages, eh? What about her case?"

"Sorry?"

"Did it look as if she'd packed it herself? Had anyone been through it?"

"No, sir. Neatly packed, they said. Everything nicely folded. Woman's packing. Oh, and there were a couple of bottles of gin."

"Souvenirs," said Dalziel, thinking that it all fitted. Annie Greave hadn't rushed off in a hurry. No, she'd made up her mind to go, got ready, then slipped away when everyone else was too busy to notice. The last time she'd been seen at Lake House was mid-afternoon, as far as Cross's questioning had been able to discover. But Dalziel felt that she had probably delayed her departure till the post-presentation party was well under way.

What had happened then? Had someone come to collect her. A taxi, perhaps. Doubtless this was being checked. Or had she arranged with someone in the house to drive her to a bus or railway station?

He tried to arrange in his mind the inmates of the house during the period of hard drinking after the presentation, but found it almost impossible. Bonnie had looked for and been unable to find Mrs. Greave round about five, but all that meant, of course, was that she'd vacated her room by then. She might still have been close by, waiting for her lift.

"The question is," said Balderstone. "Did she mean to head south? And if she did, did she know who she was going with or did she just get herself picked up and come unstuck?"

"You mean some fellow who had his fun and then started arguing about the price? Possible," said Dalziel, adding diffidently, "You'll be covering transport cafés, that kind of thing? And local taxi services."

"Yes, sir, thank you," said Balderstone politely. "Er, look, sir, what do you think? Could this have anything to do with what's going on in Lake House?"

"You tell me," said Dalziel. "What *is* going on in Lake House?"

"Well, those points you asked us to check. You were right in just about every respect."

Dalziel showed no surprise, but sipped his beer cautiously to see if it had reached a drinkable temperature.

"First we checked on Henry Uniff. Liverpool fire service had a record of his fire and someone had made a note of his insurers. A company called Royal Oak."

"Oh," said Dalziel, disappointed.

"Who are a subsidiary of Provincial Traders."

"Ah," said Dalziel. "Get on with it, man. It's not a Book at sodding Bedtime."

"Who," continued Balderstone unperturbed, "as you know, were for a time Mr. Bertie Fielding's employers. His ambitions, it seems, were managerial to start with, but the parent company found him unsatisfactory. It was thought his peculiar talents might be better suited to the more outward-growing atmosphere of an insurance office and he was offered a transfer to Royal Oak. He dealt personally with the Uniff fire. There was a medium-sized amount involved. A few thousand all told, most of it on film equipment. They dictated us a list. Not much help except that this item, the rostrum-camera, has a serial number."

"Useful," said Dalziel. "I'll take that. Thanks."

"Lastly, we've contacted Anchor Insurance. It seems that Mrs. Fielding has already been on to them, expressing sympathy for Spinx's accident but great indignation that it should have taken place while he was unlawfully trespassing on her property—especially as it seems likely that he was there on Anchor's behalf. I think she's got them worried. It could be a bit embarrassing. As for what you asked, yes, there's a whacking great fire insurance. The building, I mean the restaurant and kitchens not the main house, plus contents is covered for fifty thousand pounds."

"Jesus wept!" said Dalziel. "It's nowt but a ruined stables!"

"Yes indeed. The thing is, it's not just intrinsic value that's covered, but potential loss of revenue, you follow? But there's no theft insurance at all. They felt that until the place was completed and properly covered by alarms, it was too easy a target. Premiums would have been very high, so the Fieldings put all their eggs in one basket."

"Big bloody basket," said Dalziel. "And the rat?"

"Just as you thought, sir," said Balderstone. "I had to pass all this on to my superiors, you understand, sir."

"I wouldn't understand if you hadn't," answered Dalziel. "What do they say?"

"Well, the way things stand, we've got no kind of case at all. In fact, we've not really got any crime. This woman's death belongs to the Met, the man Spinx will almost certainly get a verdict of accident, and that just leaves the theft . . ."

"Which I lay odds you won't have for long."

"No, sir. And that's all. Isn't it, sir?"

"As far as I know," said Dalziel, looking him straight in the eyes.

"Good. Well, sir, we'll be asking more questions up at Lake House, of course. And we're keener than ever to get hold of this man Papworth. But I can see us coming out of the other end of all this with nothing but a lot of time wasted. I just wondered, well, my super wondered, how long you intend staying in the house."

"Why?" asked Dalziel.

"Well, it might be useful having someone on the inside, so to speak. Till we see how things go."

"Jesus wept!" said Dalziel. "I bet he didn't mention expenses! And I'm supposed to be on holiday."

It didn't sound very convincing. He didn't even really try.

"All right, I can spare another day or so," he said finally. "But I'll have to tell them what I think. It's got to be stopped. I think it has been, but they've got to know we know, just in case."

Balderstone looked dubious.

"I'm not sure, sir . . ." he began.

"Look," said Dalziel. "What're you hoping for? Conspiracy? Christ, there's no hope. I know 'em. No. Frighten the bastards, that's what. I'll do that, but I'll leave it to you to tell them about Open Annie. I'll have another chat with 'em first. Once they know she's dead, they'll clam up. Form a defensive ring! But I'll be inside and if anyone knows more than they should, I'll see they get an arrow up the arse!"

Feeling very pleased with his metaphor, Dalziel tipped the remnants of his beer into a pot holding a tired-looking rubber plant. The assistant manager stood in the doorway, looking disapproving. Dalziel addressed him as they passed.

"The reason the best barmaids have big tits," he said, "is for warming up pots of cold tasteless beer."

The man's expression did not alter but Dalziel was entertained to notice that Balderstone looked distinctly embarrassed.

Hereward Fielding had slumped across the driving seat in their absence so Dalziel pulled him upright and wound the seat-belt round him with all the ferocity of a devout executioner straping a heretic to the stake.

"That should hold the old sod," he grunted to Balderstone through the open window. "Oh, by the way. You won't forget there were six, no five, other people who left Lake House last night, probably heading for London. All pissed and two at least horny with it."

Balderstone looked nonplussed. Dalziel hoped he was pretending.

"Butt, the feature writer and his dolly photographer, Penitent the BBC man, and the two Yanks. I'd try Penitent first, he had a car to himself. His sidekick was too stoned to travel. Which, as it turned out, may have been lucky for someone."

"How's that?"

"Well, someone tried to get into bed with him, thinking he was Annie. Which means that whoever it was thought that Annie was alive and well and ready for fun."

The thought of Arkwright's black face rising from the pillow made Dalziel laugh again and it kept him amused all the way home. Or rather all the way to Lake House, which is not my home, he reminded himself. Though the sight of his own car parked at the head of the drive made him feel pleasantly lord-of-the-manorish as he halted the Rover alongside.

The garage had delivered it at lunch-time, Tillotson informed him. Bonnie had paid the bill, so would he please settle up with her?

Dalziel nodded his approval of this young gentleman's protection of a lady's interests. It was good to know that there were still young men who recognized that a lady of breeding should find it impossible to ask for money. Not that he approved of the elitism implicit in the recognition (as an elite of one, he felt that most other elites were puffed-up crap) but he disapproved even more of women being like men.

"I hope the sods haven't charged for cleaning it," he said, looking disapprovingly at the tide-mark left round the paintwork by its recent immersion.

"I wouldn't be surprised," said Tillotson cheerfully. "Still, drop Pappy fifty pence and he'll give it a polish for you. Does it quite nicely too."

"If he was here, I might do that," said Dalziel.

"Oh, he's here," said Tillotson casually. "Turned up shortly after you left."

"What!" bellowed Dalziel. "Has anyone told Sergeant Cross?"

"No, I don't think so. Should they have done?"

Could he really be so thick? wondered Dalziel, looking darkly at Tillotson across whose face signs of uneasiness were passing like the movement of a field of wheat at the first breath of the approaching storm.

"Would you like to see him? Shall I fetch him?" offered Tillotson, eager to be somewhere else.

"No," growled Dalziel who had paused in his efforts to ease the still-sleeping Fielding out of the car. "You look after the old man."

"Oh. Is he ill?" said Tillotson, concerned.

"No," said Dalziel. "He's unconscious. Which means he doesn't know he's back in this bloody nut-house. Which means, for my money, he's very well indeed. Here, get hold."

He found Papworth in his room, stretched out on his bed apparently asleep. He was fully clothed except for his boots which lay on the floor as though they had been kicked off and dropped over the bed end. The room smelled of tobacco, sweat and something else rather unpleasant which Dalziel couldn't place.

"On your feet, Papworth," commanded Dalziel.

The man didn't move, but Dalziel sensed that he was awake. He lifted his right foot, placed it against the bed end and thrust with all his weight. The bed moved a couple of inches and crashed against the wall.

Papworth jerked upright, his face taut with anger.

"You stupid fat bastard!" he said.

"Temper," said Dalziel mildly. "You look as if you'd like to kill me."

"Don't give me ideas," said Papworth, swinging his legs off the bed.

"You think you could kill a man just because he woke you up?" asked Dalziel. "That's interesting."

"Your words, not mine. Why don't you sod off?"

Dalziel grinned horribly.

"I ought to warn you, Mr. Papworth, that I am a police officer."

"Don't bother. I know," said Papworth. "It's not hard to smell 'em out."

"In here it would be bloody miraculous," said Dalziel, sniffing. "What else do you know, Mr. Papworth?"

"What do you mean?"

"Come on!" snapped Dalziel. "Don't play the thick ploughboy with me. That tube of tool-grease you've been passing off as your daughter, she took off last night. Where'd she go?"

"Mrs. Greave? I don't know. She's a free agent. What's up? Didn't she give her notice?"

"It's not what she gave. It's what she took."

Briefly Dalziel listed the missing items. Papworth, fully in control of himself now, was unimpressed.

"All that? She must have had a big bag."

"Oh no," said Dalziel who had also settled down. "This lot's been going for a long while. And you never noticed?"

"I'm the outdoor man," said Papworth. "If she'd taken any trees, I'd have noticed."

Dalziel smiled inwardly. There was nothing he loved better than a joker. In his experience of interrogation, wit was the last defence of the guilty and generally it sprang from deep uncertainties rather than the confidence it claimed to demonstrate.

"Look," he said in a voice unctuous with reasonableness. "Look. There's nothing for you to worry about. Don't take any notice of me if I shout a bit. It's my upbringing. I'm like you. Good solid working-class stock. I've no time for these fancy fal-da-rils. Look. This woman, Annie Greave, now we know what she's not. She's not your daughter. And we know what she is. She's a Liverpool whore. What we don't know is *where* she is. And it might help us to find her if you told us how you came to meet her in the first place."

"If she's a pro," said Papworth, "I'd have thought that were obvious."

"True," said Dalziel, looking pleasantly surprised as though the thought hadn't struck him. "So you picked her up. Where was this—Liverpool?"

"That's it," said Papworth.

"I thought so. What were you doing in Liverpool? It's a good way. Not the kind of place you go for a holiday." Dalziel laughed as he spoke, inviting Papworth to share the absurdity of the thought.

"I went there a few times with young Master Bertie," said Papworth. The feudal phrase came awkwardly from his lips.

"Did you? As his valet?" said Dalziel, unable to restrain the sarcasm. But it appeared to pass unnoticed.

"He worked up there. Didn't have a car, so when he was going back after a stay at Lake House, I'd sometimes drive him in the Rover and bring it back the next day."

"And spend the night screwing Annie," said Dalziel with a wink.

"That's it."

"And you got to enjoy this so much that when the chance came to install her here in Lake House, you thought, *why not?* But for decency's sake, and to save the bother of testimonials, you said she was your daughter?"

"Right again," said Papworth. "You needn't have woken me up, seeing you've managed to work it all out by yourself."

"I like a nice chat," said Dalziel genially. "So. Let me see. Bertie was how long in Liverpool? Just over a year, I think. Fifteen months, say. And he came back here to start the restaurant project early this year. How often did he come home while he was away? Every weekend? Once a month? Twice a year?"

"Once a month, six weeks at the outside," said Papworth cautiously.

"And you drove him back and screwed Mrs. Greave. That'd make between eight and twelve jumps you had with her last year. Enough to give you a taste for it?"

"I didn't count," said Papworth. "Does it give you a thrill, these questions?"

"No. No," said Dalziel thoughtfully. "I was just thinking how advanced the prison service in Liverpool must be. Nowt like it in Yorkshire, I tell you, else there's some would be queuing up."

"What do you mean?"

"I mean Annie Greave spent eight months last year in gaol, that's what I mean. And if you were getting on board each time you drove bouncing Bertie back home, then you must have real influence. Yes indeed."

It was, of course, a lie. Criminals lied all the time and Dalziel saw no reason why this useful privilege should be reserved for them alone.

Of course, all Papworth had to do was say *you must be daft!* and indeed the man was looking at him with what might be honest puzzlement as he rolled another of his revolting cigarettes.

"Well?" prompted Dalziel.

The door burst open and Bertie Fielding entered.

"Hello, Pappy," he said. "I've been looking for you. Ah, you're here, Dalziel. That's useful. It'll save ringing up Cross."

"We're having a private conversation," growled Dalziel. "Do you mind?"

"In *your* house with *your* employees, you can have all the private conversations you wish," said Bertie. He was feeling confident enough to say it as a joke rather than make it as nasty as he was capable of, observed Dalziel.

"Pappy, now the water's going down, we really ought to start cleaning up the bottom bit of the lawn. The flood's left an awful mess. I've got Hank out there earning his keep, but we need your expertise."

"Right," said Papworth. "I'll come now."

"Hold on!" said Dalziel. "I'm not finished with you yet."

"Is this some kind of official interrogation?" enquired Bertie. "What's it all about, Pappy?"

"He's asking me about Mrs. Greave. Something about some missing stuff."

Bertie laughed. The sight of his soft fleshiness gently shaking filled Dalziel with revulsion. At least at his age I was nothing but bone and muscle, he thought.

"Is that it? Well, consider your constabulary duty done, Mr. Dalziel, sir. That's what I was going to ring Sergeant Cross about. It's all been a mistake."

"What?"

"A mistake. Look, it's a bit complicated, but what it boils down to is this. There's nothing missing."

"What?"

"That's the long and short of it, I'm afraid. I've done a careful check this morning and in fact all the missing stuff can be accounted for. The booze has been stored elsewhere. It's silly, really."

"And you didn't know?" demanded Dalziel.

"Not in the least. Not till this morning."

"And who was it that altered your arrangements without letting you know? And why didn't he or she speak up last night?"

"Well, that would have been a bit difficult," said Bertie, grinning broadly. "It was my late father, God bless him. Who else?"

"So now you've tracked the drink down? And the ovens? Had he fiddled with them too?"

"Oh yes," said Bertie. "Security. Very distrustful man was my father."

It was of course unanswerable. And even though Dalziel had forecast this turn of events to Balderstone that morning, he felt angrily frustrated.

"You can see for yourself if you like," offered Bertie.

"No, thanks," said Dalziel to whom another thought had occurred. Was this why he had been steered away from the house that morning?

"So come on, Pappy," said Bertie. "Mr. Dalziel doesn't need to question you any more. Do you, Superintendent?"

Dalziel hesitated. Now would be a dramatic time to reveal that Annie Greave was dead. If he were in charge of the case and could have followed up his revelation by getting Papworth and Bertie into a nice neutral interview room for the next couple of hours, he wouldn't have hesitated. But it wasn't up to him.

In any case, as he had stated to Balderstone, his ambiguous position in this house was a positive advantage. Once launch into a full-scale interrogation and he would have stepped outside the wagon ring and joined the other redskins whooping around in the darkness.

He decided to compromise.

"Don't forget," he said to Bertie. "It wasn't just a nonexistent theft we had here last night. A man got drowned."

"What's that to do with me?" demanded Papworth.

"Depends what time you left the house last night and where you went," said Dalziel. "You might have seen him on the road."

Papworth considered for a moment.

"No," he said. "I saw nothing. I've no time to gawp at passers-by."

"That's a little bit vague," said Dalziel "Let's see if we can help you. What time did you leave the house?"

"Latish. I'm not a man for clocks," said Papworth.

"All right," said Dalziel understandingly. "Let's try the other end. Where'd you go and what time did you get there?"

"Well," said Papworth. "I had a wet in the village."

"In the Green Man?" said Dalziel. "But you were away all night, Mr. Papworth. Don't the pubs around here ever close?"

"Not so's you'd notice," said Papworth, standing up and making for the door. "I'd best be getting to work."

Bertie stood aside to let him by, but Dalziel blocked his path.

"You're not telling me you were boozing all night," he said incredulously.

Pappy grinned slyly.

"Not *all* night," he said. "These are long nights for a country woman if her man's away. They like a bit of company. You ought to try it, Mr. Dalziel. Have another look round my room if you want to."

He squeezed past Dalziel and went out. Bertie

followed and closed the door behind him, leaving
Dalziel in the fuggy room.

Dalziel wrinkled his nose in distaste as he considered what the man had said. With typical economy
he found a word to cover both experiences.

"Chickenshit," he said.

CHAPTER XV

Pictures of Innocence

As Dalziel began to climb the stairs, Tillotson appeared on the landing and stood there looking down at him like a young hero ready to oppose the rising of the Creature from the Black Lagoon.

"You got him to bed?" asked Dalziel.

"Yes. He woke up a bit and started to sing."

"That's bad. Has he got a bucket?"

"Sorry?"

"A jerry. A piss pot. Something to spew into. When they wake up and start singing, it usually means they'll be honking their rings eventually."

"You're jolly expert," said Tillotson.

"I should be. I've bedded plenty of drunks in my time."

"An interesting taste," said Tillotson. "Mrs. Fielding was asking whether you were back. She's in her room and would like to see you."

"Right," said Dalziel. "I won't be a moment. You going out to help tidy up?"

"What for?"

"Well, after the flood. Make the place look nice and please the customers. You ought to be protecting your investment, son. How are the builders getting on?"

"Oh, pretty well, I suppose."

"Good. It looks as if you were right after all," said Dalziel heartily. "The place'll open on time."

Tillotson shrugged.

"I suppose so," he said and made his way downstairs looking disconsolate.

What's up with him? wondered Dalziel. Another row with Louisa or is he just unhappy about all those lovely birds they won't let him shoot?

He put the youth out of his mind and proceeded quietly upstairs. The interview with Bonnie would have to wait a while longer. There was something else to do first. While everything he knew pointed in one direction, it was always best to cross check thoroughly.

Uniff's studio was in darkness and it took him a moment or two to find the light switch. The blinds were down over the windows, double and tight fitting to exclude all daylight. Uniff must have been working in here recently.

Dalziel moved lightly across the room to the rostrum camera. He examined it as closely as possible without touching it. If he respected anything it was expertise and he had no desire to do anything which might spoil the setup. In the end, however, he had to undo a couple of clamps and twist the camera upwards to see what he was looking for. A line of polished brightness in the dull metal of the base-plate.

He made no attempt to return the camera to its former position but wandered around the room whistling tunelessly to himself. He stopped before the old fireplace and knelt down. Something had been burnt here recently. He let the ashes flutter through his fingers, then with a grunt of effort pushed himself upright.

Next he made for the open shelf unit which stood between the windows. There were four large buff envelopes on one of the shelves, three with photographs in them, the fourth empty. He examined the prints in each envelope with interest. Most of the pictures in the first seemed to have been taken in and around Lake House. In some of them a man

appeared whom he did not know, but there were
sufficient of Hereward Fielding's features in the smiling self-confident face to make him sure this was the
dear departed Conrad.

The second envelope contained shots of the funeral, the coffin being mounted on the punt, the
watery cortège, misty and ghostlike in the rain-soaked
atmosphere; and then one of a solid but sinister
figure standing at the end of a half-submerged bridge
and gazing impassively over a waste of waters. It
was quite a shock to recognize himself.

Pictures taken at the funeral came next. No wonder the poor sodding vicar had got annoyed! The
variety of shots and angles indicated that Uniff must
have been hopping around like a blue-arsed flea.
Dalziel laughed quietly at the thought and looked in
the next envelope.

The mood changed though the sequence was main-
tained. Tillotson falling into the water; Dalziel, full
of wrath, preventing him from getting back into the
punt; Dalziel examining his dripping suitcase. The
man had a flair, there was no denying it, thought
Dalziel sourly. Then came the shots taken at the
Gumbelow presentation. As a record of the progres-
sive effects of alcohol, they were superb. But their
interest to Dalziel was of another kind. He examined
them closely and when he had finished was still
not quite sure what he had seen.

Finally he picked up the fourth envelope and
checked to make sure it was empty. It was. But
when he turned to go, the room no longer was.

Mavis Uniff stood by the door watching him curiously. She was so still that she gave the impression
that she might have been there all along and Dalziel
had to re-run his actions on first entering to convince himself she hadn't been.

"Hello," he said. "I was looking for your brother."

"He's down by the lake," she said. "Can I help?"

"No. Nothing really. He showed me some photographs this morning." He held up the empty envelope.

"Yes. The ones of me."

"Oh no," said Dalziel. "These were—well . . ."

"Me," she said calmly. "In close-up."

"Jesus Christ," said Dalziel. "You mean you've got a tattoo?"

"No. But we use transfers. The skin-mags like a gimmick. That's all it is, Mr. Dalziel. A commercial proposition. Nothing incestuous."

Dalziel looked at her and shook his head.

"Shocked, Mr. Dalziel?" she said. She was as impassive as ever, but observing him very closely.

"Hardly. Surprised a bit. Where are the photos?"

"Burnt," she said, pointing to the fireplace.

"Why's that?"

"Hank got worried, thought you might remember your civic duty and speak to the local police. It didn't seem worth having a confrontation about a few pictures, not when we can replace them any time. So to be safe, he burnt them."

"I told him they didn't bother me," said Dalziel.

"Yes, I know. Seems you changed your mind."

She turned and left. By the time Dalziel reached the door, turned out the light and stepped into the corridor, she had disappeared.

Quickly he ran downstairs and into Herrie's sitting-room where the telephone was. Balderstone and Cross were planning to leave for Lake House in another fifteen minutes.

"Make it a bit longer," suggested Dalziel. "I've got things to do. Oh, and there's something else you can find out for me."

Before he went back upstairs he looked out of the window. Bertie, Uniff, Papworth and Mavis were standing in a little group, talking earnestly together. Tillotson was sitting alone in the duck punt gazing out over the still-swollen waters of the lake.

Grinning broadly, Dalziel climbed the stairs once more and knocked on Bonnie's door. There was a long pause, then, "Come in," she called.

She was sitting in front of her dressing-table as if she had not moved since he left her there that morning.

"Sorry I'm late," he said.

She smiled at him, a cautious tentative smile, not the full beam.

"All alone?" he said.

"Till we get some things sorted," she said.

"I'm all for that."

He took his jacket off and laid it on the bed.

"Do you mind?" he asked.

She looked at his broad khaki braces with wry amusement and shook her head.

"Right," he said, sitting on the bed and beginning a complicated two-handed scratch down the line of his braces. "Sort away."

"Andy," she said. "There's something going on here I don't know about."

Dalziel grunted in disbelief.

"They must be doing it underground then," he said. She ignored him.

"I'll tell you what I know if you tell me what you know."

"Do we spin a coin for first off?" he asked.

"No. If you agree, I'll trust you," she answered. "I'll start."

Dalziel held two fingers up, like a gun.

"On your mark," he said. "Bang."

"It's hard to know where to begin," she said. "It's all so mixed up. Listen. This theft business. I suppose you know all the stuff's been accounted for? Well, they wanted you out of the way this morning to sort things out."

"Who's *they*?"

"I'm not sure. Bertie certainly. Herrie said he wanted to go into town to arrange about the money and naturally I offered to take him. But Bertie said no. It had to be you. He rang the garage later, you know, and asked them to deliver your car. He wants rid of you altogether."

"I'd noticed," said Dalziel. He arranged the pillows as a back rest and stretched himself out on the bed. The brandy fumes were rubbing like a cat against the inside of his eyeballs and sleep would be very easy.

"But why, Andy? I can't get any sense out of him."

"Perhaps he doesn't like my after-shave lotion," yawned Dalziel.

"No! I mean what's going on? Has there or has there not been a robbery? Where's Mrs. Greave?"

"Questions, questions," murmured Dalziel, his eyes half closed. "You've told me nowt and already you're asking questions. Tell me this, why'd the old man change his mind?"

"I don't know. Family loyalty; God knows. Herrie's mind doesn't work like other people's."

"Oh aye. He's a poet. Some folk used to think that was a defence in law. Like being daft. It's a lot like being daft, isn't it? I mean, if you're wise enough not to put cash into a half-baked business scheme when it's got some faint chance of succeeding, you've got to be daft to put it in just after a robbery's removed most of the visible assets. Don't you agree?"

"Why the hell didn't you ask Herrie yourself?" demanded Bonnie. "You're his big mate at the moment."

"Oh, I did, I did," said Dalziel. "But he's very close. Talks a lot but says nowt. That's what comes of being a poet. Tell you what I think, though."

"What?"

"Come and sit beside me," said Dalziel, patting the bed. "Don't want to risk being overheard."

Bonnie glanced uneasily round the room then brought her chair close to the bedside.

"This'll do," she said in a low voice. "You ought to get one thing straight in your mind, Andy. I bed down for pleasure, nothing else."

"Me too," said Dalziel. "Here's what I think. I think Herrie must have known that the stolen stuff was going to be returned. And he must have known because someone told him last night. You had a long chat with someone in here last night."

"So you listen at bedroom doors too!" she said scornfully.

"Only for pleasure," he said. "Nothing else. Anyway I heard nowt, just voices. *Did* you tell him?"

"How could I tell him what I didn't know?" she demanded.

"All right. So Herrie came to tell you he'd changed his mind, which means someone else had been talking to him already. What made him change his mind? Two things, I think. One selfish. The poor old sod's shit-scared of dying. He wraps it up in words, but that's the bottom of it. Which is interesting, eh? He thinks there's someone in this house capable of knocking him off."

"And the other thing?"

Dalziel's eyes were fully closed now. Repose did nothing for his face.

"Unselfish. I've got this lad works for me in Yorkshire. Bright. Got degrees and things. I listen to what he says, pick the pearls out of the pig-crap. He'd say that most people doing something selfish like to find some unselfish reason for doing it. Not that you're going to change your crime figures much by saying things like that! No, but sometimes . . . anyway, what's old Hereward got to be unselfish about? I tell you; one thing only that I've observed."

"What's that?"

"Nigel."

Dalziel opened one eye and squinted at Bonnie.

"Why don't you fetch him in?"

He closed his eye again, heard Bonnie rise and walk across the room, heard the bathroom door open.

When he opened his eyes again, Nigel was standing at the foot of the bed.

"Where's the grapes, son?" asked Dalziel.

"What?"

"You're standing there like a reluctant relative on a sick visit. For Christ's sake, make yourself comfortable."

The boy came round the bed and sat in the chair vacated by his mother. Bonnie pushed Dalziel's feet aside and sat at the foot of the bed. She opened her mouth to speak but Dalziel shushed her.

"I'll do the talking," he said. "You listen. Both of you. I'll be brief. Don't interrupt. This whole project was never a serious attempt to get a restaurant going. At least not on your dad's part, Nigel. I mean, think about it! A medieval Banqueting Hall! Did you ever hear of owt so daft! So what was going on? I'll tell you. Bertie came home from Liverpool one fine day with a bright scheme for burning this place down and picking up the insurance. Only, it had to be a bit more complicated than that. To really collect you need something worth insuring, not just a tatty old house.

"He'd got a taste for this when he was in Liverpool and he was dealing with Uniff's bit of fire trouble. They recognized fellow spirits and came to an arrangement by which Uniff claimed for ten times more stuff than got damaged. It was so easy, they reckoned they could make a good living out of it.

"So they work out this scheme. It's ingenious. Launch what looks like a genuine business venture, so you're insuring not only a building which has rocketed in value since it got refurbished, but also the business itself. I haven't seen the policy yet, but I gather they're covered for six months' loss of estimated profits. Plus, of course, a little bonus. You're covered for all fittings, furnishings, stock etc. But why burn it? Why can't it, like Uniff's equipment, just be moved elsewhere? Resold later? I wondered why anyone should want to store all that junk I found. But I soon caught on. If you're going to claim for expensive reproduction furniture and hangings, not to mention costumes, you need lots of ash of the right kind. It's a grand scheme. Really grand."

Dalziel shook his head in reluctant admiration. Bonnie let out an incredulous sigh.

"I don't believe it," she said. "I don't believe it."

Dalziel put on his favourite-uncle look and reached across to pat her knee with one hand while with the other he squeezed Nigel's arm reassuringly.

"I know it's hard," he said. "I'm sorry. They didn't tell you; knew it would be no good. You wouldn't have gone for anything like that. Aye, the criminal mind recognizes honesty when it sees it."

Bonnie looked at him sharply but his expression matched his tone of vibrant sincerity.

"No, I reckon that in on the deal were Bertie and his father, the Uniffs, and Mrs. Greave and Papworth, of course."

"Why Mrs. Greave?"

"Obvious. You wanted to take on someone who'd look after the skivvying behind the scenes. They couldn't risk you getting hold of some nice ordinary kitchen manager who'd spot something funny was going on right off. So they brought in Mrs. Greave. As Papworth's recently widowed daughter, she wouldn't be asked for references, that kind of thing. And she was very useful to have around. No doubt she and Papworth were going to start things burning while the rest of you were giving each other nice alibis a good distance away. A big fire like this, you see, they'd look very closely at it. That's where your husband came in."

"How?"

"Well the REME's one branch of the Army where they let officers know things. With his electrical know-how, it must have seemed a good idea to have some kind of electric fault causing the fire. Now in an old place like that, especially an old stables, you must have had a lot of rats. Stands to reason. Right then. A big hungry rat comes along, sees some nice new wire, decides to have a chew. What happens? It sinks its teeth in, gets electrocuted and sets up a short. I won't get technical, because I know bugger all about it, but it's possible. It has happened. A little glow becomes a big fire. When the fire-invest-igation officer has a look, what does he find? Well, the charred remains of a rat for one thing. And if there's enough left to do any tests on, he finds it's been electrocuted. Problem solved. Insurance coughs up. Everyone's happy."

"How do you know all this, Andy?" asked Bonnie quietly.

"I'm guessing. But it seems likely unless Mrs. Greave kept frozen rats in your fridge to make pies with. Frozen *electrocuted* rats."

"What happened to Mrs. Greave?"

"Simple," said Dalziel cheerfully. "She spotted me right off. Didn't need to search my pockets. Her kind know a bobby when they see one. So she got cold feet in the end and took off. She was scared that Bertie and Uniff might still go ahead even with me around. She wanted no part of it, so off she went to sell her wares down Lime Street again."

Nigel shifted in his chair and Dalziel looked at him thoughtfully.

"Of course, if you suspected some of this, it might explain why you decided to run away, lad," he said. "You're a puzzle to me, I must admit."

"I just wanted to be by myself," said the boy unconvincingly.

"Like Garbo," guffawed Dalziel. The boy flushed and began to stand but the big hand caught hold of his arm again, not reassuringly this time, but like a clamp.

"Sit still, lad. Visiting time's not up yet. I've not finished my story. You see, everything was fixed to go ahead. All that was needed was to get at the wiring and plant the rat. So first they got the workmen out of the way. Someone, the Uniff girl I think, rang Gibb and said there was no money in the kitty. Gibb remarked how badly Conrad conducted the interview, not his usual persuasive self at all. You see, he wanted the workmen out of the way so he could work at his leisure. And also having Gibb off the job gave him the excuse for carrying on himself so that no one i.e. you, or Herrie, or Louisa or even Charley Tillotson, would be surprised to find him up a ladder with a drill. But then he did something very silly which spoilt everything."

"Yes," said Bonnie.

"He had his accident and got killed. Jesus! I bet that upset everybody. Careful, son!"

He spoke sharply to Nigel who had forced himself upright and glowered threateningly down at the recumbent policeman.

"Never hit a man when he's down," advised Dalziel. "Not unless you can hit him so hard, he'll stay down. Stand if you want, but don't go away."

"Why are you doing this, Andy?" asked Bonnie.

"Because he's got as much right as you have to know what his dad was up to. Frankly I don't think either of you find it too hard to believe. He sounds a likely lad, does old Conrad. But it's better you hear about it now, straight, than that you get it through some roundabout questioning later on."

"Questioning? Who from?" asked Bonnie. "You mean that the police can still do something about it, even though nothing happened?"

"Mebbe," said Dalziel grimly. "There's a thing called conspiracy. Hard to prove if people keep their mouths shut. Me, I reckon that Bertie's got sense enough to try to cut his losses and actually make a go of the business. I think that's the other reason Herrie has decided to invest his money. I don't know how much he knew, but he must have had a shrewd idea of what his son was like. But then so must you."

He eyed Bonnie thoughtfully for a moment before going on.

"Anyway, now the only way of protecting the investment and protecting your and Nigel's interests is to make a go of things, I don't know if it's possible but it looks as if they're going to have a try. I just want to be sure there aren't any fires around here in a couple of months' time when everybody's forgotten I ever existed. Well, that's it."

He made to rise from the bed, but Bonnie restrained him.

"You run along, Nigel," she said to her son. "There are one or two things Mr. Dalziel and I have to talk about."

The boy rose and left without speaking.

"He looks as if he could do with two good nights' sleep," commented Dalziel.

"Couldn't we all?" said Bonnie. "Andy, why are you doing this?"

"Doing what? I'm doing nowt except having a private chat."

"Private chat nothing! You know damn well Bertie will screw everything you've said out of Nigel in ten minutes flat. And if he didn't talk, well, I'd have to."

"That's honest," said Dalziel. He eased his braces off his shoulders, settled back on the pillow and inserting his hand into his shirt began to scratch his belly. Impatiently she snatched his hand away. He opened one eye and looked at her. With a sigh she leaned forward so that her head rested on his chest, pulled his shirt out of his waist-band and began to scratch for him.

"Oh Andy," she said. "What are you up to?"

"What do you mean?"

"Well you're a policeman, and I think you believe in it. But you seem to be giving us a warning."

"I'm on holiday," he said. "A little bit to the left. That's grand."

"Well," she said dubiously. "I suppose there's a bit of the Sydney Cartons even in the nastiest, most cynical of us."

"Of the what?"

"Oh, do stop pretending to be pig-ignorant! Yes, I suppose one generous, unselfish act might squeeze even you into heaven."

"I'm at it all the time," protested Dalziel. "Farther down please. Ah!"

She kneaded away at his flesh with strong fingers.

"Oh Andy," she said. "I need someone to trust and rely on. I really do. I'm tired of trying to hold things together single-handed."

Dalziel reached over her shoulder and cupped her right breast in his broad palm.

"Why don't you take two hands to it?" he asked.

*   *   *

Forty-five minutes later after a perfunctory tap on the door, Tillotson burst in and halted, red with embarrassment, when he saw the two heads on the pillow.

"What is it, Charley?" asked Bonnie in an exasperated tone.

"I'm sorry," said Tillotson, retreating. "It's just that the police are here again. They want to see everyone. They say that Mrs. Greave is dead."

He left and Bonnie poked Dalziel hard with her forefinger.

"You knew about this?"

"Aye," he said, sitting up and yawning.

She watched him in silence as he got out of bed and began to dress.

"Listen, love," he said as he peered in the mirror and dragged her silver-backed brush through his greying and retreating stubble. "It's no good lying there looking suspicious. My shoulders are no good as public leaning posts. I either carry you or I drop you. Partnership means doing things my way."

She laughed at this, realized he hadn't intended a joke, frowned, then flung back the sheets and jumped out of bed.

The brush paused in mid-stroke as Dalziel regarded her in the mirror.

"All right," she said. "You're the boss. Lead on, Sydney. Even if we are travelling by tumbril."

CHAPTER XVI

Dead Ducks

After a brief preliminary consultation Dalziel kept very much in the background as Balderstone and Cross worked their way steadily through everyone in the household taking statements about the events of the previous day with particular reference to conversations with and last sightings of Annie Greave.

Papworth excited particular interest, of course, but even old Hereward was fed with black coffee and interviewed in his own bed. Dalziel meanwhile wandered outside to see how Gibb and his men were getting on. The progress they had made was not perceptible to the inexpert eye, but the little builder assured him that all was proceeding to schedule.

Dalziel continued his perambulation, returning eventually to the front of the house where he stood looking out over the lake. It really wasn't much of a lake, he realized, now that the sinking of the flood waters was making its normal limits much more clear. Not your Windermere or your Loch Lomond. But it might be a useful adjunct to the restaurant if you knew how to exploit it. A floating bar perhaps. Or gondolas.

He laughed to himself. It would be easy to start thinking in the nutty fashion of the Lake Housers.

Suddenly a dull explosion shattered his thoughts. Birds screamed and rose from the trees and the lake.

But a couple did not rise and lay instead staining the water with dye as bright as their bills.

From behind the small island which Dalziel had examined for signs of Nigel only two days ago emerged the duck punt. The gun in the bows was still smoking and Tillotson waved triumphantly when he saw he had a spectator.

"Great," said a voice behind Dalziel. "Roast duck stuffed with lead for supper."

"The buggers'll sink before he reaches them," said Dalziel.

"You were looking for me earlier," said Uniff.

"Not really," said Dalziel. "I was just poking round your room."

"Hey, man," said Uniff, grinning through his tangled beard. "You're too honest to be honest. What'd you find?"

"Tell you what I didn't find. I didn't find a serial number on your camera and I didn't find those dirty pictures you showed me."

"Dirty? Those weren't dirty! Man, I could show you pictures that would blow your mind!"

"I doubt it. Your sister said she posed for 'em. She's a liar."

Suddenly Uniff drew himself upright, placed his left hand on his hip and thrust the other forward as if holding a sword.

"Call my sister a liar, sir? Zounds, you besmirch our family honour. On guard!"

The change of accent was very good, rather better on the whole than his American.

"I got Sergeant Cross to check with Epping," said Dalziel. "Annie Greave had that tattoo on her inner thigh."

"Ain't you the clever one," said Uniff, reverting. "So what?"

"So why did Mavis lie?" said Dalziel. "You know the question I'm really asking myself, Mr. Uniff? Why did you get so worried after you'd shown me those pictures?"

"Like I said, you're the law."

"Never forget it. No. Two answers are possible. One: you were worried in case Annie blabbed when we picked her up. If you and Bertie were forced into a position of your word against hers, it wouldn't help matters if it could be shown that you knew her well enough to use as a model. So get rid of all the photos. Two: if you knew Annie was lying like one of the babes in the wood all cold under a pile of leaves, then you'd be even less keen to let me find a connection."

"What're you trying to say, friend?" asked Uniff uneasily.

"I'm not your friend, friend," said Dalziel. "And you don't need an interpreter. Now, I don't know what time you went missing from the little party last night, but I do know what time you got back. Empty roads, fast car. You could get to Epping and back in five hours easy."

"I told you, I was drinking after hours," said Uniff.

"That's what they all say round here," mocked Dalziel. "I'll tell you something else for nothing, seeing as this is one of my helpful days. You can file, file away at a number stamped in metal; we've got machines in our labs that'll bring it up like chicken pox."

"Man, I'm shaking," said Uniff. "What's it to be— the rubber truncheon or the water torture?"

He sounded quite recovered from his momentary uneasiness.

"Tell you what," said Dalziel thoughtfully. "I think I understand you. You really do think that money's just a game."

"No. An evil," said Uniff.

"Oh aye. But you need it."

"Yeah. *That's* a game. Getting it, spending it. But I don't like the game so I won't play to the rules."

"You'll commit crimes?"

"Not against people. Just against the money system," said Uniff. "Look, man, money's immoral, right? Then all activities aimed at getting hold of money are immoral, right? Your pay-cheque at the end of the month is just as immoral as . . . as . . ."

"As defrauding an insurance company," suggested Dalziel.

"Nice example, Andy," grinned Uniff. "That's about the strength of it."

"So when I suggest you're crooked with money, all I get from you is a laugh. But when I suggest you might have something to do with Annie Greave's death, you begin to shake."

"Hurting people's something else," said Uniff seriously. "You gotta see that. Humanity makes me shake."

"Is that it? Or guilt?"

Suddenly their conversation was interrupted by two sodden, bleeding birds thrust between them by Charley Tillotson.

"You two look very serious," he said cheerfully.

"Not as serious as those things," said Uniff. "I thought Bonnie said no shooting."

"Yes. I believe she did. But she didn't seem to mind when I gave her a couple earlier for dinner. There's plenty to spare just at the moment with the flooding. Think of what it must have been like in the old days."

"You need a licence for that thing," warned Dalziel.

"Do I really?" asked Tillotson. "Well, Bonnie might have one. It's her gun, after all. I'll go and ask her."

"Have you made your statement?" said Dalziel.

"Oh yes. First in," said Tillotson proudly.

He went into the house dripping blood and water.

Dalziel turned to follow him, but Uniff placed a restraining hand on his arm.

"Would you answer me a question for a change, Andy."

"Mebbe."

"Well, man; like, you keep dropping hints and making threatening noises, but I just had a little talk with the prodigal son and what he said made you sound more like a mother hen than an avenging angel. This fire business, which is all fantasy, you dig, I mean I admit nothing, but if that's what you believe, then shouldn't we all be down at headquarters having our fingernails pulled out? What's the name of the game, man? Or can I guess?"

Dalziel didn't answer, but turned away and went back into the house.

Behind him Uniff laughed provocatively but Dalziel ignored him. Very soon, he was beginning to realize, he would have to make a decision. In fact he supposed that already that afternoon he'd taken very definite steps towards making it. At the moment he could examine his professional conscience and find it pretty clear if you ignored those small shifting misty areas which always swirled around on the periphery. What he knew to be relevant he had passed on to Balderstone and Cross. And what he merely suspected to be relevant he had not yet consciously decided to withhold.

Ideally Balderstone and Cross should sort things out for themselves without reference to his own special knowledge gained as a guest in this house. Yet they felt, as he would do in their shoes, entitled to share this knowledge. The only way to remove himself from this pernicious position was indeed to remove himself and that might be as painful as remaining.

The interviewing had taken place as nearly all semi-formal activities seemed to in this house in Herrie's sitting-room. At least with the old man sleeping the sleep of the stone upstairs, there should have been no indignant outbursts.

He met Nigel coming out of the door.

"All right?" said Dalziel genially.

The boy said nothing but looked at him with an expression which might have been accusation or fear. As he moved on, Dalziel watched him with a troubled mind.

Inside Cross and Balderstone sat drinking tea. Bonnie must have made it, thought Dalziel with absurd possessive pride. She was the only one in the house who would even have considered making the policemen comfortable.

"Finished?" asked Dalziel looking at the pile of statement forms which lay on the table by the teapot.

"Yes, sir," said Balderstone.

"Except for one," said Dalziel.

"What?"

"Mine." He produced from his inside pocket a foolscap sheet folded in quarters and placed it with the others.

"I was here too, don't forget."

"We hadn't forgotten, sir," said Balderstone.

"Tell me then. What's new?"

"Well, nothing much, sir," said Cross. "As far as we can make out, Annie Greave was last seen about the place at two-thirty yesterday afternoon. It was Mrs. Fielding that saw her. That was just before the presentation ceremony. So any time after that she could have packed up and gone. We've checked with taxi services, bus and train ticket offices, but no joy yet. She could have been picked up by a passing motorist, of course."

"Passing where?" asked Balderstone. "The road past the gate runs between Low Fold and High Fold and it's still under a foot of water most of the way."

"Yes, sir," said Cross. "So either she walked to Low Fold and got a bus there, which no one recalls. Or she was given a lift by someone in the house though no one admits it. Now this could have been just before the ceremony . . ."

"No," interrupted Dalziel. "I was walking back from the village between two-fifteen and two-forty-five and no cars passed me coming from the house. And everyone was gathered in this room when I got back."

"Except Papworth," said Cross reprovingly. "But the rest were all here till the drinking started. No one's so sure who was where doing what from about four o'clock on."

Dalziel felt they were both regarding him significantly. His shoulders rose in a small non-typical Gallic shrug.

"The thing is," said Balderstone. "No one would surely be much bothered by admitting they'd given her a lift and just dropped her in Orburn, say, or even farther afield. So I think we've got to accept that nobody did this. Which raises the much more important question. Could anyone have taken her all the way to Epping, either dead or alive, and got back here within the known period of their absence? The answer is, only two. Papworth and Uniff. Now they're both vague enough to be suspicious. Uniff won't give us the name of the pub he claims he was drinking in after hours and Papworth won't give us the name of the woman he claims he was rogering. They both have highly developed senses of honour, it seems. Well, I've tried to avoid waving the big stick . . ."

"Why?" interrupted Dalziel. "They shouldn't give us big sticks if they don't want us to wave 'em. Any road, that's up to you. I tell you this, though, on my patch we wouldn't need to ask. We'd know the pub and we'd know the woman."

Cross and Balderstone exchanged glances in the face of this large and unmannerly claim. Dalziel glowered at them, recognizing in himself a desire to fall out with them and then let ill-temper cut the ties of co-operation.

"Of course, we're approaching it from that side too, sir," said Balderstone calmly. "Now, the other possibility, and this looms very large in view of the statements we have received, is that Mrs. Greave left with one of the visitors."

"Visitors?"

"The people here for the presentation. You can't recall when any of them left, sir?"

"No," said Dalziel, shaking his huge head slowly. "They'd all gone, except Arkwright, when I came back downstairs."

"After your . . . discussion with Mrs. Fielding," said Balderstone, glancing at Dalziel's statement. "It's a pity, but they all seem to have got away fairly quietly. Lots of cheeriohs inside the house, but no one seems to have escorted them to the door."

"Do you know *where* they went?" asked Dalziel.

"Your own surmise, London, seems very likely. But we've passed on the information to Epping and no doubt they will be checking down there. Well, I think we've done all we can here and it's getting on."

He began to gather up the sheets of paper from the table. Dalziel glanced at his watch. It was after six.

"By the way, sir," said Balderstone, "Mr. Albert Fielding while we were talking to him made enquiries about the procedure for bringing a complaint against a police officer."

"What did you do to him? Forgot to kiss his arse?" asked Dalziel.

"No, sir. The complaint, I gathered, was aimed at you."

"*What!*"

"He seemed to think that certain insinuations you made in the presence of his young brother, Nigel, were slanderous. I indicated that as you were not here in an official capacity, he would be best advised to seek redress through a civil action, when the police, I assured him, would investigate the alleged offences thoroughly. This seemed to quieten him down."

"The puffed-up nowt!" said Dalziel. "He needs to be locked up for a few months."

"Perhaps. But it seems unlikely now. Conspiracy is very difficult to prove, especially when the conspirators are forewarned." His voice was studiedly neutral.

"It would never have stuck," said Dalziel.

"You're probably right," agreed Balderstone. "This boy Nigel puzzled me a bit, though. The one you talked to."

"Yes?"

"Well, we just had him in as a matter of form. So we could say we'd seen everyone in the house. His mother had told us he just came back this morning. That struck me as odd. He's how old? Fifteen? Sixteen? And she hadn't been bothered when he ran away. Strange, even in this day and age."

"He'd done it before," said Dalziel. "And he did ring."

As though on a cue the telephone rang and Dalziel grabbed it. It was the uniformed sergeant at Orburn Police Station wanting to talk to Cross. Balderstone and Dalziel moved across into the window bay to avoid disturbing him.

"The lad seemed very disturbed by it all," continued the inspector.

"He's very young," offered Dalziel. "I suppose from his point of view, Annie Greave was almost one of the family. And he still hasn't got over his dad's death."

"You're probably right," said Balderstone. "It can't have helped for him to hear you saying what you thought his father had been up to, either."

"No," said Dalziel. "An error of judgement, that. I'm sorry."

"There's been a sight too much death about this house," said Balderstone. "Mr. Fielding, Mrs. Greave. And Spinx, of course. We found his car by the way. When he came through the gates he turned right and ran it down through the trees to the lake edge. good spot to hide. You haven't picked up any hint of what he was after, have you?"

"No. Everyone seemed baffled. Probably he was just trying a last desperate snoop before reporting failure."

"It was his last, sure enough," said Balderstone. "Tell me, sir, you said you'd leave it to us to break the news of Annie Greave's murder so you could chat with the people here before they knew about it. Did anything come out of this?"

"Not really," admitted Dalziel, thinking guiltily of how he had spent a great deal of his time since getting back to the house. "I had a good go at Papworth, but got nowhere. He says he picked Annie up one night in the Pool, struck up a regular liaison with her and brought her out here when the chance presented itself."

"It's possible, I suppose," said Balderstone. "When they're getting on a bit, some of these girls fancy a steady relationship even if it means a cut back in pay. But not out here, I shouldn't have thought. You indicated to Sergeant Cross that you were pretty certain Papworth was knocking her off, though."

"Yes, I did," agreed Dalziel. Another prevarication.

"So there might be something in it. What about connecting the others with her?"

"I think there's a chance Uniff might have been using her as a model for some candid camera shots. Hard to prove, though. Liverpool CID might be able to establish a connection, but what would it prove?"

"I don't really know, sir," said Balderstone blankly. "So no one said anything which suggested a foreknowledge of Mrs. Greave's death."

Dalziel shook his head. He could do this quite honestly.

Cross put the telephone down and joined them in the bay shooting a quick glance at Balderstone. It seemed to Dalziel that the inspector nodded almost imperceptibly as though indicating to the sergeant that it was all right to go ahead. If true, this both piqued and alarmed him

"They've been on from Essex again," he said. "Trying to baffle us with speed, I reckon. But fair dues, they've done well, or the Met has. They found the Yanks at Claridge's and seem pretty convinced they're in the clear. Penitent, the BBC man, they got hold of also. He started talking about his civic rights a bit quick, but in the end they were sure he hadn't seen Annie Greave."

"Pity," said Dalziel, feeling much more disappointed than the single word showed. He was surprised to find how much he wanted Annie to have been seen alive and well and a long way from Lake House.

"You fancied him?" asked Balderstone.

"He was alone."

"No, he wasn't," interrupted Cross. "I think that's what bothered him. It turns out that he gave a Miss Nicola Sugden a lift back . . ."

"Who?" asked Balderstone.

"The lass in the green tunic!" said Dalziel. "The photographer."

"That's her," said Cross. "And she seems to have spent the night in Penitent's flat. His wife and two kids arrived home from a visit half-way through the interview."

"No wonder he abandoned poor Arkwright!" said Dalziel. "That means Butt was by himself."

"Yes, sir," said Cross, looking at his notebook. "They contacted the paper he was doing the feature for and got his address. It's in Chigwell, Essex, only five or six miles from Epping."

Dalziel began to scratch his ankle, bending forward to conceal the relief on his face.

"Butt," he said. "Nasty bastard. I'd have said touching up typists on the Underground was his limit but you can never tell."

"We mustn't jump to conclusions, sir," said Balderstone in a tone of admonition too mild to be insubordinate. "What did Mr. Butt have to say for himself, Sergeant?"

"Nothing, sir," said Cross. "They couldn't get hold of him. It seems he flew out to Brazil first thing this morning. On an assignment. They checked, of course, and it's genuine."

"Damn!" said Dalziel. "Yes, he was going on about it yesterday. You'd have thought it was a royal visit. Here, what about his car?"

"Yes, they thought of that as well, sir," said Cross. "It was parked at the airport. They opened it up, had a good look. In the boot they found an old travelling rug. On it were traces of make-up, some hairs and a small patch of blood. They're doing tests on them, of course. Also in the boot was a small spade, the kind of thing motorists sometimes have in case of heavy snow. This one had traces of fresh earth on the blade. They're cross-checking that too."

"It sounds promising," said Balderstone. "When's he come back?"

"He has a return flight booked for a week on Saturday," said Cross. "But they won't wait that long, will they?"

Dalziel shrugged.

"I don't know. They won't want to alarm him. There's no extradition treaty with Brazil, remember. And after that balls-up with Biggs, everyone will be treading very carefully."

"In any case," added Balderstone, "they haven't finished their tests yet. Mind you, it would all fit very nicely. Very nicely indeed. Now we must be off, Sergeant. Mr. Dalziel will be wanting his dinner. Goodbye, sir. We'll keep in touch."

Dalziel walked with them to the front door and watched them drive away with much unprofessional relief. When he turned to re-enter the house, Bertie was standing there.

"All right, Dalziel," he said. "You've got your car back now, so there's nothing to stop you following your friends."

Dalziel pushed by him with enough force to make the stout youth stagger. He made for the kitchen, followed closely by Bertie who talked incessantly.

"This isn't a fascist state, Dalziel. You can't go around bullying people and slandering them without being made to pay for it. Just shove off, get out of our lives, go and decompose somewhere else."

They were all in the kitchen except Hereward. There was a smell of roast duck in the air and Louisa was setting the table.

"Have they gone?" asked Bonnie.

"Yes, just," said Dalziel. "They asked me to say cheerioh and thank you for the tea."

"How frightfully polite," mocked Uniff.

"Wasn't it?" agreed Dalziel. "More than I can say for laughing boy here."

He sat down and smiled at Louisa.

"Don't forget to lay a place for me."

Bonnie looked coldly at Bertie.

"What have you been saying?"

"I told him he'd outstayed his welcome. His car's back on the road and there's nothing to keep him here. There's enough to bother us without having to lock our doors because we've let a creeping spy into the house."

"He's right, you know, Andy baby," said Uniff. "Nothing personal, but, hell, we'd be crazy to keep you."

"Wait a minute!" interjected Louisa. "Who's giving orders? Let me remind you whose house you're in. If anyone decides who goes, who stays, it's Bonnie and me."

"And what do *you* say, love?" asked Dalziel.

"I'm not sure."

"Well, while you're deciding, shall we eat?" asked Dalziel.

He almost fell out of his chair as Bertie seized it from behind and pulled.

"To hell with this!" cried the stout youth. "Just get packed, Dalziel, and get out."

"Quieten down, lad," said Dalziel soothingly. "It's ill-mannered to talk like that to a guest. It's downright stupid to talk that way to a business associate."

Something in his voice quenched Bertie's wrath. "What do you mean?" he asked uneasily.

"What I say," Dalziel said. "Earlier this afternoon I accepted your chairman's invitation to invest a couple of thousand of my hard-earned savings in your business. Ask your mam. So you're no longer just my friends, you're my colleagues. And I'll tell you what, Bertie. I'll be worth my weight in fire-insurance."

No one spoke for a moment, then Uniff began to laugh.

"Bonnie!" cried Bertie. "It's not true?"

Slowly his mother nodded.

"Right," said Dalziel, seizing a knife and fork and holding them in clenched hands. "Madam Chairman, if the meeting has been called to order I think I'm ready for item number one."

CHAPTER XVII

Opening Night

It is a truth universally acknowledged by all married men that their wives are rational, understanding, submissive and amiable only in proportion as they are distanced from their mothers.

"For God's sake, Ellie," protested Peter Pascoe. "We've only called in to pick up the presents. It's Saturday. I start work on Monday. I need all of tomorrow to get myself organized!"

"We can still be home by mid-morning," said Ellie firmly. "If you keep off the booze, that is. Which might not be a bad thing."

"What's that mean?"

"Well," said Ellie maliciously, "that was a nasty case of brewer's droop you caught last Tuesday. I understood CID men were immune. You'll be back in uniform if you're not careful."

"It was that southern beer," protested Pascoe, grinning. "That's why I want to get home really. Surely they'd understand?"

"No," said Ellie. "Mum and Dad have gone to a lot of bother. Just look at the way they've done up this bedroom. As for tonight, the table's booked and it's not been cheap, I can tell you. They're not all that well off and I'm not going to let their efforts be wasted. So resign yourself to it. And let's go downstairs before they start worrying. In my family decent folk don't screw in the afternoon."

"All right," sighed Pascoe. "They said it would be like this but I never believed them. You know, I wouldn't mind so much if we were being treated to the best French cuisine in Lincolnshire. But a medieval banquet! Jesus wept!"

It was even more hideous than he anticipated. For a start the car parking was chaotic. A tall blond youth in a see-through tunic and knee-breeches was directing operations with a fine disregard for the laws of space, time and dynamics. Leaving the car was almost as dangerous as remaining in it, but they finally reached the bar where even Ellie's isn't-this-nice expression fractured momentarily when she found they were attached to a gaggle of Townswomen's Guild members, many of whom insisted on dredging up anecdotal treasures from her distant childhood. Fortunately their simultaneity made them mostly incomprehensible.

Pascoe caught Ellie's expression and smiled; and smiled yet again when he saw his father-in-law demand confirmation of the exorbitant prices the striking middle-aged barmaid had charged him for their apéritifs. He suddenly felt that the evening might prove ghastly enough for an objective student of the social sciences to be able to enjoy himself.

Inside the alleged medieval Banqueting Hall, which was more like a parody than an imitation, goodies continued to spill out of the cornucopia. The room was illuminated by electric candles whose dim religious light showed rows of benches and tables set with wooden platters, plastic-handled daggers and goblets made of some alloy so light that once filled to the brim with unctuous mead they became dangerously unstable. Which, decided Pascoe after a careful sip, was more than he was likely to do. The diners were packed close on the benches. Pascoe had Ellie's mother on one side and on the other a statuesque townswoman from whose close-pressed thigh he might have derived much harmless pleasure had it not felt strangely corrugated.

From a gallery at the far end of the hall came music vaguely Elizabethan in style, and a girl so slightly built that in the best Elizabethan tradition she might have been a boy was singing about the pleasures of her hey-nonny-nonny-no. The assembled diners, who seemed not to have been much deterred by the price of pre-dinner drinks, joined in the chorus with prurient enthusiasm.

Pascoe leaned over to Ellie who sat opposite.

"I was wrong," he bellowed. "I think I shall enjoy this."

Behind him someone was beating a tin plate and a strangely familiar voice was shouting, "My lords and ladies, pray be silent for the entry of the first course."

No one took much notice except Ellie who ignored Pascoe's words and stared over his shoulder with an expression of pantomimic incredulity.

"Peter," she said. "You'll never believe this."

Slowly Pascoe turned. What he saw came as such a shock he had to use the townswoman's thigh as a support.

"My God!" he said.

Standing at the far end of the hall clad in a green velvet gown and wearing a floppy blue cap embellished with a peacock's feather was Detective-Superintendent Andrew Dalziel.

Pascoe laughed so much he couldn't drink his Baronial Brose and was still having difficulty by the time he reached the Cavalier's Capon. The townswoman fortunately put this down to her own rib-tickling conversation. Only Ellie understood his amusement, though after an initial outburst she no longer seemed to share it.

"What's he *doing*, Peter?" she asked under cover of an outbreak of screams as some wit, immediately imitated, demonstrated the Tudor method of chicken-bone disposal.

"God knows," said Pascoe. "But he hasn't spotted me yet. Here!"

He beckoned to a bearded youth in a jester's outfit who was going round taking flash photographs at fifty pence a time.

"Right, man. Grab hold of the little lady and smile."

"No, no. Not me," said Pascoe. "I'd like a picture of *him*. The portly gent in the green nightie."

"No, Peter!" protested Ellie. But the photographer after a quizzical raising of the eyebrows had moved away.

"Andy, baby, you've got fans," said Uniff.

"What?"

"Guy over there wants a pic. So make with the medieval merriment. Say cheese."

"Shit," said Dalziel as he followed the direction indicated by the jerk of Uniff's head.

"What the hell are you doing here?" he growled into Pascoe's ear a couple of minutes later.

"Just having a lot of fun," grinned Pascoe, on whom the mead was having a greater effect than anticipated.

"It's about time you had a piss," said Dalziel. He nodded sternly at Ellie and moved away.

"Everything going OK, Andy?" asked Bonnie whom he met outside the door.

"Fine," he said. "What are you doing?"

"I just stepped out of the kitchen for a quick drag. It's red hot in there."

Dalziel could believe it. It was a close, humid night with wreaths of mist rising from the unmoving lake.

"Back to it, I suppose," said Bonnie. She rested her hand on his arm for a moment and raised her face to his. As he kissed her the door to the hall opened and someone came out.

"See you later," said Bonnie and moved away.

"Hello, hello, hello," said Pascoe.

"You'd best sober up before you say summat you'll be sorry for," said Dalziel grimly. "Let's go outside."

They stood together in the cobbled yard hardly

able to see each other in the dim light which forced its way out of the Banqueting Hall through the stained plastic windows. Noise escaped more successfully and the overall effect was rather like overhearing an orgy in a church. Pascoe took a deep breath and tried to think of something inoffensive to say.

"Having a nice holiday, sir?" was the best he could manage.

"Grand," said Dalziel, and then repeated the word with a note of surprise in his voice.

It was in many ways true, he realized. Certainly in this past week he had been almost totally immersed in getting the restaurant into operation. After the initial reaction to his involvement, they had settled down quickly into a remarkably good team. There were various kinds of expertise present in Lake House but what Dalziel had had to offer was momentum. He got things moving and kept them moving, generally by brute force.

The hard work involved served a double function. It distracted his attention from both the past and the future. The Dalziel whose nights were filled with doubt and sorrow had retreated into some limbo with that other Dalziel whose constabulary soul would shortly have to go marching on.

Or perhaps not. He had always been a liver in the present, never one of those who tried to take the golden moment and beat it out thinly to cover more ground. But just as his mind in the past months had gradually started to plague him with visions of vacant futurity, so in these last few days, unbidden and almost undetected, an insidious optimism had begun to rise in his subconscious like curls of mist on the lake. He still woke early but now Bonnie was by his side. As one who had long opined in many a Yorkshire club and pub that there was nowt wrong with most discontented and unhappy women (e.g., all female politicians, jockeys, journalists, etc.) that couldn't be cured by application of a healthy well-endowed man, he should not have been surprised to find the therapy reversible. He was not a man given to self-analysis, however, but he knew that a future with Bonnie felt a much better prospect than a future without her.

Now here was Pascoe to remind him of the realities of his life starting next Monday morning.

"Something going on here, is there, sir?" enquired Pascoe.

Before Dalziel could reply the door into the yard opened again and another figure emerged and joined them.

"Evening, sir," he said.

"Hello, Cross," said Dalziel. "Bowls Club enjoying themselves?"

"Yes, thanks. Sorry if I'm interrupting. I thought you might be with Mr. Balderstone, but he can't have arrived yet."

He looked with open interest at Pascoe. Dalziel introduced them, then said, "Look, I'd best get back inside. I'm supposed to be working and we're a bit short-handed. Cross, would you fill in Mr. Pascoe here before he pees himself out of curiosity."

He turned abruptly and left them.

"Smoke, sir?" asked Cross.

"No, thanks," said Pascoe. "Just tell me all."

Briefly Cross outlined the course of events as he knew it which had resulted in Dalziel's involvement in Lake House.

Pascoe listened avidly and when Cross finished his relation he said, "Yes. Good. That's the police evidence bit and very nicely done too. But what about the rest?"

"Sir?"

"Look, Sergeant. I know Mr. Dalziel well. Fair enough, if he sniffs out some dirty business, whether he's on holiday or no, he'll worry away at it. But it'd take more than you've told me to get him to invest money with a gang of people he suspects to be crooks and to go around dressed up like Henry the Eighth's butler."

Cross considered carefully before replying.

"Well, sir. I think he feels a bit protective towards Mrs. Fielding. In a way by staying on he's looking after her interests."

"Mrs. Fielding? The big good-looking woman behind the bar? Ah yes, I saw them together just before."

Pascoe grinned broadly for a moment, then loyalty wiped his amusement from his face.

"Now, this fellow Butt?" he enquired.

"Due back from Brazil today, sir. The police over there were asked to keep an eye on him, just in case he showed any signs of slipping away. But it was felt best to leave him alone till we had him back on British soil."

"A bit dangerous, isn't it? If it's not down to him, then the trail will be damned cold," said Pascoe.

"Not really, sir," said Cross politely. "If Butt didn't do it, then the trail leads right back here. They went over his car with a fine-tooth comb. Annie Greave was in his boot all right, there's no doubt about it. And Butt has probably spent the last hour explaining how she got there. Mr. Balderstone, Chief Inspector Balderstone, was going to contact Mr. Dalziel as soon as he heard anything. I thought he might be here by now."

So, thought Pascoe. Dalziel is hanging on here in the hope that this guy Butt will cough up everything and life at Lake House can go on undisturbed.

How deep is he in? he wondered uneasily. He had not liked the way Cross now and then had seemed to be lining the fat man up with the Lake House gang rather than with the forces of law and order.

Yet it was Dalziel who had stirred things up, he reassured himself. He couldn't believe that he would ever have anything to do with the suppression of evidence. Though, of course, technically there was nothing illegal in the suppression of theory. But the Dalziel who had been his mentor these many years would not indulge in such hair-splitting.

"We'd better go back inside," said Pascoe. "Our wives will be getting worried."

"I've been married fifteen years," said Cross. "After the first ten, policemen's wives stop getting worried. They start getting angry instead. Come on."

But inside the building they encountered Dalziel once more. He looked anxious and uncertain, expressions which Pascoe had observed on his face as rarely as smiles on an undertaker's.

"Balderstone just rang," he said without preliminaries. "The plane arrived, but no Butt."

"What?" exclaimed Cross.

"He was taken ill at the airport, it seems. Ambulance took him to hospital in Rio."

"Very convenient," observed Cross. "That seems to wrap it up, I'd say. It looks as if we'll have to do it the hard way from now on in. I don't suppose they'll be asking for volunteers to spend a couple of days in Rio chatting him up, will they, sir?"

Dalziel didn't answer but turned away and disappeared towards the kitchens. Cross shrugged at Pascoe and the two men re-entered the Banqueting Hall.

"Thought you'd got lost," observed Ellie's father.

"There was a queue for the loo," lied Pascoe as he attempted to squeeze back on to the bench beside the townswoman whose thighs seemed to have settled and spread like wedges of ripe Brie.

"You missed the Sir Toby's Syllabub," observed Ellie.

"I don't think I did, really," said Pascoe.

They had now reached the stage in the evening when the historical was at war with the nostalgic—a war it could not hope to win. The bearded photographer had reappeared armed with a guitar and though the mead-sodden audience were happy enough to listen to one verse of "Drink to Me Only," further than that they would not go. The guitarist read their mood and gauged their taste perfectly, and soon the composition rafters were ringing with such fine medieval songs as "Bless 'em All," "She'll Be Coming Round The Mountain," and "The Rose of Tralee."

After some thirty minutes of this, during which time the tables were cleared completely (a pre-empting of the souvenir hunters in which Pascoe thought he detected Dalziel's hand), the guitarist announced that coffee was available and the bar would be open until ten-thirty. Clearly authenticity stopped at the licensing authorities.

Ellie and Pascoe sat fast while all around them their fellow diners scrambled for the exit.

"They'll be able to charge a quid a drink from now till closing time," observed Pascoe. "That should please Dalziel."

"Why?"

"He's a shareholder."

Quickly he passed on all he had learned that night. Ellie whistled speculatively when he finished.

"What's she like?" she asked.

"Who?"

"This woman, Bonnie Fielding is it?"

"I don't know, do I? I've only seen her distantly. Your dad thinks she overcharges."

"Let's hope she doesn't overcharge big Andy," said Ellie. "Come on, let's take a look."

"He can look after himself, you know," said Pascoe, rising to follow her.

"Huh!" she snorted.

"What's that mean?" he asked as they squeezed through the crowd towards the bar.

"It means that the way he was babbling on at our wedding reception, he was ripe for plucking. He no longer deems his soul immortal. I've seen the symptoms developing. You getting married was the last straw."

"Bollocks!"

"Well, one of them," emended Ellie in the face of this forceful argument. "I don't mean he fancies you. And I don't think he objects to me like he used to. But he's unsettled. I mean, wasn't it a bit odd that he should take his first holiday in God knows how long at the same time as your honeymoon?"

"No wonder you can't flog your novel!" said Pascoe.

They had finally reached the bar at which all hands seemed to be manning the pumps, or rather taps, optics and bottle openers. Dalziel was among them. Pascoe watched his technique for a while with interest. He poured the drinks with swift efficiency then charged eighty pence for a round of two, one pound forty for three, one ninety for four and three pounds for anything over. It seemed to be generally acceptable. Pascoe studied the list of prices, took from his pocket the exact amount required for two scotches, ordered them from an old man in a black doublet and passed over the money.

"That's Hereward Fielding," whispered Ellie.

"Who?"

"The poet. I knew he lived locally, but I didn't link him with this lot."

Somewhere behind the bar, a phone rang. The big woman who Pascoe supposed was Bonnie Fielding retreated to answer it.

"It's for you, Andy," she called a moment later.

Dalziel was a long time on the phone and though the bar service went on efficiently as ever, Pascoe sensed an awareness among the servers of what was going on in the background. Finally Dalziel reappeared and beckoned to Bonnie and the two disappeared from sight.

"Let's try to find somewhere less crowded," suggested Ellie.

Again Pascoe followed her, but he protested when she opened a door marked "Staff" and led him through.

"Friends of the proprietor," she grinned.

"Can't you read?" demanded a most unfriendly voice. A stout youth had appeared at the other end of the corridor they were in and was glowering at them.

"We're friends of Mr. Dalziel," said Ellie firmly.

"Are you? Well, I'm sorry, but we don't let our

staff socialize during business hours," said the youth pompously.

"You're Bertie Fielding?" said Pascoe.

"Yes. Why do you ask?"

"No reason. Someone described you to me, that's all."

Fat and nasty had been Cross's words. To another auditor he might have used the same words of Dalziel, thought Pascoe.

"You might tell Mr. Dalziel I'd like to see him," continued Pascoe, resolved not to retreat before this creature. "Inspector Pascoe."

"Not another!" groaned Bertie. "What do you do? Breed from mud?"

But he went all the same and a moment later Dalziel emerged from the bar. He shook Ellie's hand formally.

"Nice to see you," he said.

"Hi," she answered.

"Come on through," said Dalziel. "I'll be glad to take the weight off my feet."

They followed him into the main house. He moved around, observed Pascoe, with the familiarity of the inmate.

"We'll go in here," said Dalziel. "It's the old boy's sitting-room, but every bugger uses it."

"Cosy," said Ellie. "You seem to be enjoying your holiday."

"Aye," he grunted looking at her ironically. "He'll have told you everything, I suppose?"

"I wouldn't know that," said Ellie. "He may be holding something back."

"He's daft if he doesn't," said Dalziel. "The practice'll come in useful later."

"If I may interrupt this curiously oblique conversation," said Pascoe. "Look, sir, is this private business or a case? I mean, I don't want to stick my nose in . . ."

"Why not?"

"Because if it's private, it's private, and I've no

right to interfere," said Pascoe steadily. "Unless re-
quested, of course. But if it's a case . . ."

"Cross gave you a run-down, didn't he?" said
Dalziel. "How'd it look to you?"

"It looked like you were dancing on a tightrope,
sir," said Pascoe. "With a high wind blowing up."

"Did it? Well, I'll tell you what, Inspector, I'll just
put you right in the picture, you and your missus
both, and we'll see what the combined might of two
university educations can make of it."

Dalziel lit a cigarette. He looked, thought Pascoe,
a bit like Cardinal Wolsey might have looked in a
private moment, worn down by, rather than relaxed
from, the cares of office.

"There's a possibility that this man Butt may have
given Annie Greave a lift from Lake House, fallen
out with her somewhere along the road home, killed
her and dumped her in Epping Forest. We mustn't
discount this."

"But you don't believe it?" said Pascoe.

"I wouldn't say that," Dalziel answered. "There's
another possibility though. Only one other, really.
Annie Greave was killed here and hidden in the
boot of Butt's car. Butt didn't find her till he was
nearly home. He stopped for a drink and a sandwich
just before closing time at a pub just off the A1 at
Baldock. They back-tracked him there. Perhaps he
opened the boot for some reason when he came out
of the pub. There was Annie's body. Now he'd be
very bothered. I mean, Christ, who wouldn't? But
he'd be particularly bothered. First he was half-cut.
He'd got stoned here to start with. I bet he hadn't
got much idea how he'd driven to Baldock! So he
didn't fancy talking to the police in that state.

"And second, he was off to Brazil in the morning.
A big job, lots of prestige. Now, you and me, we
know a hundred reporters who'd just love to get so
close to a murder enquiry. But not Butt. At best, if
he rang the police it'd mean cancelling his Brazil
trip. At worst, it could mean a lot more. For all we

know he was so stoned that he couldn't positively remember that he *hadn't* given this woman a lift and perhaps even killed her! Remember, he hadn't seen Annie Greave up here, so he had no direct link in his mind with Lake House.

"So the stupid sod, half pissed still, does the obvious stupid thing. Drives to Epping, scrapes a bit of a hole, drops Annie in it, covers her up, and goes home. Next morning he flies off to Brazil."

"Well, it's a theory," said Pascoe dubiously. "It is only a *theory*, isn't it, sir?"

Dalziel ignored him.

"There was another person died here that night," he said. "Spinx, an insurance claims investigator. It looks like an accident. It looks to me less like an accident if Annie died here at the same time."

"The old police text," observed Ellie. "Wherever two or three die together, there shall Old Bill be also."

"What's the connection, sir?" asked Pascoe with a warning glance at his wife.

"Spinx came to the house for some reason," said Dalziel. "Suppose Annie rang him? She'd decided to take off, not liking the look of me. But Annie's kind like to make a bit of money wherever they can. So she rings Spinx telling him she's got a bit of information to sell him. She fixes for him to come out to the house. That'll mean she'll get a lift as well, very useful. He turns up, parks his car at the agreed spot by the lake. But she doesn't come. He waits an hour, then goes looking. He's been to the house before, of course, so he knows his way around. When he gets to her room, there's someone in the bed, so he gives them a shake."

"How do you know this?" demanded Pascoe.

"I've talked to the guy in the bed," said Dalziel. "He can't identify Spinx, of course, but it fits. You see, everybody else in the house knew Annie had gone by then."

"So why should anyone kill Spinx?"

Dalziel lit another cigarette. *He's back up to forty a day,* assessed Pascoe.

"He ran into the killer perhaps. Said he was looking for Annie. That made him dangerous. What had Annie said to him on the phone? Perhaps he hinted at more knowledge than he had. He was an absurd little git. Bang, he gets hit on the head with a lump of wood. And drowned."

"Out there, on that landing-stage?" asked Pascoe incredulously. He had risen and was peering out of the bay window which overlooked the lake.

"It's pretty black tonight, but I think I'd still notice any funny goings-on," he said. "And this would be earlier than now, I take it?"

"Yes," said Dalziel. "I think it probably happened by his car. I think that someone then took the punt along the shore to those trees where the car was parked, loaded the body in it and brought it back to the landing-stage to fake the accident. I noticed that the water where I found the body was pretty oily. I've had a quiet look at the lab report on Spinx since then. His suit was badly stained with oil. So was mine. I got it from sitting in the punt."

"Why did you take a *quiet* look, sir?" asked Pascoe.

"Because," said Dalziel slowly, "because this is all guess work. Because I don't want to stir things up for the people in this house if I don't have to."

"Mrs. Fielding in particular?" asked Ellie.

"Have you seen owt else here I'm likely to fancy?" snapped Dalziel. "Any road that's my business."

"You said," interrupted Pascoe in a thoughtful voice, "that Annie might have had some info to sell Spinx. Would that have been about fire insurance? Or the theft?"

"What's it matter?"

"Well, the allegedly stolen stuff wasn't insured, Cross said. And there was no fire claim pending, was there? I mean, even the fraud scheme had gone into abeyance because (a) Fielding had died and (b) you had come to life."

Dalziel looked at Pascoe with a faint smile.

"I taught that lad," he said. "Well, that's my business too."

He's still not telling us everything, thought Pascoe, peering out of the window again. There was someone down there by the landing-stage, he observed, only a shadow moving darkly against the misty grey of the water's surface. One of the Townswomen's Guild keeping a lecherous rendezvous? More likely one of the Bowls Club honking his ring.

"Well, it'll be settled one way or another soon enough," he said.

"How's that?"

"They won't leave Butt to his own devices now, will they? It looks damn suspicious already, having a nice convenient illness just before coming home. He'll have read about the discovery of the body in the English papers and probably thinks the longer that he takes to come back, the safer he'll be. No, it'll be the old bedside interrogation technique. A man on his back soon cracks. I wonder which he'll go for when the first British copper walks through his door— the sudden relapse or the miraculous recovery."

He laughed as he spoke.

"He went for the relapse," said Dalziel.

Pascoe stopped laughing.

"I'm sorry . . . ?"

"Butt's dead. That's what the second phone call was about. Heart attack. He never recovered consciousness."

"Oh," said Pascoe, rapidly considering the implications. "You've got to give it to him. If it was an act, then he really died the part."

"What've you been feeding him on?" Dalziel asked Ellie. "It's a joke a minute."

"I suppose we'll never know now," continued Pascoe. "One thing's certain, if anyone up here does know anything about Annie Greave's death, this must have been a happy bit of news. You'll have talked to Mrs. Fielding?"

"Yes," said Dalziel.

"Oh," said Pascoe, keeping disapproval out of his

voice with difficulty. "Then all you've got to do is arrest anyone with a big smile. Sir."

He reverted to peering out of the window and musing on the mutability of things.

"I don't really see what difference it makes," said Ellie, puzzled. "Even if Butt had come back and was questioned, surely he was bound to deny killing the woman and you'd be no further forward?"

"That'd be right," agreed Dalziel. "If it wasn't for the diary."

"The *what*?" asked Ellie.

"Butt was sober enough when he buried Annie to attempt to lay a bit of a false scent. He helped himself to the contents of her purse to make it look like robbery. But as well as her cash he got hold of a notebook she kept which gave details of her relationship with everyone in this house."

"Oh," said Ellie, nonplussed. "I didn't know that. In fact, come to think of it, how do *you* know that?"

"She's got the makings of a jack," said Dalziel to Pascoe who had been listening in puzzlement to the conversation. "No, of course it's not true. But it's not too unlikely a story, is it?"

"It is if you know that Butt's lying dead on the other side of the world," said Pascoe.

"Right," said Dalziel. "Fortunately that's not common knowledge in this house. No, I told Bonnie, Mrs. Fielding, that Butt was alive and well and waving his notebook under the noses of our interested colleagues at Heathrow."

It was at best a compromise, he admitted that. And like most compromises, it was a fusion of small betrayals. Lying to Bonnie was one; holding out on Balderstone another. As a trap it was too feeble; he saw this in Pascoe's face. But as a way of treating those who trusted him, it was too brutal; he saw this in Ellie's.

But it was the best he could do. Having decided that, no bugger was going to get in his way.

"What do you think's going to happen, sir?" asked

Pascoe in the kindly voice he reserved for lady magistrates and Ellie's relations.

"Likely nothing," said Dalziel. "I told Bonnie that the Essex police were pretty satisfied that Butt had nowt to do with the murder and that Balderstone would be coming out here tonight. And I asked her to let everyone know that they should hang around after the bar closes and the customers go home."

Pascoe glanced at his watch. It was twenty past ten. The bar closed in ten minutes.

"Ellie," he said. "Your mum and dad will be wondering where we've got to. It would be kind to reassure them."

"When policemen start being kind to their in-laws, let wives beware," said Ellie. "What are *you* going to do?"

"I'll hang on here for a while. Look, if they want to head for home, tell them not to worry. I'll cadge a lift into Orburn later."

Ellie glanced from her husband to the fat man in the floppy hat.

"OK," she said.

After she had gone the two men kept their silence for a while. Dalziel lit yet another cigarette and Pascoe prowled lightly round the room peering at the old man's books and examining the furniture.

"None of your antiques here," said Dalziel finally. "But if yon cupboard's open, you'll mebbe find a drink in it."

The cupboard was indeed open and Pascoe straightened up with a bottle of Rémy Martin in one hand and Glen Grant in the other. Hereward had not put all his money into the business. The scotch had been purchased in recognition of Dalziel's personal taste and the fat man had acknowledged this kindness by spending at least an hour each night sitting here with the old poet drinking and exchanging tales of the criminal and the literary underworlds.

Pascoe poured Dalziel a scotch and helped himself to a generous measure of cognac.

"This man, Balderstone," said Pascoe. "What's he like?"

"Not bad."

"Is he relying much on you? For inside information, I mean?"

"He'd be bloody daft if he was," said Dalziel avidly.

Pascoe sipped his drink thoughtfully. At least there was no self-deception here.

"So what happens tomorrow when nothing happens tonight?" he asked.

"You're a detective," said Dalziel. "They've questioned everyone twice, taken statements. What'd you do?"

"Well, normally I'd go and solve some easier crime, and thank God this one was down to Essex, not me!"

"Now suppose you're the killer. What then?"

Pascoe considered.

"Unless I was very stupid, I'd laugh myself to sleep at this all-revealing diary story. Then when I discovered that Butt was actually dead, I'd laugh myself awake. If I wanted to be *really* clever, I might just start recollecting that I caught a glimpse of Butt driving away that night with someone beside him in the car. But that'd be gilding the lily a bit."

"There you are then," said Dalziel. "There's nowt to be done."

"Not quite," said Pascoe. "You haven't asked me what I'd do if I were *you*."

Dalziel reached up one voluminous sleeve and began to scratch under his armpit.

"No, I bloody haven't," he said uninvitingly.

"I'd be worried sick," said Pascoe, "in case by not telling the investigating officer that I suspected, I was impeding the course of justice."

"What's suspicion?" asked Dalziel. "Bugger all. It's what you know that counts."

"And what makes you think that Balderstone's told you everything *he* knows?" demanded Pascoe. "Have you given him cause to take you into his confidence? Put what you suspect and what he knows together and bang! you may have a solution."

Dalziel glared at him angrily and Pascoe realized he had gone further than he intended. He sank the rest of his drink quickly in an effort to anaesthetize himself, but before the storm could break, the door burst open and another high pressure centre flowed in on a wave of distant noise like the honking of a flight of geese.

"Andy," cried Bonnie. "Have you seen that halfwit Charley anywhere? God Almighty, it's like Brand's Hatch out there! Where the hell has he got to?"

The noise he could hear wasn't geese, Pascoe realized, but the gabbling of human voices raised in anger commingled with a variety of car horns.

"What's up?" asked Dalziel.

"It's the car park. He got in such a muddle that he told the last people to arrive just to leave their cars on the drive with the keys in and he'd sort them out. Well, they're still there, blocking the way, but the keys have gone. Some twit tried to go round them across the garden, but it's so wet with all this rain that he's got stuck. God, what a mess!"

"And Charley's gone?" asked Dalziel, very alert.

"I've been telling you, yes! You must have directed traffic sometime, can't *you* do anything?"

They all make cracks about a cop's job in the end, thought Pascoe. But she was a fine-looking woman. A bit long in the tooth perhaps, but what she'd lost in youthful athleticism she could probably more than make up in expertise. Which was a male chauvinist pig thought he'd do well to keep hidden from Ellie.

"Come on," said Dalziel, rising and making for the door. Pascoe realized that he was being addressed, not Bonnie, and rudely pushed past her in the fat detective's wake.

"This Charley," he said. "Could he be the one?"

Dalziel didn't answer but began to climb the stairs.

If so, he's probably long gone, thought Pascoe. All those cars to choose from. Unless . . .

He caught Dalziel's green velveteen sleeve.

"Those keys," he said. "You've got 'em!"

"Right," said Dalziel. "No bugger drives out of here till I'm done."

He flung open the door of a room which was in darkness. Neither of them needed the light to know it was empty.

"It doesn't look as if he's taken anything," said Dalziel, puzzled. "He won't go far in his fancy dress surely."

"Where'd he go anyway?" asked Pascoe. "I mean he'd hardly set off walking to Orburn if he thinks Balderstone's coming driving along that road any moment. Hang on, though. Downstairs when I was looking out of the window, there was someone by the lake."

"Oh no!" groaned Dalziel.

They turned, met Bonnie looking bewildered halfway up the stairs, pushed by her once more and ran out of the front door.

The night was warm and almost windless. The mist on the lake surface had crept a little further up the garden in the last fifteen minutes and the rail of the landing-stage was barely visible, an indistinct line of faded runes scratched on a limestone wall. Though the noise of the car park chaos was more clearly audible here, its effect was to increase the feeling of isolation, like traffic heard beyond a prison wall.

"Andy!" called Bonnie from the doorway. But Dalziel did not pause.

"Careful!" he said to Pascoe as he ventured out on the landing-stage. "This stuff's rotten."

With sixteen stone going before me, what have I got to worry about, thought Pascoe.

Dalziel stopped short of the broken and still-unmended section beneath which he had discovered Spinx. The duck punt had gone.

Pascoe began to speak but Dalziel gestured impatiently and peered out across the lake, his head cocked to one side. Like a St. Bernard on an Alpine rescue mission, imaged Pascoe.

"Do you hear anything?" asked Dalziel.

"Only the waters wappe and the waves wanne."

"Come on."

Grasping Pascoe's arm for support, the fat man clambered down into the rowing-boat which rocked dangerously under his weight.

"You want me to come in that?" asked Pascoe incredulously.

"Someone's got to row," said Dalziel.

"But what's the point?" protested Pascoe as he stepped down. "If you think he's out there, just get the locals to start a search. I mean, what's at the far side "

"America," said Dalziel. "Just row."

Grumbling, Pascoe unshipped the oars and began to pull away from the shore while Dalziel sat in the stern with the tiller in his hand. It took only a few strokes to put the house and garden out of view and the sense of being alone on a limitless expanse of water grew rapidly.

"I'm sorry, sir, but what *are* we doing?" demanded Pascoe for the sake of hearing his own voice rather than in hope of an answer. But to his surprise, Dalziel laughed, a short bark reminding him once more of his St. Bernard image.

"We're on the track of a very dangerous man."

"Dangerous?" said Pascoe in some alarm. "The car park man?"

"You'd be surprised. Look there!"

Dalziel put the tiller hard over so the boat came round as sharply as a shallow-bottomed leaky rowing-boat could. Pascoe glanced round in alarm as he felt his left oar strike something. He would not have been too surprised to see an arm reaching out of the water and brandishing a sword. Instead he saw a punt pole, its top pointing drunkenly at the sky and its other end presumably buried in the sludge at the bottom of the lake.

"I told you he was dangerous," said Dalziel. "Listen."

They listened. After a while out of the other small water noises Pascoe picked an intermittent slapping noise, as though some aquatic creature were beating the lake with its flippers.

Dalziel nodded imperiously and Pascoe began once more to strain at the oars. This form of exercise was not one he was accustomed to and his arms and shoulders were already beginning to ache.

"Who's there?" a voice suddenly called out of the darkness. "Is there anyone there?"

"Aye, is there," answered Dalziel.

"Is that you, Mr. Dalziel? Could you give us a tow? I'm afraid I've lost the pole."

Pascoe glanced over his shoulder and saw the silhouette of a punt. In the stern a lanky figure was pushing himself upright, his hands dripping. The halfwit must have been paddling with them since he lost his pole, thought Pascoe. His feeling of superiority was almost immediately dissipated as he caught a double crab and fell backwards over his bench. From this undignified position, he heard another voice.

"No closer please, Andy. Just pass over your oars and we'll be on our way."

Pascoe struggled upright. The punt had now swung round, or perhaps the boat had moved as a result of his mishap. In any event, they were now broadside on to the bow of the punt and in it, sitting behind a formidable looking gun, was a second man.

"Evening, Herrie," said Dalziel.

"Just the oars, Andy."

The old man's voice was steady but not quite right, thought Pascoe. Strain showed through it. It was like Gielgud playing Little Caesar.

"Come on, Herrie," said Dalziel jovially. "What's all this about?"

"I couldn't get the car down the drive," said the old man. "Charley said he'd shift some of the visitors' but the keys had gone. That'd be you, I suppose, Andy. So I rang up a taxi, arranged to be picked up on the road at the far side of the lake. I'd have been there by now if my Charon had not proved more than usually incompetent."

The two craft had moved almost to the point of touching and Pascoe, upright once more, was able to view the strange tableau in all its absurd detail. The fact that he was the only one present in normal twentieth-century garb accentuated his sense of being an audience. The old man was the center of the tableau. His finely sculpted patrician head was perhaps more suited to a toga than a black doublet, but he made a good Duke Vincentio or even a Hamlet played by some English actor who had left it too late. Dalziel, standing now looking down at the punt, was an imposing figure in his long green gown, but his was not a head for philosophy and suffering; beneath the absurd cap flopping down over his brow, his eyes were calculating and shrewd; Ulysses assessing a tricky situation, or even an overweight Prospero, feeling a bit regretful that he'd drowned his book.

As for the third figure whom Pascoe had already seen at work in the car park, he too was one from the magic island. Ariel and Caliban combined, grace and awkwardness, look at him now as he began to advance down the punt; his first couple of steps movements of ease and elegance, he looked as if he had been wearing thin silks and pink hose all his life. He spoke.

"I say, I don't know what's going on . . ."

Herewind Fielding turned his head, Dalziel saw his chance and stepped from the rowing-boat into the punt, Ariel took another step and became Caliban, stumbling over a loose cushion and falling heavily to the deck. The punt rocked violently; Dalziel standing precariously on the gunwale swayed like a clipper's mast in a gale, Hereward rose from his gun and reached out a saving hand but it was too late. Like the undermined statue of some deposed dictator, the massive bulk of the man toppled slowly sideways and entered the water with a mighty splash. Tillotson and Fielding knelt anxiously at the side of the punt eager with apologies and assistance. And Pascoe, feeling it was time the twentieth century asserted itself, stepped calmly into the bows and took possession of the gun.

It struck Pascoe as odd that a man who had recently been threatening to blow a hole in his boss should now be so solicitous about his health, but Tillotson's words as he helped drag the waterlogged Dalziel aboard seemed to explain this.

"I'm so sorry, but really all I was going to say was there's no need for any fuss. I mean the gun's not loaded, you don't think I'd leave the thing loaded do you? I told Herrie, he knew it wasn't loaded; please, what's going on? Oh gosh, you are wet, aren't you?"

Pascoe squatting by the duck gun began to chuckle quietly. The unloaded gun doubled the comic dimensions of the thing by removing altogether the heroic element. Of course, if there had been a risk . . . idly he pressed the trigger.

The resulting blast tore the mist apart for about five yards in all directions. More devastatingly, the rowing-boat which was in the direct line of fire at very close range had a hole nine inches across punched in its side close enough to water-level for each rocking motion to ship some water. Very quickly the craft began to settle and the lake poured in.

"Not loaded," said Dalziel to a dumbfounded Tillotson. "Jesus Christ. Pascoe, grab those oars!"

Pascoe obeyed just in time. As he began awkwardly to paddle the punt back towards the shore, the rowing-boat sank with a quiet burp, leaving only a few bubbles and Dalziel's floppy hat to show where it had foundered.

Back at the house they found the car chaos was now under control. Cross had taken over and the only cars now remaining where those stranded by Dalziel's removal of the keys which fortunately had survived his immersion. But the confusion in the car park seemed now to have been internalized by the members of the household who hung around in their fancy dress like actors uncertain of their cue. Pascoe was particularly sorry for Bonnie Fielding whose anx-

iety about her father-in-law and distress at Dalziel's
half-drowned state were doubled by the discovery
that her son Nigel had decided to run away again.
Another note had been found saying that one night
of working in the restaurant had convinced him that
this was no life for a sensitive spirit, or words to that
effect.

Pascoe tried to keep Hereward apart from the rest
of the household but his effort was in vain without
resorting to the strong arm of the law and as Dalziel
had retired to dry himself without firm instruction,
he contented himself with keeping the old poet in
sight. He was not at all surprised to find Ellie waiting at the landing-stage. She had sent her parents
home by themselves and returned just in time to
hear the boom of the duck gun. The look of relief on
her face as she saw them emerge from the mist had
been a great boost for Pascoe's ego, even though her
first words to him were, "You've got oil all over
your best suit!"

Now they were all gathered in the old man's sitting-
room. Hereward had poured himself a large brandy
and Pascoe was interested to notice that he filled up
a glass with Glen Grant also. Cross came into the
room accompanied by a new figure whom he introduced to Pascoe as Chief Inspector Balderstone. Briefly
Pascoe outlined what had taken place. Obscurely he
felt the need to somehow cover up for Dalziel, but he
had no idea how to do this. The fat man would have
to look after himself.

Balderstone listened carefully but ventured no comment and a couple of minutes later, Dalziel reappeared.

He had changed quickly into sports jacket and
slacks. On his feet incongruously he wore a pair of
multi-coloured carpet slippers. But casual though his
garb was, Pascoe realized it separated him from the
medieval/Tudor costume of the Lake House people
as clearly as if he had come down in full police
uniform.

He greeted Balderstone and spoke quietly to the

two local policemen for a few moments, after which Cross slipped out of the room.

"Andy," called Hereward Fielding. "There's a drink waiting your attention here. And for your friends too."

The atmosphere had subtly changed, realized Pascoe. From confusion and doubt a kind of optimism had emerged. He felt he could guess its source and the next minute confirmed this.

"Thanks," said Dalziel, taking the drink. "I need that."

"I'm sorry about your soaking," said Hereward. "And about that gun! When I think what could have happened, my blood curdles."

He shivered and took a long pull at his drink.

"My fault really," added Tillotson. "I'm so sorry."

"But even with the gun empty, it was a silly joke," resumed Hereward.

"Joke?"

"Holding up like that! It's true what they say about second childhood. I never thought I'd start playing pirates!"

He laughed and all around him the others laughed too.

Dalziel didn't laugh.

"Where were you going, Herrie?" he asked.

"I told you. I couldn't get out of the gate because of those damned cars, so I organized a taxi."

"At the other side of the lake."

"That's so. You see I wanted to get into High Fold and as you'll recall from our first encounter, that's over that side."

"And why did you want to get into High Fold?" asked Dalziel. He was speaking very calmly and with hardly any inflection, as if, thought Pascoe, he merely wants to get this out of the way so he can get on with the real business. Pascoe had no doubt that this was Dalziel's intention, but where he could go from here he could not see. It was clear that the truth about Butt had been unearthed, probably from Sergeant Cross who would have no reason to withhold it. This is what came of acting alone, as Dalziel had often warned him. Almost certainly this stupid pretence about the diary had been exploded also. So Hereward had now learned the truth. There was no need to run. The evidence such as it was pointed to Butt and no one else.

Pascoe wondered uneasily if Dalziel *had* assumed he would keep the old man incommunicado, but he himself had made no effort in this direction when they first re-entered the house.

"I wanted to get to the pub there and buy a couple of bottles of cherry brandy. Revolting drink, I know, but very popular with the lower orders. We had run short. Bonnie asked me to see what I could do."

He glanced at Bonnie who met Dalziel's disbelieving gaze full on and nodded.

"Why go to High Fold. Why not Low Fold? It's a mile closer."

"It's the licensing hours," said Hereward. "Different authorities. They have an extra half-hour at weekends in High Fold."

It all fitted together rather nicely, thought Pascoe in whose mind a little doubt had begun to stir. Could it be *true*? No! He had been there, had heard the exchange between Dalziel and this man. But what had he heard? A joke. Why not?

Dalziel had remained silent since Fielding's last answer and the old man decided to press home his advantage.

"What's all the fuss, Andy? Is it the gun? I'm sorry about that, but you have to make allowances for the mentally handicapped. Hank has promised to dismantle it tomorrow. He's good with his hands."

Uniff waved them before him like a Negro minstrel.

"Yeah, man," he said.

Balderstone coughed gently.

"Excuse me, sir," he said to Dalziel. "Have you any instructions?"

"It's your case, Chief Inspector," said Dalziel. "I'm a guest here. Though there's one suggestion I could make."

"What's that, sir?"

"Arrest the bloody lot of them," snarled Dalziel. "Charge 'em with obstructing the police and with being accessories before, after, and during the fact."

"What fact is that, sir?"

"The fact that Open Annie Greave was done to death in this house ten days ago."

He glared malevolently at the group before him. Their reactions all looked to Pascoe like bad acting, but perhaps it was their amateur theatrical costume which gave this impression. Only Hereward remained firmly in character.

He laughed disbelievingly.

"Can that be it, Andrew? You think that absurd story you told Bonnie made me start like a guilty thing surprised and set off across the lake like Lord Ullin's daughter? For God's sake, you know me well enough by now. Even if I were guilty, if in my age I had found sufficient strength first to roger then to strangle this unfortunate woman, can you imagine that I would take flight in such a futile and undignified fashion? Dressed like this?"

His hands touched his doublet, his face lengthened in amused surprise, till finally he began to laugh at the self-evident absurdity of the idea. It was an infectious laugh and gradually, one by one, the others joined in. Even Pascoe felt tempted. Dalziel's face didn't change.

"Come on, Andy," said Bonnie. "Let's have a drink and count the takings. Your friends can help. At least it'll be an honest count with the law so well represented."

She advanced smiling. She was an extraordinarily attractive woman, thought Pascoe. Something of this must have shown on his face as a sudden sharp kick on the ankle reminded him that Ellie was standing close by.

"I'm sorry," said Dalziel.

"Sorry? Never apologize," laughed Bonnie.

But Dalziel stood aside and pushed open the door.

The smile faded and with it ten years from Bonnie's face.

"Oh, Andy," she said. "Whatever happened to Sydney Carton? This is a far, far shittier thing than you have ever done."

Dalziel considered this while Pascoe's eyes flitted from the stricken woman to the even more devastated visage of her father-in-law. Then he looked through the door.

Standing in the hallway with Sergeant Cross's protective or retentive arm around his shoulders was Nigel Fielding.

"No, it isn't," said Dalziel to Bonnie.

CHAPTER XVIII

The Last Days of Pompeii

"Was she your first?" asked Dalziel.

"Yes."

"And Hank fixed you up?"

"Yes."

"Well," said the fat detective with an effort at jocularity, "we've all got to start some time and it's best to start with an expert."

The room had been cleared except for Nigel and his mother. They sat on the sofa while opposite them Dalziel and Balderstone lounged in armchairs. Cross had gone upstairs with Hereward who had folded up like an evening daisy when the boy appeared. Pascoe stood quietly in the window bay.

"So you had been intimate with Mrs. Greave since she came to this house?" asked Balderstone delicately.

"Come on. Inspector," said Bonnie scornfully. "I didn't bring up my children to be mealy-mouthed!"

"Did you know of this relationship, ma'am?" enquired Balderstone.

"Not till too late," said Bonnie.

"And when you found out, what did you do?"

"What should I do?" she asked. "I saw no harm in it. I thought she was Pappy's daughter, remember. A nice respectable widow who happened to have hot pants. Like the Superintendent says, we've all

243

got to start somewhere and it was better than getting some local kid into trouble.''

Dalziel took up the questioning again. His voice had a strange quality which puzzled Pascoe, who had attended the fat man's interrogations more times than he could remember. But this intonation was new to him.

"After your father's funeral you decided to run away?"

"Yes," said Nigel. He had spoken only the minimum necessary to answer questions. He looked pale but composed. Only occasional quick flickers of his eyes from one extreme of vision to the other hinted at agitation.

"But you didn't get far. It was too wet. You came back to shelter."

"Yes."

"And you hid in Mrs. Greave's room?"

"Yes."

Dalziel nodded and scratched his nose.

"I thought it was Papworth," he explained to Balderstone. "Only, when I searched his room, I couldn't find any suede shoes. Any road, I doubt if he eats doughnuts for breakfast! We nearly bumped into each other once or twice, eh, lad?"

The boy nodded.

"So you were here all the time. And when I found you in the billiards-room with your rucksack, you hadn't just come back. No, you were just on your way out then. I wondered how you knew my name! You were waiting till Herrie got me safely out of the way to Orburn, then off you would go and as far as I was concerned the one person who could know nothing about Annie's death was you. Right? But you did know something about it, didn't you Nigel?"

The boy nodded. His mother put her arms protectively over his shoulder. They were large shoulders, Pascoe realized. The large frame of the elder brother was all here, though unhung as yet with Bertie's superfluous flesh. He was a powerful young man, powerful enough to . . .

"I killed her," he said blankly.

"Tell us about it," said Dalziel gently.

Why doesn't his mother intervene? wondered Pascoe. There's no need to let him answer these questions now. She could get her solicitor here for a start.

"She just packed up and said she was going. I found her getting ready and when I tried to persuade her to stay, she just laughed at first. I tried to stop her and we had a fight. We ended up on the bed and, well, I thought it was going to be all right then. But after we'd finished, she just went back to her packing."

He fell silent and glanced at his mother.

Dalziel coughed phlegmily.

"You were fond of her?" he said.

"Yes," said Nigel lowly. "I told her I loved her. I thought she felt the same. But she laughed again, told me to grow up. She'd never treated me like a child before. I started unpacking her case and she got angry. She pushed me away, I hit her, she said things about my father . . ."

"What things?" demanded Balderstone.

"About your father making love to her?" said Dalziel quickly.

"Yes. She said that. She said that I was being a bloody nuisance now like he'd been. I didn't believe her, but then she started saying nasty things about my mother too. We had another fight, only this time . . ."

His agitation was quite clear now. His mother's arm tightened around him, but still she didn't speak.

"But you didn't mean to kill her," urged Dalziel.

No wonder Bonnie doesn't bother with a solicitor, thought Pascoe. This was the unfamiliar intonation in Dalziel's voice. Defence counsel trying to lead his witness.

"No. I was just angry."

"And afterwards you went out and found Herrie?" said Dalziel. He was recalling the photos he had looked at in Uniff's room. In one of them Herrie had been standing by the door, apparently talking to someone in the corridor. In the subsequent shots, the old man had disappeared. Everyone else was accounted for except for himself and Bonnie, upstairs on the bed (his mind quickly suppressed the image), Papworth allegedly drinking in the Green Man, and of course Annie Greave, already by this time he now knew lying dead in her room. His mind had been toying with the limited permutations for ten days now. Nigel had made an appearance at a subconscious level long before he would permit him to take the lead.

"Yes," said the boy. "I locked the door. Charley tried it, but I just kept quiet. Then I slipped out and nearly bumped into you and my mother."

He turned to Bonnie and said, "I was going to look for you but I couldn't say anything when I saw you with him, could I?"

Bonnie shook her head slowly.

"No. I'm afraid you couldn't, darling."

Balderstone took up the questioning.

"Why did your grandfather and yourself put the body in Butt's car?"

"He wanted to use the Rover, but Mother had the keys and she was with Mr. Dalziel. Mr. Butt had left the keys in his car. Herrie thought that Mr. Butt was so drunk he'd be hours. But just after we'd got the boot shut, he came out of the house. He didn't see me, but he saw Herrie by the car. They talked for a moment, then he drove away."

No wonder the old man had believed he could offer himself as a decoy. If Butt's memory had been stimulated by interrogation, then the meeting with Hereward by his car would have been strong circumstantial evidence. Pascoe wondered how far he had intended to go. Would his actions have been merely diversionary or was he willing to go the whole hog and confess in order to protect his grandson?

And how far would Nigel have let him go? There was in this boy, Pascoe suspected, a broad vein of the tough self-interest which characterized both his brother and, by report, his father.

"What about Mr. Spinx?" Balderstone now demanded. "Hadn't Annie rung him and asked him to give her a lift?"

Pascoe wondered if Dalziel had outlined his theory to Balderstone or if the local man had arrived at the same conclusion independently.

"I don't know anything about Mr. Spinx," said the boy emphatically.

"All right, son," said Balderstone unexpectedly. "That'll do for now. Mrs. Fielding, we'll have to take Nigel down to the station with us, you realize that. You may accompany him, of course, just as you or your representative may be present at any further interrogations. Perhaps you'd like to put some overnight things together for the lad."

As Bonnie left the room, Cross entered.

"I've got a statement of sorts from the old man," he said. "He doesn't half ramble on! The doctor's here now and he's given him a sedative. I thought there'd be plenty of time for another go later, when he's more himself."

"Yes," said Balderstone. "Plenty of time. Would you take Nigel out to my car, Sergeant?"

The boy turned at the door and said very formally, "Good night."

"Watch how you go, son," said Dalziel. "By the way, Sergeant Cross, I've been meaning to ask, you ever catch your chicken thief?"

"No, sir," said Cross.

"We served chicken tonight. I've a notion Papworth supplied them. We never did find where he was the night Mrs. Greave disappeared. And his room stinks. A word to the wise."

"Thanks," said Cross, ushering the boy out.

"Well, sir, that seems to wrap it up," said the Chief Inspector. "I was surprised that the mother was so cooperative, but it looks as if we'll have a nice detailed confession all signed and sealed before we get to bed."

"It's good for the soul," answered Dalziel. "What's your guess—manslaughter?"

"Not for me to say," answered Balderstone. "You'll call to see me tomorrow, sir, and we'll get what you've got to say down on paper too? Then it's back to your own patch."

"That's it," said Dalziel. "Eight sharp on Monday morning."

"Right then. I'm sorry how it's worked out, all this," said Balderstone making a vague gesture with his hand. "Tell Mrs. Fielding we're waiting in the car."

He left and Pascoe came out of the bay.

"You still here," grunted Dalziel.

"You forget, my in-laws have gone off home in my transport. Perhaps I should ask Balderstone for a lift."

"No. He'll be crowded. You come along with me. I'll just put my gear together."

"You're leaving?" asked Pascoe in surprise. Such diplomatic gestures were not unusual in his superior.

"I can hardly stay on, can I?" said Dalziel. "Not after . . . well, anyway, it's back to the Lady Hamilton for me. Fitting, really. That's where it all started. Which reminds me."

He stuck his head out of the door and shouted, "Charley!"

After a few moments, Tillotson appeared. With him was Louisa. On the whole, Dalziel decided, studying the effect of their almost identical silk tunics, Tillotson was the curvier of the two.

"Is it true?" asked Charley. "That you've arrested Nigel, I mean?"

"Yes, it is," said Dalziel. "I'm sorry."

"Poor sprout," said Louisa. "I told you no good would come of it."

"But you couldn't foresee this!" protested Tillotson.

"Not precisely. But I could foresee *something*, which is more than you could do. It takes you all the time to foresee past your stupid pointed nose!" snapped Louisa.

"Don't be ridiculous, Lou," said Tillotson. "All Hank did was fix Nigel up with a bit of sex. My God, I sometimes wish he'd fix *me* up."

The fist came snaking out in the same fierce, uninhibited punch as before. Tillotson, in whom familiarity seemed to have bred faster reflexes, managed to duck and take the blow on his temple. Even so he staggered a pace backwards and the girl had gone by the time he recovered. Dalziel wisely avoided involvement this time.

"Why did she punch you in the Lady Hamilton?" he asked. It was a question that somehow he had never got round to asking.

"Much the same thing," answered Tillotson, gingerly touching his head in search of a wound. "She said it was disgusting, especially as Conrad, her step-father, had been having it off with Mrs. Greave too. I told her I didn't blame him, I wouldn't mind myself, and bang! I was knocked flat."

"You mean you knew? You all knew? About Nigel and Conrad and Annie? Then you must have suspected what had happened when Annie's body was found?"

"Certainly," said Tillotson. "You didn't have to be a detective to work that out. Nigel will be all right, won't he? He's only a boy. I say, we made a hell of a lot of cash tonight. We've just been counting it up in the kitchen. Shall I show you the figures?"

"Go away!" said Dalziel. "Just go away."

He went upstairs to pack. In the hall he passed Ellie who glowered at him inimically from the shadowy corner she was sitting in. They did not speak.

Before going to his own room he went along the landing and tapped at Hereward's door. There was no answer and he peered inside. The old man's head lay on the pillow, still majestic in repose. He breathed deeply and regularly. It was good to see him looking so peaceful, thought Dalziel approaching the bed.

"I'm sorry about all this, Herrie," he said. Apologies were easy to the sleeping and the dead. He turned to leave but as he did so, the old man's eyelids flickered and his thin tenor piped almost inaudibly.

"Oh the life of the spirit's a very fine thing
But you can't be a monk without flogging your ring."

Then the regular ebb and flow of his breathing resumed.

Downstairs with his case, Dalziel found Pascoe and Ellie waiting for him. Bonnie had left with Balderstone, Pascoe told him.

"Did she say anything," asked Dalziel pointlessly.

"No."

In the car on their way to Orburn, the trio sat in silence for the first five miles. It was Ellie who broke it.

"I suppose we should congratulate you," she said suddenly.

"What for?" asked Dalziel.

"Coming through with flying colours. All these temptations to act like a human being and you still managed to be true to yourself. The patron saint of policemen must be proud of you. You've told the truth and shamed the devil!"

"Aye," grunted Dalziel. "I'm glad to see marriage has mellowed you."

He pressed viciously on the accelerator and the car leapt forward. Pascoe sitting in the back rammed his knees into the back of Ellie's seat, partly as a safety precaution and partly as a warning. His married life was going to require many such warnings, he told himself. He didn't rate his chances of being a Chief Constable by forty very highly.

"There are still some things I don't understand," he said in what Ellie called his let's-change-the-subject tone of voice.

"Me too," said Ellie.

Pascoe ignored her and ploughed on.

"This business of Nigel running away and then coming back and hiding round the house. I mean, why do it? You're not telling me his mother didn't know."

"No," said Dalziel. "Old Herrie didn't at first, though. We almost got ourselves drowned looking for the lad, so Bonnie faked a phone call from him saying he was safe and sound. Quick thinking, that. Someone rang, Spinx I think, and she must have pressed down the rest and pretended she was talking to Nigel."

He spoke admiringly.

"Yes. But why?" pressed Pascoe. "And why did Annie Greave ring Spinx? What was she going to tell him? And what really happened to Spinx? You said you thought he might have been lugged around in the punt? What does Balderstone think?"

"You know me," said Dalziel. "I wouldn't presume to tell anyone else how to run their case."

Jesus wept! thought Pascoe. He'd tell God how to run heaven if he got the chance.

"And I still don't understand why Hereward really decided to invest in the business," he went on.

"Pressure," said Dalziel. "You heard Charley Tillotson. I bet they all knew what was going on. I wouldn't be surprised if Big Brother Bertie hadn't threatened to shop Nigel if Herrie didn't shell out."

"Happy families," said Pascoe.

"God, you two are so smug and superior!" exploded Ellie. "They're *people*, some nice, some nasty."

"I know it," said Dalziel.

"But you don't let the distinction bother you?" she demanded.

He didn't reply and they completed the journey in silence.

"See you on Monday morning, sir," said Pascoe as they parted outside his father-in-law's house.

"Good night," said Dalziel and drove away.

"Ellie," said Pascoe. "Why don't you practise what you preach some time."

"Meaning?"

"Meaning that you might try to understand rather than just judge."

She slammed the front gate so hard that a light went on in her parents' bedroom. Pascoe smiled. It was a small sign of remorse. Slowly, thinking about Dalziel, he followed her up the garden path.

Dalziel had been in bed an hour when the phone rang. He answered it instantly.

"I've just got back from the police station," said Bonnie. "The night porter at the Lady Hamilton didn't sound pleased at being woken."

"Sod him," said Dalziel.

There was a long pause.

"Andy," she said finally. "Will they find out?"

"About Conrad? I don't know."

"Anchor are going to pay up, did I tell you?"

"Are they?"

"Yes. Andy, why didn't you say anything?"

"Because I don't know anything. Not for certain."

It was true. He did not know for certain that the Propananol tablets in the bathroom cabinet had been prescribed to Conrad Fielding for his heart condition, though he did know for certain that no mention of the condition had been made to Anchor Insurance. All Conrad had to do to get the life cover required by the finance house for a short-term loan was to sign a declaration that he was in perfect health and give the address of his local doctor. The tablets had been obtained in London, where no doubt the diagnosis had been obtained also.

Nor did Dalziel know for certain that Conrad had had an attack while up the ladder in the banqueting hall. Nor that Nigel had found him and fetched his mother. Nor that Bonnie, realizing that death from a long-established heart condition would invalidate the insurance policy, had taken the still running drill and held it to her husband's chest. Perhaps it *had* caught him as he fell, perhaps that was what gave her the idea. In any case, Dalziel knew none of these things for certain. But, if true, they explained much. They explained why once she discovered he was a policeman she wanted to keep Nigel out of his way.

They explained why Mrs. Greave, who could have seen Conrad taking his pills on one of the occasions he slept with her, had felt her knowledge might be worth money to Spinx.

This was all reasonable supposition.

But some things Dalziel did know for certain. He had seen the pathologist's report on Conrad Fielding's post mortem examination. The doctor had had no inducement to examine the tattered remains of the man's heart for any damage other than that cause by the drill. Told of a suspected heart condition, he might indeed have been able to find traces. But it wouldn't have mattered.

For beyond any doubt, Conrad Fielding had died from the cause stated. When the drill plunged into his heart, he was still alive.

Bonnie could not have known that, Dalziel assured himself. She had believed that the physical effect of mutilating a dead man was the same as a live one. Her crime (if there were a crime) had been an attempt to obtain insurance money fraudulently.

But he could never be certain of this without becoming certain of all the other things he did not care to know.

"When will we see you again, Andy?" she asked.

"I don't know," he said. "I'm a busy man."

"Lots of crime in Yorkshire," she said with an effort at lightness.

"Aye."

"But you've got business interests here."

"Happen Bertie would be pleased to buy me out."

"If that's what you want," she said.

"That's it."

"Well then. We'll be in touch."

He put the receiver down without saying good night and let his great grey head relax on the pillow. Thoughts fitted madly through his mind. He lay there waiting for their mad whirling dance to exhaust itself. In the end, as always, the last to fade was a policeman's thought. What had been the circumstances in which Bonnie's first husband had drowned in the lake—and how much insurance did he have?

He didn't want to know that either. He felt exhausted but reluctant to sleep. With a sigh he turned over on his side, reached out to the bedside table, picked up *The Last Days of Pompeii* and opened it at his place.

Reginald Hill has been widely published both in England and in the United States. Among his novels are *A Fairly Dangerous Thing* and *A Very Good Hater*, and in the famous Pascoe-Dalziel series, *Deadheads*, *A Clubbable Woman*, *An Advancement of Learning* (all available in Signet). He lives with his wife in Yorkshire, England.

SUPER SLEUTHS

(0451)

☐ **ACCIDENTAL CRIMES by John Hutton.** It was the perfect place for murder... a lonely road through a desolate moorland. And in the killer's twisted mind, they'd been the perfect victims: young and pretty, hitchhiking alone after dark..." A dazzling psychological thriller..."
—*Publishers Weekly* (137884—$3.50)†

☐ **NIGHTCAP by J.C.S. Smith.** Someone had taken Lombardo's reputation for drop-dead chic too literally—but to have gotten up to the penthouse without using the locked elevators, the killer would have to be deadlier and far more cunning than the subway rats Jacoby was used to chasing... (137736—$2.95)*

☐ **THE GREAT DIAMOND ROBBERY by John Minahan.** There were twelve diamonds, famous and flawless. And three suspects, all no-name, Class B hoods. There had to be a Mr. or Ms. Big, pulling the tangle of strings that leads Rawlings all the way to England... and a spooky aging beauty with a family secret that makes the Godfather's look tame...
(135717—$3.50)*

☐ **JUNKYARD DOG by Robert Campbell.** Is the debris from a blown-up Chicago clinic the perfect cover-up for murder? When an anti-abortion demonstration ends with a bomb blast that kills a pretty young girl and an old woman, precinct captain Flannery takes it personally. But when the killer goes after Flannery's lady, he gets as mean as a junkyard dog—on the scent of dirty politics mixed with passion and revenge, a very deadly combination...
(143965—$2.95)

☐ **THE 600 POUND GORILLA by Robert Campbell.** It becomes a jungle out there when Chicago politicians get tangled up in monkey business—and the result is murder. When the boiler in the local zoo goes kaput, Chicago's favorite gorilla, Baby, gets transferred to a local hot spot. But things heat up when two customers are found beaten to death and everyone thinks Baby went bananas. But precinct captain Jimmy Flannery is about to risk his life to prove it's murder... (147103—$2.95)

*Prices slightly higher in Canada
†Not available in Canada

Buy them at your local bookstore or use this convenient coupon for ordering.
NEW AMERICAN LIBRARY,
P.O. Box 999, Bergenfield, New Jersey 07621

Please send me the books I have checked above. I am enclosing $_____
(please add $1.00 to this order to cover postage and handling). Send check or money order—no cash or C.O.D.'s. Prices and numbers are subject to change without notice.

Name_____

Address_____

City_____ State_____ Zip Code_____
Allow 4-6 weeks for delivery.
This offer is subject to withdrawal without notice.